I0822348

Clamorite
Bellicose
Delaisse
Eastmeade
Equivox

New Territory
Fallmont
Avid
Nortown
Rockhallow
N
W
E
S

Dawn

Dawn

BOOK THREE OF THE EOS DAWN SERIES

Jen Guberman

UGM Publications

ISBN: 979-8-9851781-5-9

Any references to historical events, real people, or real places are used fictitiously. Names, characters, and places are products of the author's imagination.

Printed by Ingramspark in the United States of America

Dust jacket first edition printing 2022.

Edited by: Amy Guberman, Kylie McGee, and Megan Dellinger

www.UberGuberman.com

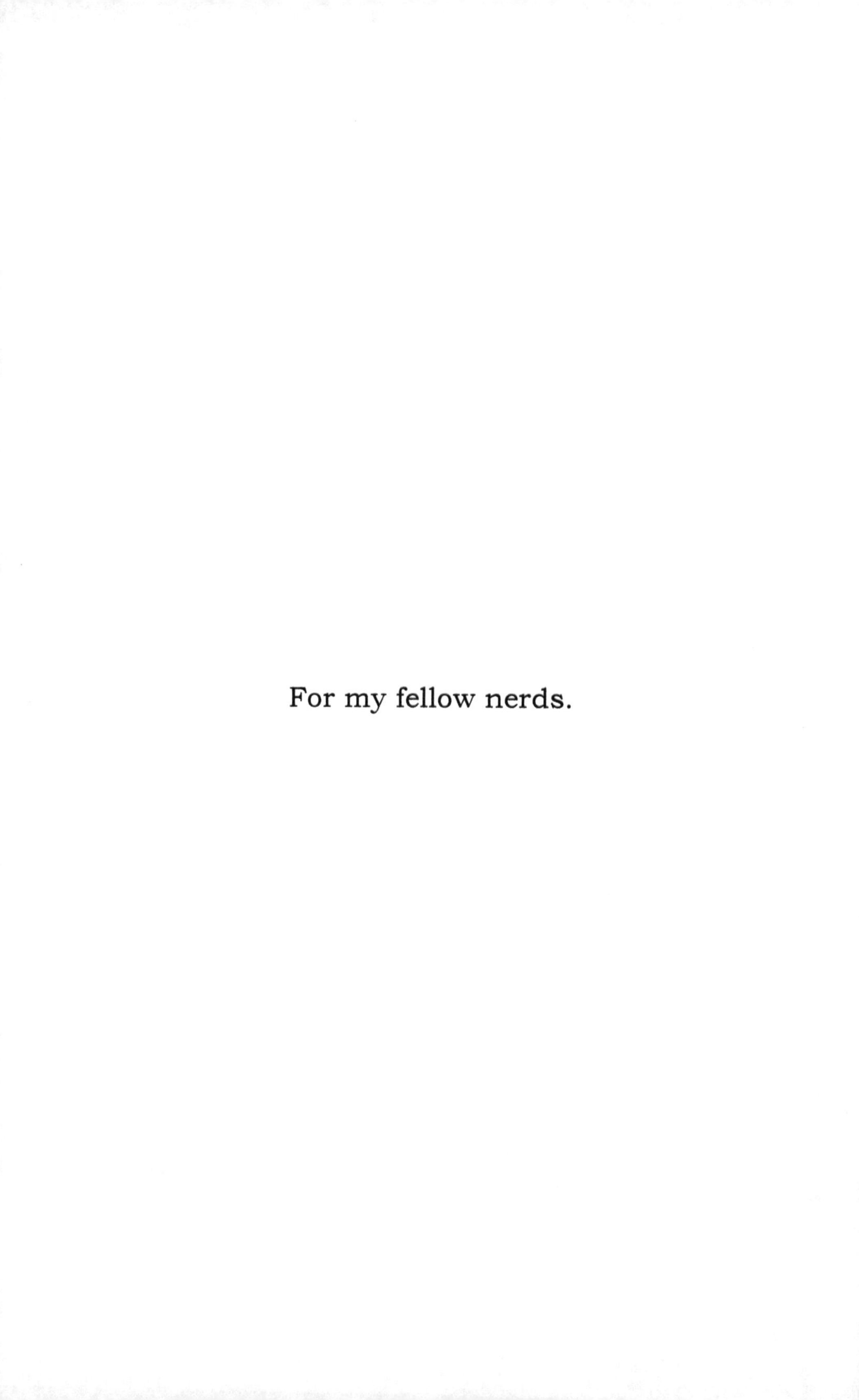

For my fellow nerds.

ONE

I lay there in the grass, my eyes squeezed shut, half-expecting and half-hoping I would wake up. All I wanted was to wake up and see Zane leaning against the tree beside me, peacefully eating breakfast. When I opened them, Braylin and Skylar sat at a pathetic fire, still half-asleep. Desperate, I quickly shut them again.

"She's been out for hours," I heard Braylin murmur to Skylar.

"Wake her up, then."

"She's been through a lot—"

"We all have."

It all started because I stole some expensive rum from a local bar with the hopes of selling it. From there, I was exiled to Avid, a town full of thieves. It was in Avid that I met Zane, and ever since then, each day had been a little brighter than the last—until Raine shot him and ended everything.

Skylar paused for a moment before speaking again. "You and I don't get to sleep in. Why should she?"

Dawn

"We've been walking for hours, Sky, let her rest. You know as well as I do—she isn't handling it well."

"Handling *what* well, Braylin? Walking? She's walked all the way to Fortitude before. She's fine."

"You know what I meant."

"Zane's death? Is that what you meant?"

"You don't have to be so blunt."

I felt my heart sink at their words and decided to end their discussion immediately.

"I'm awake, guys."

"Oh."

With a groan and an exaggerated stretch, my eyes flickered open, blinking back the sunlight. Towering trees with thick, rough bark and yellowing leaves surrounded us like a complicated maze. In last night's remaining glow of sunlight, we arrived at the gates at the base of Clamorite—the exile town for the noise polluters and general nuisances of the New Territory. We figured one night in an exile town would be safer than the middle of open desert. Considering we were in an exile town, Clamorite was the most beautiful of them—it was located behind a waterfall along the side of a mountain. The base of the mountain was full of trees and was the only place I have found wildlife in the New Territory.

"Your fire is stinking up the fresh air," I teased, fanning myself. "Isn't someone going to notice this?

"People in Clamorite have little fires all the time," Braylin said. "It's fine!"

"Why do we even need a fire? It's not cold," I said.

"*Someone* wanted toast this morning," Skylar said, her eyes flicking toward Braylin.

"My bread is stale, so I just wanted to make the best of a mediocre breakfast!" Braylin defended.

"Mine isn't," Skylar said. "You suck at keeping your food preserved, don't you?"

"I do not!"

"How do you store your bread?" she asked.

Braylin dug around in his backpack, his sleeve pulling up and revealing some of his simple black tattoos. He pulled out a loaf of bread, wrapped in a plastic bag that was merely tucked over on itself.

"You're lucky it doesn't have mold yet!" Skylar said, her petite nose crinkling. "You have to squeeze the extra air out and twist the end of the bag! You don't know the next time we can get more food, so we have to make this stuff last."

When we ran low on food, we had to steal from the cities or the exile towns. The best option was to keep our food as sealed and safe as possible.

After the war years ago, the survivors rebuilt four cities: Fallmont, Eastmeade, Rockhallow, and Nortown. The population was a lot smaller than people were used to, and the government they once knew was destroyed with the rest of the country. Because of this, we ended up with the exile town system. In the past, if a citizen was caught committing a crime, he or she would be arrested, tried, and either fined or sent to prison. Now, people are given a trial that they have almost no hope of winning, and after they inevitably lose the case, they are shipped out to the appropriate exile town. Avid was created for the thieves and has also conveniently become the literal dump of the New Territory. Bellicose is located inside caverns, mocking the "caveman" qualities of the violent criminals. Delaisse, an abandoned industrial town, is where the leaders and government officials stick the drug addicts and the vandals. Equivox, my personal least favorite, is located at the bottom of what is essentially a huge crater where they keep the liars. Then, there's Clamorite. The "noise polluters" and rioters living in Clamorite are surrounded by beautiful, untouched greenery, and their camp is near a stunning waterfall.

"So, besides toast, what's for breakfast?" I asked, running my fingers through my hair and wincing when they tugged on a stubborn tangle. "Please don't say eggs."

"Eggs? Where would we get eggs?" Braylin asked, his head spinning around as if implying a market was hidden in the trees.

"The birds around here might've laid some eggs. Please don't eat them," I moaned, remembering when Zane and I were in Clamorite and I woke up to him preparing to cook a songbird's fertilized eggs over a fire.

"Birds? There are birds here?" Braylin's freckle-framed eyes widened.

I grunted in affirmation, forgetting that he wouldn't know about the wildlife since the birds had quieted by the time we arrived last night.

"How do you know?" He narrowed his gaze, as if expecting me to reveal a clever joke.

"I was here a while back. I found a key here that helped unlock the Skeleton Key box."

"You never did tell me much about that Key. Did you have it when you met me and the rest of the old group?"

"I did," I said as I picked at my split ends, never looking up to meet his eyes.

"Don't pick at your hair, Skunk," Skylar warned. "You'll make it look worse."

"Stop calling me that," I said, dangling a loose black hair over her. I was tired of Skylar calling me that stupid nickname because of my long, platinum and black hair.

"You had a key that could unlock anything, and you didn't share with the group?" Braylin asked, fixated on the conversation at hand.

"I didn't know if I could trust you guys. Now I know, so now you know."

"How did you find it?" he asked.

"It's a long story," I said, finally turning to face him.

"I'll take the summarized version."

"I found some documents in Avid that mentioned that there was a single key in each of the exile towns that could open the box containing a key that could open any lock, so Zane and I found each of the exile town keys. Then, we found the box in Fallmont, unlocked it, stole *the* Key, and that's it."

Except it's not. I decided he didn't need to know that Raine *Velora, the leader of Fallmont, the largest city in the New Territory, caught us and tortured Zane in order to get me to tell her everything I knew about the Key and how I travelled between exile towns.*

"Huh," Braylin muttered. "Can I see it again?"

"Skylar's got it," I answered.

Skylar reached into a pocket on her bag and pulled out the Key, handing it to Braylin. He ran his fingers along its cool metal, holding it up to the light as the sun shimmered through the green, purple, and blue glass of the head.

"We need a plan," Skylar interrupted Braylin's trance.

"For what? Taking down Raine and the entire exile town system? Eh. No big deal," I said.

"Eos, I'm being serious right now. We can't just camp out here forever and hope this resolves itself."

"I'm aware of that, but we've also only been here for a few hours. We don't want to rush into this. I tried that already—clearly it doesn't work."

Skylar and Braylin shifted their gazes away from me and everything went silent.

"Guys," I said. "I'm fine. It's fine."

"That isn't something you just get over," Braylin said, his head hung low. "Does everyone who made it to Fortitude with you even know?"

"How would they?" I asked, my lip snarled unintentionally. "They're in Fortitude. I can't exactly mosey over and tell them."

I thought for a moment about my friends—the team that helped Skylar and I make it all the way to Fortitude. I hated that I never had a chance to say goodbye to Bexa before I left, and I wished Cindee was here to see her brother alive and well.

Upon seeing me sitting in silent thought, Braylin decided to throw in his two cents again.

"I think it would really help you to talk about it," he said.

I turned slowly to face him, staring dead into his eyes.

"Zane and I tried to convince Raine to change her mind. We didn't have a solid plan and we rushed things. Raine shot Zane. Zane's dead. Now we know better. What more do you want me to say?"

"Seriously?" Skylar looked back at me in dismay.

"You loved him, E. It's okay to grieve."

I turned away from them, my eyes locking on a tiny crimson bird in a lush tree. When I locked eyes with the bird, it tilted its head at me, as if waiting for my response.

"Yup. I loved him, but I'm fine. Moping around isn't going to kill Raine Velora. Creating a rock-solid plan is going to kill Raine Velora, so believe me, I understand the importance of a plan, but for now? For now, I just want breakfast."

Without letting them respond, I retreated to my bag, lying at the base of a tree a few yards away. I dug out a walnut muffin and nibbled at it mindlessly. I looked up at the crimson bird, still perched in his tree, staring at me.

"What?" I mouthed to him, as if he could understand.

Just then, the little bird relieved himself, letting a small white puddle spatter against some rocks at the base of the tree before he flew away.

Nice talking to you, too.

My attention returned to my muffin, but I still felt Braylin and Skylar's stares on my back, so I turned on my heel and tucked off between some of the trees.

Truthfully, it didn't feel real. It was strange, not travelling with Zane—

it almost felt as if he had gone on a supply run and would return soon. The few days I was in Ironwood, the only prison in the New Territory, were the worst of it. The city leaders only send criminals to Ironwood as a last resort because they don't have the staff to manage it. If it weren't for Braylin being in the cell across from me, I would have gone mad from the grief compiled with loneliness. *I made it*, I told myself. *I did my grieving, and now it's time to move on.*

When I finished choking down the dry muffin, I wandered back to the makeshift campsite, walking in on an enthusiastic brainstorming session.

"It would work though!" Braylin said, his dimpled grin giving him a childish look, despite his silvery hair.

"But what about the officials? They were already all over the place, and if you think Raine doesn't have them on some kind of super alert after I broke you two imbeciles out of the only prison in the New Territory, you're delusional."

"Skylar's got a point," I said, sitting on a rock beside Braylin. "I didn't hear what the plan was, but whatever it is, we need to be mindful of the officials. We don't know what kinds of orders Raine has given them—whether it's to shoot on sight or to capture—but we do know they are definitely looking for us. That's why we picked here to hide out, isn't it? It's less likely they're going to check an exile town, so it at least buys us a little time."

Braylin crossed his arms defiantly. "You didn't even listen to my idea, so you can't discredit it!"

I motioned with my hands for him to present his case, and he straightened his posture, locking eyes with me before proceeding.

"Propaganda."

"What?"

Skylar jumped in. "He's got this crazy idea to deliv—"

"Hey! Don't steal my spotlight!"

"Okay, okay. Keep going," Skylar rolled her eyes. "Child…" she muttered.

"If we write letters that reveal the terrible, corrupt things Raine has done and how flawed the exile town system is, we can deliver them under people's doors, and maybe we can at least begin to convince people to stop supporting her. Maybe we could gain followers who can help us with supplies or give us shelter. If nothing else, we would be sneaky about delivering them, so even if it doesn't work, the only thing we lose is some time."

"Like I said, it's crazy—"

I hummed to myself as I visualized the logistics of such a feat.

It could go terribly wrong. Then again, when have we ever done anything that didn't have the potential to make everything worse? We always take risks—there isn't a safe route, but this one is about the closest thing we have. Like Braylin said, we just need to be sneaky about delivering the letters.

Skylar stared at me, head cocked to the side and eyebrows raised, waiting for me to speak.

"Actually, I think it's a good idea," I said.

"See?" Braylin straightened his posture proudly. "I told you!"

"There are at least a hundred ways this could go wrong! Do you really want me to count them off?"

"Sure," I said flatly, arms crossed. I blinked impatiently at Skylar.

Her mouth hung open for a moment before she composed herself and began to speak.

"One... We could get caught and sent to Ironwood. If we're all arrested, you can forget escaping this time. Two... they might just save themselves the time and kill us. Three... even if we aren't caught by officials, residents might see us and send search parties after us all over the New Territory—"

"You think they aren't already all searching for us? We escaped the only prison in the New Territory, I killed an official, and we've escaped exile towns. Even just escaping Avid before the rest of this mess started—that alone gives them a reason to hunt me down. I took just about the only rule of the exile towns and made a mockery of it by breaking into and escaping from every single exile town. They have plenty of reasons already to be scouring every foot of sand in this hellhole," I responded.

"Fine. You know what? You want to try Braylin's propaganda idea—we'll try it. If I even catch wind that we've been spotted, I'm leaving you two behind, and I'll be gone so fast you—"

"You'll be missed," I teased.

"Damn," Braylin muttered, his eyes darting between Skylar and me.

"So, how do we start these letters?" I asked, turning to him and ignoring Skylar's stunned expression.

"There aren't any printers in the exile towns, and it's far too risky to break into one of the cities to try to casually print off thousands of letters. So, first we need paper and pens."

"Sounds simple enough," I said.

"Not exactly. I don't know about you, but I doubt the exile towns have much of a paper and pen supply, so we might have to really scavenge."

"Avid has pencils and paper," I said, remembering the closet under the stairs in my building in Avid. Early in my stay there, after finding the Skeleton Key documents, I had asked Lamb if she had paper and a pencil—I had intended to take notes on the documents, but I refused to tell her what I needed them for. Little did I know at the time that Lamb would join Zane and me in the hunt for the Key, ultimately leading to her death in Equivox at the hands of a deranged exile.

I felt my stomach burn, dragging me from my thoughts.

"What? Really? Alright—I guess we'll go to Avid. About how far is it from here?" Braylin asked.

"It's on the other side of Fallmont."

"Crap. Is there anything closer?" he asked.

"Delaisse and Fallmont," I said. "Everything else is just as far or even farther."

"You were from Delaisse, right?" Braylin turned to Skylar, who already had her arms crossed and eyes narrowed at him.

"Yup."

"Did they have pens and paper?"

"No pens. And not paper for writing."

"Paper for wh—"

"Nevermind," Skylar cut him off, rolling her eyes with a subtle smirk.

I snickered under my breath.

"All jokes aside, no. Not as far as I ever saw," she said.

"Fallmont has to have pens and paper," he thought aloud.

"Yes, they should," I said. "And officials. Probably some citizens who would love to turn exiles in to those officials as well."

"Touché."

"So, Avid is our next best option?" Skylar asked.

"I think Bellicose is just about as far, too. It's also a lot harder to break into and out of, and I don't really know if we'd find what we need there."

"I also don't really want to be surrounded by murderers, thanks," Braylin said, his leg twitching.

"That's a generalization," I corrected him. "They aren't all murderers and you know that."

"I know," he grumbled. "Still don't want to go there."

"It sounds like that wouldn't be logical anyways, so stop whining about it," Skylar snipped.

"Well, I guess we should be on our way?" He stood and adjusted his socks around his ankles, which had become uneven as he sat.

Skylar and I groaned in unmotivated unison.

"It's nearly lunchtime already," Braylin observed. "*Someone* decided to sleep in, so we've already lost a few hours, and it took us about a day to get here from the last ruins we stayed in. It'll be a couple days before we reach Avid, so I'd rather get going."

"I hate that we came all this way just to turn around and go right back in the same direction," Skylar said.

"I know," I agreed. "But this was just the best option at the time. I thought they'd be less likely to check the exile towns for us first, and this one was close and seemed like the best option at the moment."

"But why not just make this our permanent camp?" Skylar asked. "It's so much better than the desert for so many reasons, and like you said… who's going to look for us in an exile town?"

"Eventually they might think to, and in the event that someone was to spot us, there aren't limitless escape routes here like there are out in the ruins. There's one exit. If they find us here, we might not have a chance to escape."

"Let's get moving!" Braylin called, already walking toward the gates.

"You heard the man," I signaled to Skylar, sarcastically saluting Braylin with a teasing smirk.

Braylin beamed at me as he spoke, throwing his bag over his shoulder.

"Darn skippy."

TWO

We cleared camp in a matter of minutes, scattering the remains of our fire and covering the ashes with sand.

Our campsite wasn't far from the entrance gate of Clamorite. When Zane and I were here trying to find the Clamorite Key to help open the Skeleton Key box, we had to use a button inside an official's truck that we had stolen in order to get out of the town. This time, however, we had the Skeleton Key, and in our experience thus far, every gate in the New Territory has a manual lock override as well. Fortunately for us, that meant we were able to leave Clamorite with ease.

Growing up, our history classes taught us that Clamorite was one of the few places untouched by the war. Instead of building a city there and demolishing some of the remaining natural life, they decided to put the noise polluters and rioters there, where the sounds of the waterfall could drown out the sounds of their protests. Equivox also had some natural life; however, according to history, it was still damaged by weapons of war. Some of the greenery around it was there originally, but much of it has had to regrow over time.

Passing through the gates of Clamorite was like crossing from one world into another. Inside the fences, the terrain is covered in a blanket of lush grass and colorful leaves, but outside, nothing but sand and endless blue skies. If we were lucky, we'd find brambly bushes or tall palm trees peppered through the sand—other than that, the outside world provided minimal visual stimulation, and virtually no cover from being seen.

I'm getting really tired of sand, I thought to myself after a couple hours of walking. I let out an audible grunt.

"You good?" Braylin asked.

"Sure, we'll call it that."

"What?"

"Nevermind. Let's keep moving."

After about an hour of walking, it seemed the only way we could measure our progress was to gauge how much the mountains of Clamorite shrank in the distance behind us.

"We need a plan," Skylar broke the silence.

"We've got one," I said. "Where were you when we decided this?"

"No, not that one. A plan in case someone spots us while we're passing Fallmont."

"I thought you said you'd run?"

"I might. You two are pretty pathetic on your own though, and I feel like that'd be like a mom losing her kids in a grocery store and leaving them for good."

"Are you trying to imply that you're motherly?" I choked back a laugh.

"Heck no," she scoffed with a playful smile. "But I am saying you two are needy and I feel moderately responsible—especially since, even though we each have guns now, you two are still new to ranged weapons."

"Hey—I'm a good shot!" I defended. "I knocked over all ten targets you set up that last time!"

"True, but will you be able to aim it at a person if needed? And what about Braylin? The only time he hit one of the targets was on accident while aiming at the target beside it."

A few steps ahead of us, Braylin shrugged without looking back.

I pondered aloud. "As far as a plan goes, if someone spots us, my vote is that we run if we can."

"And if we can't run?" Skylar asked.

"We'll do what we have to do."

The air grew heavy, despite the warm breeze making a thin layer of sand dance at our feet. A few minutes passed in quiet contemplation, only for Skylar to break it, mumbling angrily to herself.

I peeked at her as she walked beside me a couple feet from my left side. I cleared my thoughts for a moment in hopes of deciphering her indistinguishable mumblings. Her pace seemed to quicken the more she rambled. With an exasperated sigh, she smoothed her long, chestnut hair, which was growing frizzy with the wind.

The only word I could definitely make out was "Raine."

Her cat-like, olive green eyes squinted in extreme concentration, as if she was questioning every step she took despite how determined she appeared as she walked.

"Why are you staring at me?" she asked without turning to break her concentrated gaze, her nose crinkling in disgust as she spoke.

"I thought you said something," I said. Suddenly aware of my nosiness, I looked forward again.

If I'm being honest with myself, Skylar used to intimidate me. After spending this much time with her, I've realized she's not that scary—she's just another girl who has been cheated out of a good life by Raine and her twisted government.

"What are our goals with this propaganda thing?" Skylar asked.

"What do you mean, 'what are our goals?'" Braylin asked.

"Well, what's the long-term goal here?"

"To show the people of the New Territory that their leader sucks," I answered.

"That's short term. I mean, it'll still take a while to get that word across, but is that all we want?" Skylar asked.

"I want to end Raine Velora," I said stiffly.

"That might be a bit unrealistic unless you really want to screw yourself over with the officials," Braylin said, turning to look at me over his shoulder. "Even if you help everyone realize that Raine is a horrible human being—if she even qualifies as a human—the people might not take kindly to murder, especially when some have been exiled for life for far less than that. Just saying."

"They deserve justice. Every single person who lost their freedom because of Raine—they deserve justice," I grumbled. "She needs to suffer."

"We can work on that. I'm sure we can come up with some kind of social justice that doesn't involve killing her. Killing her almost seems too humane," Braylin scoffed. "What else do we want?"

"She needs to be kicked out of office, if nothing else," I said, clenching and unclenching my fists. "But we don't need someone else corrupt taking her place. We need someone who agrees that the exile town system's outdated—someone who will initiate the reinstitution of the prison system… someone who doesn't send people away for life for petty crimes."

My words trailed off as my mind drifted, thinking of Zane, Paren, Lisette, and so many of the other exiles I had met.

"You know who I think Raine might have screwed over the most?" I asked. "A girl named Lisette. I met her in Clamorite. She was from Rockhallow, but she was engaged to a guy from another city. Her fiancé was a driver, so he was able to travel between cities legally, unlike average people. She met him during one of his trips. Eventually, she fell in love with him—someone the city leaders would never allow her to be with just because people can't move to other cities. Understandably, Lisette protested in the streets until she was arrested and exiled to Clamorite for her 'unruly public behavior.' All of this just because she wanted to marry a guy from another city."

"That's horrible!" Braylin lamented, kicking a lump of sand as he walked. "I remember meeting her when I was in Clamorite, but I didn't know her well. I had no clue that's why she was there!"

"Raine's a witch," Skylar grumbled.

I began to think about other people Raine had unfairly allowed to be exiled, and my mind naturally floated toward Zane. I felt a stinging in my eyes, which I stubbornly forced back.

Much like myself, Zane was arrested in his early twenties—he had only lived in Avid for a short time longer than me before we went looking for the Skeleton Key. His brother was incredibly ill, and his parents couldn't afford the medication on top of usual household expenses, so Zane took to stealing in order to help his family stay afloat. At the particular time of his arrest, he was stealing a bracelet for his mother, but even though it was more of a materialistic target, he still only ever had his loved ones in mind. He was exiled after that, never to return to his family.

I missed Zane, but no matter how much I allowed myself to think about him, it felt like he would just be hiding in some ruins somewhere, waiting for me to find him.

Paren's story was similar to Zane's in the respect that neither of them had malicious intentions, but his story was completely unique in its details. I had met Paren during my short time in Bellicose, where he told me about his "crime"— he "attacked" a man who was getting handsy with a girl in a bar. Seen as an aggressive, dangerous man, he was sentenced to spend the rest of his life (and he only appeared to be a few years older than Zane and me) living in caverns.

"You okay?" Skylar broke my thoughts. I had been so fixated on my memories that I didn't realize until then that we were walking toward some ruins.

"Oh, I'm fine." I shook myself out of my trance.

"You looked like you were about to snap or something, maybe even start foaming at the mouth," she teased. "Thinking about that 'justice' for Raine?"

"Yeah, something like that."

"Hey," Braylin spoke up. "Let's talk about something less depressing for a bit!"

"Like what?" I asked.

"Like… what's your full name? I don't know if you ever told me. Is Eos short for anything? What's your last name?"

"You want my blood type and old address while you're at it?" I laughed.

"I just figured I should get to know you guys better if I'm going to be spending so much time around you," he defended.

"Eos isn't short for anything. It's Eos Dawn."

"That's interesting!" Braylin said. "Do you know any Greek mythology?"

"Not one for staying on topic, are we?" Skylar asked.

"It's relevant," he retorted. "Eos was the Greek goddess of the dawn. So, it's kind of like your parents named you Dawn Dawn."

"Hilarious." I scoffed.

"Random question," Braylin asked.

I threw him a quick glance.

"Why doesn't the New Territory just limit sentences to the exile towns? Wouldn't that be a fair compromise?"

"We were just talking about names. Where did that come from?" Skylar asked.

"I dunno," he said. "Just popped into my head."

"I guess because the exile towns are anarchy. I remember reading in history books that prisons used to have rehabilitation programs. It'd be cool if we could do something like that but build on what people in history discovered—what worked, what didn't work. The exile towns just reinforce the negative behaviors though," I said. "While I was in Avid, I feel like I got even sneakier than ever."

"Hey, kid," Skylar called up to Braylin.

"Me?" he asked.

"Yeah. I'm done talking about this. Change of subject. How old are you? I never asked. You've got a major case of baby face going on, but you've got grey hair. Your hair says 60, but your face says 12. Which is it?"

Braylin snickered. "I'm 32."

"What?" Skylar and I both said, exchanging surprised looks.

"There's no way!" I exclaimed.

"Yup. Why? How old did you think I was?"

"I don't know. Like Skylar said, your face and your hair really contradict each other."

"I've had grey hair since I was about 28. Almost a full head of it! Can you see some of the roots? Some of them still come in black," he parted his hair, revealing some black roots. "My mom always said it was stress—"

"I hate to interrupt," Skylar said, "but did either of you hear that? It sounded like a voice."

"Don't start hearing voices now," I teased. "We can't have you going crazy on us."

She urgently pursed her lips, throwing a finger against them in a hushing motion. She squatted to the ground, motioning for us to follow suit.

Braylin and I crouched beside her, exchanging confused glances with each other and then directing our confusion at Skylar, waiting for answers. After a few moments of silence, I spoke softly.

"I still don't hear anything."

"I thought I heard people laughing," she hissed back. "Stay quiet for a moment."

"Sky, I think you're imagining things—" I started.

"She isn't," Braylin interjected. "Look!"

I followed his pointed finger, spotting two blurry figures along the horizon.

Is it naïve to hope they're friendly?

Skylar stood, pivoting to face the oncoming figures. The one on the left was considerably taller than the right one, and they both appeared to be carrying something that looked alarmingly like rifles.

"Run!" Braylin hissed from beside Skylar before he took off toward the ruins.

I started to follow Braylin but stopped in my tracks, digging my heels in the sand to halt my momentum. Skylar was still standing there, but now, she was reaching for her gun, which she kept tucked into the back band of her jeans.

"Skylar! Let's go!"

"No!" she growled. "Go with Braylin!"

"Are you kidding me? You'll never hit them from this distance," I argued. "We've still got a chance if we go *now*!"

The two figures grew slightly more distinct in the distance, clearly coming our direction as Skylar stood, clutching her gun and stretching her arms out, trying to find her target with the sights.

"Don't!" I charged at her, my feet kicking up thick clouds of sand with every step.

When I was a few feet away from her, I pushed up from the ground and launched myself at her back. She stumbled, dropping her gun and falling to her hands and knees as I rolled off of her and into the sand.

"What'd you do that for?" she asked, furious as she pawed around the ground until she could reach her gun.

"Don't shoot them! We don't know if they're officials or just other exiles."

"Are we really willing to risk it?"

"Yes!"

"We have every official in the New Territory hunting us down—I'm not so sure we want to take our chances. Let go!" She kicked her foot back at me as I tried to tug her away from the gun. Her heel slammed into my shoulder. I instinctively pulled back in pain.

"Skylar! Listen to me! What if they're just like Bexa, Cameron, Yulie, me, Braylin, or even you?"

She let out a frustrated sound—an unflattering mixture between a snort, a snarl, and a groan.

"Fine—let's go. We don't have much time," she observed, tucking away her gun and scurrying to her feet.

The figures were becoming alarmingly clear—one was a man, one was a woman. They were in typical all-black uniforms. The woman's strawberry blonde hair was pulled back in a tight ponytail. She took longer strides than the man beside her, despite the fact that he was considerably taller than her. *I'm positive that's an official. The way they walk with that disgustingly familiar air of cockiness is a dead giveaway. If they could drown in their own sense of authority, there wouldn't be any officials left for me to worry about.*

When Skylar and I caught up with Braylin, we were nearing the compact cluster of charred ruins. Just as we slowed our pace to an exhausted trot across the gravel road, a loud *crack* rang out behind me.

"Go!" Skylar yelled, pushing Braylin and me forward, urging us to run.

Just then, there were more cracks as bullets ricocheted off of warped metal and aged brick in the ruins around us. I quickly turned to scramble behind one of the buildings, my shoes grinding against the gravel. My body, unable to keep with the momentum of my feet, lurched forward. I caught myself by throwing my palms in front of me, scraping my hands and wrists on the gravel in the process. With a sharp inhale, I stood and shook it off, continuing to run deeper into the ruins, making as many turns as I could to lose our pursuers. When I rounded another building, I spotted the female official, her rifle butted up against her shoulder as she crept down the empty street. Unfortunately, she must have heard the gravel crunch under my feet. I stopped, unable to decide where to run. She swiveled on her heel and pointed the barrel at me. Frozen, I clenched my teeth and tensed up, preparing for the worst.

Bang.

My eyes instinctively shut, as if to say, "If you can't see her, she can't see you." A few seconds passed, and I felt unscathed. I opened my eyes and spotted Skylar wrestling the rifle from the official's body, which was now crumpled in an unnatural position in the gravel. She threw the strap over her shoulder and turned to face me.

"You're fine. Let's find Braylin."

Speechless, I nodded and followed after her down the alleyway, only stopping when we heard another gunshot.

"This way!" Skylar beckoned, changing her direction and taking off down the street to our left, toward the sound.

We knew we were getting close when we could hear the pained wails of a male voice. I felt my heart drop as I imagined an official letting Braylin bleed out slowly. *They wouldn't be that cruel, would they?* Then I remembered when Raine had her officials force-feed acid to Zane just to get me to talk. *Yes, they would be that cruel.*

When we finally found Braylin, he was clearly distraught, but not because he was injured. The same couldn't be said for the male official, who was writhing against the gravel, clutching his left shoulder with his right hand, which was coated in thick crimson.

"I missed," Braylin admitted in a half-whisper.

The official let out a horrific scream, and the sun glistened off of the blood pooling on his black shirt in his helpless flailing.

Skylar stood there, her mouth gaping open as she turned her attention from the official to Braylin.

"You *missed*?" she asked, dumbfounded.

"He had me cornered, and I had my gun out, and I tried to aim quickly and shoot. I didn't think I had time to carefully aim, and it hit his shoulder instead. I can't bring myself to try again. He's dying, isn't he? I let him die a slow, agonizing death! I didn't mean to put him in any pain—he was just doing his job!"

"You probably shattered his shoulder, too," Skylar observed, crossing her arms and glaring at him.

"Make it stop!" the official wailed.

"Did somebody send you after us?" Skylar interrogated the official, her eyes full of hate as she stared down at him.

"Wh-what?" he managed through gasps. "We were just sent on routine foot patrol!"

"Did somebody—"

"I don't know who you are!" the official insisted, his eyes travelling from Skylar, to Braylin, to me. When he made eye contact with me, he began to speak again. "*Her*. Raine wants *her*."

"So, you've been looking for us," Skylar concluded impatiently.

The official let out another pained yell, thrashing on the ground.

"Do something!" Braylin begged, his panicked eyes apologizing to the man he shot.

Without another word, Skylar pulled her pistol from the back of her jeans, effortlessly aimed at the man, and pulled the trigger. The official slumped backward, releasing his grip on his shoulder. The bullet wound in his shoulder, now exposed, looked far less gruesome than the fresh entry in the man's skull, despite the significant amount of pain it had caused him only seconds ago.

I stared at the body, feeling numb.

I shouldn't feel this way. Why doesn't this hurt? The first time I killed an official, it was also in self-defense, but that time I was so upset I vomited in the back of a truck. I know I wasn't the one who killed this one, but I should still feel something—he was a person. What's wrong with me?

"I said 'do something,' I didn't say kill him! What if he had a family? Don't we have some medical supplies or something?" Braylin's hands shook as he spoke.

Braylin, on the other hand, clearly feels a large range of emotions to make up for my lack of any.

"Some bandages and alcohol wouldn't have fixed a shattered shoulder, Bray," I said.

"No, but it would have at least bought him time to get to one of the cities, right?" he asked, his eyes welling up. "Right?"

"I don't think so," I admitted. "Skylar put him out of his misery—"

"Misery?" he wailed. "I didn't mean to cause him misery! I was just scared, and I thought he was going to kill me, and I didn't think I'd ever see my sister again—I didn't mean to hurt him."

"What did you expect to happen when you fired a gun at the guy?" Skylar bluntly asked.

"I—"

"If you pull the trigger, you have to mean it," Skylar said.

"I know." He sighed. "I knew it would kill him, and I didn't want to. I should have known I'm a terrible shot and just accepted my fate."

"I think you made the right move," I interjected. "First of all, you heard him. They probably have orders to arrest or kill us. But I just think we need to work on your aim before something like this happens again."

"Agreed," Skylar said. "We're going to do target practice until I trust that you're at least somewhat competent with that thing. Deal?"

"If I can't even kill one official, how am I supposed to do this?"

"We'll work on that somehow. If we can avoid being spotted in the first place, I think we can avoid killing. And I'm sure if someone you care about is in danger, it'd be a little easier," Skylar predicted. "Let's focus on staying hidden, but let's make sure you're ready with that gun in the event that it comes to self-defense."

Braylin nodded solemnly.

After an uncomfortable silence, I said, "Go ahead."

Perplexed, Braylin and Skylar looked at me, both of them with furrowed brows.

"Skylar," I started. "You were right. They were dangerous, and I put us all at risk, and I'm sorry."

"Oh, don't pull that whiny crap on me," she grumbled, taking a brief account of her surroundings before heading off toward her left.

Braylin's lips flattened as his eyes bounced between Skylar and me. After an almost comically awkward shrug, he trotted off after her.

With a groan, I adjusted my bag on my shoulder and followed. By the looks of it, we still had hours of daylight left, and we were going to need it.

Fortunately, the daylight passed quickly and without event—after being chased down by two armed officials, I had hit my excitement limit and was looking forward to stopping for the night in some ruins. When we finally spotted some as the sun was setting, I decided to speak up, hoping I wasn't the only one who was ready to call it a day.

"Let's stop here," I said, hoping my voice conveyed a tone of leadership rather than a tone of desperation.

Without any disagreements from my travel companions, we approached the ruins and selected the most structurally sound building we could find to call home for now. Of course, as I've learned with plenty of experience, "structurally sound" is an incredibly generous statement. These ruins were no different than any of the others—just a black spot on an incredibly flat, sandy map. Of all of the buildings in this particular cluster, the one we decided to camp out in simply had a full roof, which is a luxury we didn't always find.

We each picked our makeshift beds, mine being a couch that I first had to beat the dust and ash out of with a pan I found in the kitchen.

"Stop that!" Braylin coughed, fanning the air around him as if he was being swarmed by the dust, despite being on the other side of the room.

"I don't want to hear it!" I said raspily. "I'm the one who's inhaling all of this crap!"

"Clear mine off, while you're at it!" Skylar snickered, waving toward the armchair she agreed to sleep in.

When I had finally cleared off the couch and the armchair, as well as a rug for Braylin, the three of us settled down. Braylin and Skylar both seemed to fall asleep far faster than I did, but when it finally came, sleep hit me hard.

THREE

"How does it feel?" asked a familiar male voice.

My eyes fluttered open, immediately locking on his soft brown eyes as he lay beside me.

I sighed in relief. "Zane."

Relief? Why do I feel relief? I know he's dead, and I know this can't be real.

"How does it feel?" he repeated.

"It feels like everything is right again," I answered softly, reaching out a hand to feel his cheek, but stopping as he pulled back.

"What's wrong?" I asked, unable to help feeling dejected.

"How does it feel," he started again, "knowing you lost the best thing about you?"

"What?" I asked, a lump catching in my throat as I tried to find more to say.

"E? You okay?" I heard another voice as Zane's figure vanished.

I shot up from the sofa, trying to catch my breath.

"E! Hey, Skylar! Wake up! E's choking!" Braylin panicked, grabbing my shoulders to steady me as he took a hand and rapped his palm against my back.

I sputtered and drew in a long, wet breath before my breathing finally returned to normal.

"What happened to you?" Braylin asked, kneeling beside the couch, one of his hands still on my shoulder.

"Nothing," I murmured. "Bad dream."

"Bull," I heard Skylar say from her armchair behind me. "People don't wake up choking because of a simple 'bad dream.'"

"Fine. *Really* bad dream."

"About what?" Braylin asked.

"I don't want to talk about it."

"E," Braylin urged gently.

I rolled my shoulder, pushing away Braylin's hand as I threw off my blanket and rushed out the door without my shoes. I slammed the door behind me, knocking some rubble loose as it tumbled to the ground with a clatter. The rough pavement of the damaged town pricked at my bare feet as I raced behind the nearest building. My heart felt like it was rattling my ribcage with every beat as I slumped against a wall, letting myself slide to the ground with a broken cry.

The thoughts racing through my mind were changing so rapidly I couldn't understand what I was even feeling.

Mad. I should be mad. He's implying there's nothing redeeming about me now that he's gone.

I threw my hands against my face, as if I could just block everything out.

No... I should be sad. That wasn't really Zane—it was all in my head. He's gone.

I ran my fingers through my hair with an exasperated groan.

Why is this in my head? Fear. I should be feeling fear.

"Get up," Skylar commanded, tugging my wrist and pulling me from the ground and my thoughts.

Without a word, she dragged me along behind her, deeper into the ruins. I swore when I stepped on a sharp piece of rubble, but she didn't slow her pace.

"Where are we going?" I asked.

"Not far."

About a block away, she finally stopped and released my wrist, which was now red and throbbing. I rubbed it with my other hand, throwing a bitter glare at Skylar. She paid me no mind, however, and retrieved a hunk of brick from the edge of a dilapidated house.

"Throw it," she instructed, dropping the brick into my hand.

"What?"

"Throw it at the house," she said, stepping out of my way.

"Why?"

She crossed her arms and stared at me. I felt like she was about to count backwards from ten like my mother used to do when I misbehaved as a kid. *Whatever. I'll just humor her.*

I chucked the brick full-force at the blackened side of the house. The brick shattered against the wall, sending shards of rock flying in a cloud of dust.

"Now what?" I asked.

"Again." She dropped another brick into my hand.

Brick after brick, Skylar had me hurl chunks of rubble at the side of that house until my arms could hardly lift another.

"No more," I croaked. "This is pointless."

"One more," she said, holding out another brick to me. "I know there's something bugging you, and I want you to put it in this brick and throw it as hard as you freaking can."

I looked down at the lump of brick in my hand, allowing myself to play back the dream in my head. Just as the mental replay of dream-Zane said, "best thing about you," I launched the brick at the wall with such force that I fell to my knees the moment it left my hand. With a deep rumble, hunks of the wall began to crumble to the ground.

I sat there on my knees for a moment, watching the pieces of rubble tumble.

Skylar reached out a hand to me, helping me up.

"Better?" she asked, her expression genuine, lacking the smugness that I expected.

"Thank you," I muttered, brushing off my knees.

On the way back to our temporary home, I decided to tell Skylar about my dream. She didn't have much to say, but rather, she listened patiently and nodded empathetically. When we returned, Braylin was frantically pacing around the living room.

"Oh, thank God," he said breathily when he saw us. "Where did you find her?"

"She wasn't missing," Skylar said plainly.

"She ran away!"

"She's not a dog. I didn't 'find' her; she didn't 'run away.'"

"I kinda did," I admitted. "I'm sorry. I didn't mean to freak you out—I just needed some air."

"It's okay. I understand," he said with a sympathetic smile. "I made you breakfast!"

"You made me breakfast? How did you 'make' anything?" I asked, my voice coming off far snarkier than I intended.

"I mean, it isn't much. You had some bread in your bag—I'm

sorry for snooping! I found a jar of honey in the cabinets. Totally sealed! Looks brand new! I know it isn't, but it looks fresh, so I decided to drizzle a little on some bread for us." Braylin smiled proudly. "Like I said… nothing gourmet. It's a definite improvement from our usual though."

"Thanks, Bray," I smiled as he handed me a plate with the honey bread.

"Sorry about the plate," he said. "I cleaned them the best I could without using up any of our water. I already tested the water out here—it isn't running. I didn't figure it would be, but once in a while you find some ruins with functioning well water, so I was hopeful."

With his last sentence, he looked down remorsefully at my feet, black from the soot and pavement outside.

"Thank you again," I nodded, lifting the sticky piece of bread to my mouth.

That was one of the best breakfasts I'd eaten in a while.

Skylar and Braylin had target practice after breakfast before we set off for the day. After a few hours of walking, my eyes were beginning to sting from the dust in the air. Looking out across the sandscape, we were able to make out the distinct shape of Fallmont in the distance. Fallmont was the home of Raine Velora, as well as the largest population of citizens of any city in the New Territory. For us, this meant Fallmont was the main place we needed to steer clear of, but unfortunately, it was there on the horizon, watching our every move.

"Did Cindee ever tell you about the waffles?" Braylin asked.

"Yes, she did," I answered. "I feel like I already told you that when we were in Ironwood—didn't I?"

"I don't know. Maybe you did? Ironwood was awful. I try to forget the fact that I was sent to the one remaining prison in the New Territory. That makes me sound like a hardcore fugitive, though, doesn't it?" He smirked.

"Honestly, it just aggravates me," I said. "Raine knows there's a prison in the New Territory already… how is it that far of a stretch to just move the exiles into Ironwood for different sentences based on their crimes?"

"She's stuck in her ways. A lot of people are. They originally didn't use it at all because there weren't enough people to take care of it," he answered.

"But there are enough people now, aren't there?" I argued. "It's taking more people to patrol city streets and go hunting for exiles out in the ruins than it would require for a prison. Why doesn't she just go back to the prison system?"

"Just playing devil's advocate here," Braylin defended. "The exile towns only require a couple drivers to make a trip every once in a while to drop off some low-quality rations. Won't a prison need a lot more officials?"

"Did you not pay attention to the fact that I said there are officials patrolling city streets and hunting down exiles in the ruins? Take those officials and have them guard the prison. They have *plenty* of officials. Plus, the general population has recovered quite a bit."

"I still think the exile towns would require less people to make them work."

"Are you suddenly on their side now?" I asked, unintentionally raising my voice at him.

"No, I just—"

"They have *enough* people—why not just open up Ironwood fully and stop worrying about the exile towns altogether? If they had even *half* as many officials running Ironwood as they do searching and patrolling the cities and ruins, they could make sure people don't break out like we did."

"That's basically what we are trying to change, isn't it?" Braylin asked. "I mean, I'm glad we were able to break out of Ironwood, but if the justice system was actually fair, we wouldn't have to worry about any of this in the first place."

"I'm starting to think I'd rather listen to Braylin ramble about the stupid waffles," Skylar teased. "Stop bickering."

"Yes, mom," I said in a mocking tone, tossing a pebble at her arm.

"Stop that!"

"Remember the time I flicked a spider at you?" I reminded her, a wicked grin creeping across my face.

"Yup," she answered bluntly, clearly not amused by the memory.

"What?" Braylin asked with a laugh. "Tell me more!"

"She flicked a spider at me because she thought I was flirting with her boyfriend," Skylar summarized, grimacing. "Spoiler alert—I wasn't."

"Oh, please!" I said, kicking up sand as I walked. "You were all but throwing yourself at him."

"You really want to start with that? I've got a fun story about you that involves you, a handsome but sleazy man, and some drugs!" Skylar bragged.

"That's not funny," I crossed my arms.

"Woah," Braylin said, his eyes wide.

"And you still stayed friends with the guy!" Skylar exclaimed.

"He's not a bad guy, Skylar!"

"I beg to differ."

"Can we slow down?" Braylin asked.

"We're trying to make it before nightfall," Skylar reminded him.

"No," he started. "I didn't mean slow down our walking. I meant the story! What is this about drugs?"

Skylar motioned sarcastically with a curtsey and a roll of her hands for me to speak.

"When we were in Fortitude," I started. "I may have taken a pill. Only one! And it was the only time I've ever done something like that."

The playful arguments continued until Fallmont grew alarmingly close. I advised the other two to begin veering our path to the right, steering clear of Fallmont without losing sight of it. When a majority of the land is desert wasteland, cities and towns are the best landmarks we have to compare to our map.

As we walked, we made sure to keep a consistent distance away from Fallmont, frequently scanning its perimeter for any movement in case we needed to take off running. After a silent, tense few hours, Fallmont was eventually far enough in the distance that we were able to relax enough to let our guard down a bit.

"What are we going to put in the first letter?" Braylin finally broke the silence.

"I think we should say something about some of the exiles that have been unfairly treated because of Raine's outdated system," I said matter-of-factly.

"So… everyone?" Skylar asked.

"What?" I turned to her.

"You said we should write about the people who have been unfairly treated. That's literally every exile ever."

"Oh. I mean, not necessarily all of them, but that's a valid point. I've met a few people who had it really bad. That girl I told you about who lives in Clamorite—the one with the fiancé—she'd be a good subject for our letters. Or my friend Paren."

I filled them in on the details of how Paren was exiled to Bellicose for life because he defended a girl from a creep in a bar. Skylar groaned through my entire story, throwing in an occasional dramatic eye roll.

"That's just ridiculous. Weren't there witnesses who could testify in his defense or something?" she asked.

I shrugged. "Even if there were, do you think Raine would have given him the time of day? She thinks everyone who doesn't fit into her little conformist bubble is a monster and needs to be kept locked up. That's why I think we need to write about him and Lisette."

"Lisette?" Skylar asked.

"The Clamorite girl who was arrested protesting for her marriage," I clarified.

"Right. My bad."

"Sounds like a plan," Braylin agreed.

Skylar nodded.

"I feel like all of this talk about Raine and the government is making me realize how long this is all going to take. I'm up for the challenge, but I'm ready to start with the first step at least. Are we almost to Avid yet?" Braylin asked, dramatically letting his head sink to his chest.

After what felt like an endless walk, we could finally spot Avid. Once at the gates, Skylar pulled the Key out of her pocket and handed it to me.

This is so much easier than when I had to clumsily climb a tree and jump over the brick wall when I first left Avid.

I twisted the dial on the Key until I felt the pins lock into place. Effortlessly, I turned the Key and heard the gate unlock. Pocketing the Key, I ushered my friends in behind me, being sure to close the gate after us.

For a moment, it was as if I never left Avid. It still gave me that uneasy, unwelcomed feeling in the pit of my stomach—the same horrible feeling I had every moment I was there before my escape. There in front of us was the grey brick well and the town center—just as deserted as I remembered.

"Where is everyone?" Skylar asked.

"Probably inside, at the dump, or maybe the gardens," I replied, moving forward into the town circle surrounded by tall buildings that could only be compared to dilapidated hotels.

"Gardens?" Skylar scoffed. "Dump or gardens. I can't even tell if you're being serious."

"I am. The gardens and the dump are both that way," I waved my hand to the side carelessly. "We're headed to my old building though."

"Why would thieves have a garden?" Skylar asked, clearly still caught up on the idea.

"Sometimes rations weren't enough—thieves like to eat as much as anyone. Did you not have gardens somewhere in Delaisse?"

"No! Were there gardens in Clamorite?" Skylar turned to Braylin.

"Yeah. We lived in probably the greenest place in the New Territory. It'd be really stupid to not bother growing some of our own food."

Skylar stared back at him in disbelief.

"Apparently druggies and vandals don't like to eat their veggies," Braylin teased.

Skylar punched him in the shoulder and he let out a sharp yip.

"Seriously, guys?" I turned back to glare at them as I reached for the door of my past residence. "Are you trying to draw attention to us?"

I opened the door and peeked in.

Inside, there was just one boy sitting on the couches in the common area playing a card game by himself. His slight portly figure, caramel skin, and dark hair looked familiar, but the sullen look on his face was new.

Luka.

I took a deep breath.

Luka was terrible to me while I was in Avid. He stole my clothes while I was in the shower, he messed with my belongings, and he was generally rude to me. I originally thought Zane had been the one terrorizing me, but it turns out Luka was the one I should have avoided. As annoying as he was, he was harmless.

"It's safe," I whispered to my friends, opening the door for the three of us.

Luka looked up from his cards, his sunken eyes meeting mine. His expression went from one of depression to one of disbelief.

"Where the hell have *you* been?" he gaped. "And who are they? And where are Lamb and Zane?"

I felt my stomach sting as I forced down the lump in my throat at the reminder of my friends.

"They're not here," I replied vaguely. "This is Skylar, and this is Braylin."

Skylar kept a stoic face, but Braylin offered a timid and awkward wave.

Luka didn't break eye contact with me.

"What do you mean they aren't here?" he demanded, his face twitching subtly, as if trying to convey anger and intimidation, but the fear on his face was undeniable.

My eyes began to burn, and I bit my lip as I tried to think of how to put everything into words.

"Oh," he answered, running a hand shakily through his thick hair, turning away from me. "What happened to them?"

He turned back to face me as he spoke again, "Never mind." His voice cracked slightly. "I don't want to know."

"I'm sorry, Luka," I said. "I know you were friends with them both."

He shrugged. "Why are you here?"

"We need paper and pens," I answered.

"You seriously risked coming back to Avid for paper and pens? Jackson knows you ran off."

"Who's Jackson?" Braylin asked.

"Town representative," I replied, remembering Avid's creepy leader—a lanky man with gingery brown hair, a face full of tiny cuts, and a voice so shrill that the hair on your neck would prick right up.

"You do realize if Jackson sees you, he's going to report you, right?" Luka continued.

"That's why he can't see us. Please."

"Alright. But you have to fill me in on why paper and pens are worth getting caught."

"Deal."

FOUR

Shortly after we arrived at Avid, the sun had completely set. We filled Luka in on some of the things Raine had done to other exiles, and how we planned to write and deliver letters to people to expose her. His lips twisted into a thrilled grin as he muttered a "serves her right."

We decided to stick around for a day, where we'd have better access to food and water, even if only for a while. The three of us promised each other we wouldn't make it a long-term thing.

That night, Luka pointed to some of the doors of unoccupied rooms, reminding me that the locks in Avid were easy to pick.

"Shouldn't be a problem," I nodded, the weight of the Key in my pocket seemingly growing.

"I can help you write those letters in the morning if you want. I'll take my breakfast to go and share with you guys—I'm not much of a breakfast person anyways."

"Why are you being so nice to us?" I asked, crossing my arms and glaring at Luka.

"I'm sorry, I can stop." He grinned smugly.

I rolled my eyes. "I don't mean it like that. I mean, honestly, you were a jerk to me when I was here before."

"I'm not doing it for you."

"Meaning?"

"The exile town system is inhumane," he said. "If we went back to using prisons instead, I would have been home by now, or at least soon. Instead, I get to rot in this crap hole. I'm just willing to help however I can. It's not like I have a problem with you."

"Then why did you torment me?"

He shrugged.

"Whatever. I'm just glad you're helping now."

"Just being a model citizen," he said dryly. "Night."

That night, Skylar, Braylin, and I dragged a mattress from one room into another, which allowed us to stay in the same room. We slept soundly, locked in a room together.

Morning came and Luka was—surprisingly—true to his word.

"I've got a couple pieces of toast, a muffin, and some apricots," he said, holding out a plate, a few pens and a stack of paper in his other hand.

"Thanks," I said, taking the food, splitting it up and passing some to Braylin and Skylar. "Let's get some writing done, I guess."

"You should write the first one," Skylar suggested, handing me one of the pens. "I just think you know the stories of these people better than we do, so you should write the first one and we can all copy it."

"Good point."

I pulled out one of the pieces of paper and clicked the pen.

How do I even start this?

I wiggled my pen between my fingers, staring down at the paper on the floor as I sat there.

"It doesn't have to be poetic or anything—just write," Skylar said, narrowing her eyes.

I sighed, leaned forward, and began to write.

Dear friend,

Has anyone close to you ever been exiled for a violent crime? For theft? For vandalism, drug possession, lying, or noise polluting? Maybe you've lost someone to this horrible system, or maybe you're blissfully unaware of the state our government is in and how they treat criminals in the New Territory. The war was many years ago—before my time. Before your time. Our society has had time to recover, and the population is stronger than ever since the war. The exile towns are no longer a necessary alternative to prisons. Let me tell you about some of the people our government has allowed to suffer.

The words began to come to me faster than I could write, and I had to restrain myself from writing any faster—we needed these letters to be legible. I wrote every detail that I knew about Paren's story and Lisette's story.

When I had finished, I put my pen down and handed the letter to my friends.

"How's this?" I asked.

I watched Skylar and Braylin's eyes darting across the page as they read. Braylin finished reading before Skylar and kept glancing between her face and letter, impatiently waiting for her to finish it.

"So?" I pried.

"It gets the point across," Braylin said honestly. "It isn't the most eloquent thing I've ever read, but we don't need it to be. I think it'll work. It's genuine, and that's what we need."

"Let me see." Luka grabbed for the letter, taking a seat beside Skylar.

When Luka had finished reading the letter, we each reached for a pen and stack of paper and began copying the original letter, word for word. After a couple hours of writing, I had an idea, and I desperately needed a break from writing.

"I'll be right back," I said, letting out a groan as I stood and stretched my legs.

"Nuh-uh," Skylar said, looking up from her letter, brows furrowed.

"Pardon?" I asked with an uncomfortable laugh.

"Where ya going?"

"To see an old friend," I answered. "Chill."

"Excuse me?" she said, her voice defensive as she sat upright.

The boys put down their pens and watched with wide eyes.

"Sorry," I said. "I just need to get out of here for a few minutes."

"I'm coming with you," she said, standing up.

"It's easier for me to sneak from here to there by myself. More people means more chances of being seen. I'll be careful—I'm not going far, and I won't be long."

"Where are you going?" Luka asked. "That way we know where to start looking if you aren't back soon."

"It's just the building with the oldest thieves," I said with a shrug.

"She'll be fine," Luka said to Skylar, holding her pen out to her to continue writing. Reluctantly, she sat back down.

"I won't be gone long at all—I promise." I stepped out of the room, closing the door gently behind me.

I trotted carefully down the stairs and out of the building, peeking around the door to make sure Jackson was nowhere in sight. A cluster of people were lounging out in the town center around the brick well, laughing and talking. *It's a nice day out,* I tried to reassure myself. *They're probably all too busy relaxing and hanging out to notice you. Act natural.*

Tentative nonetheless, I walked briskly from Luka's building to one of the others, my goal clear in my mind. The people around the brick well continued chatting, seemingly unaware of my presence—or perhaps they just didn't question it. When I reached the door, I checked the inside for people. There were a few elderly men—two were heavily invested in a game of chess, and the third was asleep in a plush red armchair. I ran up the stairs, which looked essentially identical to the other. I stopped in front of one of the doors and took a deep breath before knocking gently.

"Mr. Montgomery?" I called softly.

A moment later, the doorknob started to turn and I heard a voice coo a hesitant, "yes?"

When he opened the door all the way, his face lit up and a wrinkled smile crept across his liver spotted face.

"Miss Dawn! What brings you here?"

"I wanted to show you something," I started. "May I come in?"

"Of course!" He swung the door open, ushering me into his room full of knick-knacks he had collected over the years from the trash mounds.

I took a seat in a wobbly wooden chair, and Mr. Montgomery sat in a tattered leather chair across from me, the cushion letting out a deep squeak as he leaned back.

Without saying another word, I dug out the Skeleton Key and held it in display in front of me.

"My word," he breathed. "It that really it?"

I nodded, handing him the Key.

"How?"

I told him about the exile town keys and some of the people I had met and things I had faced along the way. His eyes ignited with excitement as I shared details about leaping off the side of the cliffs of Equivox, learning to fight against the supervisor of Bellicose, and breaking out of Fallmont with the Skeleton Key.

"That's incredible!" he exclaimed with a toothy smile, handing the

Key back to me. "What an adventure! Thank you so much for coming to tell me about it. I can't tell you how much I enjoy a good adventure story. You've grown so much from when you were the timid new exile who stole my pudding."

"If you like adventure stories, you'd love to hear about Fortitude," I said, crossing my legs and leaning back in my chair.

"Fortitude?"

"It's a secret city full of escaped exiles. It's not in the New Territory—it took ages to walk to."

"Don't stop there!" Mr. Montgomery urged, leaning forward in his seat. "What was it like?"

"It was fantastic, really. But a bunch of criminals in a city without laws turned out to be more dangerous than I had hoped. I made a friend along the way—her name was Yulie. She was pregnant and someone had attacked her and stabbed her while we were there. Last I heard, she was doing better, and they were hoping to save the baby, but I haven't heard anything new about her. I have no way of knowing."

"That's horrible," Mr. Montgomery sighed, his smile fading.

"The city itself wasn't horrible—just some of the people in it. The city was completely functioning like any of the cities in the New Territory—there were shops and restaurants. They even had a club where people would dance and drink together. If you were careful, Fortitude was a great place for exiles to live if they wanted their freedom back."

"Why'd you leave?"

"Well," I started, my eyes stinging. "My boyfriend left with me—we wanted to break into Raine's office and tell her why the exile town system is unfair and outdated."

"Hmm," Mr. Montgomery grumbled. "That can't have gone well."

"Understatement of the century," I moaned. "Long story short, I ended up in Ironwood and one of my friends broke me out. And now we're here."

"Why Avid, of all places? Why not go back to Fortitude?"

"I gave Raine a chance to keep her dignity. I'm done with that. I've got a small group of exiles with me, and we're writing letters to slide under peoples' doors in the cities to tell them about some of the corrupt things Raine has done. People deserve to know."

Mr. Montgomery chuckled. "You're a ball of fire, aren't you? I admire your persistence. I wish there was a way I could help. I can't stand that woman. Most exiles don't deserve to be banished from their families and friends for life—I wish someone would take *her* freedom. That'd be the ultimate justice."

"I agree," I sighed. "I just hope this works."

"Even if it doesn't, you won't give up until something does," he reached out and patted my knee before standing and moseying toward a box in the far corner of the room.

He rummaged around for a minute until he retrieved what he was looking for.

"Here," he said, holding out a marbled pen. "I may not be able to do much to help, but I'd love to know that ink from my pen helped bring Raine down."

His eyes twinkled with excitement as he handed me the marbled pen. It felt cool, and it was heavier than I expected.

"Thanks," I said, twisting the pen tip out and testing it on my hand. The ink was blue and wrote smoothly. "I should probably get back to my friends and help write more letters. It was good talking to you!"

Mr. Montgomery wished me luck before I left. When I returned to the room, Luka and Skylar were still busy writing, and Braylin had been tasked with counting letters.

"We were beginning to wonder if you'd ever come back," Luka teased.

"I was betting that you'd happen to come back just as we were finishing up the last letter," Skylar said without looking up from her current page.

"Sorry—I had someone I needed to go see," I admitted, sitting and taking a blank paper from the top of the stack. "How many do we have so far?"

Braylin held up a finger and continued to thumb through the stack of completed letters.

"44… 45… 46," he muttered.

"Please don't talk to him. He'll have to start all over again, and he already whined about that a few minutes ago when Luka thought it'd be funny to spout off random numbers while Braylin counted."

"51… 52…53. We have 53—"

Skylar tossed her paper at him. "Done."

Braylin grunted. "54. We have—"

"Me too," Luka smirked, flinging his letter at Braylin as well.

"Seriously guys?" He snatched up the paper and added it to the neat stack. "We have *55* Dawn Letters done. Including the original. We're definitely going to want more letters."

"Hang on," I stopped him. "What did you call them?"

"Dawn Letters," he replied. "Taking down Raine means more to you than anyone I think. Plus, you remember what I told you about the meaning of your name?"

"Dawn Dawn?" I asked.

"Yes, but it's more than that. Eos was the Greek goddess of the dawn, but do you know what 'dawn' also referred to?"

I raised an eyebrow, not saying anything back to him.

"The coming of a new day. *That's* why I think we should call them Dawn Letters."

"I like it!" Skylar chimed in.

"I have an idea," Braylin said. "It'll only take a few seconds longer per letter, but if… *when* we deliver others later, it will unify them—it'll give people a name to remember—something that will stick with them. Let's just sign each of the letters as 'Dawn.'"

"I mean, if you guys want to. I don't want to cause more work than necessary," I said.

"It makes sense. I say we do it," Luka agreed.

Braylin was right—it only took us a few minutes with the four of us to sign each of the letters with 'Dawn.' When we were done, it was Skylar to break the silence after the frantic scratching of pens.

"Where should we deliver letters first?"

"I think we should hit Fallmont first. It's the biggest population, and they're in more direct relation to Raine anyways. It'll take longer to drag her down if we start with the cities where people never even interact with her," I answered.

"Not looking forward to going to Fallmont," Braylin muttered. "But you're right."

Skylar nodded in agreement and turned to look at Luka.

"What?" he asked.

"What about you?" Skylar asked.

Luka snorted. "I'm not going *with* you guys!"

"Why not?" Braylin asked.

"Because I'm not stupid! You guys are already deep in this mess. Me? I'm comfortable here, and no one is hunting me down. I'd like to keep it that way. I'll help however you need from here. I can keep writing letters—not like I have much else going on anyways. But I'm not leaving."

Skylar snarled, "You can't be seri—"

"—he has a point, and he can still be useful to us from here. Even more so, probably. That's one less person to watch out for and worry about getting caught, and it's a constant source of letters," I rationalized. "I'll take a turn writing for a while. You guys go ahead and take a break."

Using Mr. Montgomery's marble pen, I copied my original letter over and over again while my friends stretched out across the floor with exhausted groans.

A while later, Luka disappeared. About the time that I was sure that my hand was bound to be covered in blisters forever, Luka returned with food in his arms.

"You snagged us some dinner!" Braylin smiled warmly.

Luka set down a plate and a bowl. "Take your pick—baked potato or vegetable soup. I call dibs on a roll and half the roast chicken."

"Ditto," Skylar said.

I turned to Braylin with a shrug. "How about we split the potato and soup?" I suggested, my stomach gurgling at the spiced smells filling the room.

We spent the evening eating, hanging out, taking turns showering, and eventually forcing ourselves to write more letters. The later it got, the more my vision blurred with sleepiness and the more my hand refused to write.

"I'm calling it a night," Luka said, yawning as he made his way to the door. "You guys are more than welcome to sleep in separate rooms, by the way. The rooms on either side of this one are empty. See you all in the morning."

"Night," we called to him.

"I think I'm done for the day, too," Skylar said. When she turned to me, I could see her eyes were bloodshot. "I'll be next door."

Braylin and I tried to finish the letters we were working on, but I couldn't keep my eyes open for even one more letter.

"I think I'm going to go to bed," I said, massaging my sore hand sleepily. "Thanks for your help."

"Are you going to be okay alone tonight?" Braylin asked, setting down his pen.

"Yeah. Why?"

"I just know Zane was here the last time you were in Avid, and I just want to make sure you'll be okay."

"I'm fine," I mumbled. "Thanks."

Braylin put a hand on my shoulder in an awkward attempt to be comforting before he stood.

"You can have this room. I'll take whichever one Skylar didn't take. Let me know if you need anything."

When Braylin had finally left, there was a noticeable silence, making me consciously aware of my own loud breathing.

Well, that's obnoxious.

I tried to quiet my breathing but just ended up frustrating myself.

It's way too quiet in here.

I crawled over to the mattress and flopped over. Fortunately, I was so exhausted that even the silence wasn't enough to keep me from sleep.

FIVE

I was back in Raine's office, my hands gripped tight around the office doorknob as officials yelled at me from the other side. Across from me, Zane was beside Raine's desk, just as he had been in his last moment when he was begging her to reconsider the prison system. Instead of pounding on her desk and arguing with her as I recalled, he turned to me. His once soft brown eyes now looked void of the joy and love they used to carry. There was nothing there anymore as he stared at me. His lips curved slowly upward into a malicious sneer. Suddenly, the officials stopped yelling and it was completely silent.

"Glad to know none of this was *my* fault," he said, his voice piercing the eerie quiet.

He turned slowly back to face Raine.

"No—" I muttered under my breath as I tried to let go of the handle, tried to run and push him out of the way, but I was unable to move.

Bang.

"No!" I screamed as everything went black.

"Eos! Stop!"

I felt a strange pressure on my shoulders and something warm over my mouth. I tried to suck in a breath but felt myself choking. My eyes shot open in panic.

Braylin and Skylar squatted over me. Braylin was pushing my shoulders down, and Skylar's hand was over my mouth. Their eyes were both wild with fear as they looked from me to Luka, who was peeking cautiously out of a crack in the door.

I started flailing, breathing heavily through my nose.

"Erm rker," I tried to speak. "Ler ger! Gef ferf mmm!"

Skylar released my mouth, and Braylin pulled his hands back. I sucked in a cool breath and wiped Skylar's palm sweat from my mouth.

"What's going on?" I asked.

"Shh!" Luka looked over his shoulder and glared at me. "Jackson was doing rounds and you started screaming —now shut up!"

We sat there in silence for a moment when suddenly Luka stepped out of the room and shut the door instantly behind him.

"Hey, Jackson," I heard him say, his voice muffled from the other side of the door.

"Luka," Jackson's familiar voice rang out. It was just as cringe-worthy and high-pitched as I remembered. "May I ask what you're doing hanging out in empty rooms?"

"Hiding stuff," he answered gruffly. "People assume I'd keep things in my own room, so no one would bother breaking into an empty room looking for valuables. Can't trust these 'dirty thieves,' can we?"

Jackson let out a crackly giggle. "That's an interesting idea, and you make a great point."

I felt myself relax at his words.

Good job, Luka.

"Unfortunately, I don't believe you."

My body went cold.

"What?" Luka asked.

"I've seen you take your meals out of the cafeteria a couple times now, and I had someone from your building ask me who the 'new kids' are. We haven't had any new exiles in about a month. Are you hiding some visitors and feeding them? Answer me honestly, Luka." Jackson spoke with an unnerving calmness.

"No. I've been coming back and eating in the lobby while playing cards—see for yourself. My cards are still on the table downstairs."

"That's all well and good," Jackson was growing impatient. "But I'm going to need to inspect that room you're nervously blocking—the fact that you widened your stance just now was a bit of a giveaway!—so please move. This is the last time I'm going to ask."

I began to frantically scan the room for options—there was no window, nothing to hide in, nowhere to go.

Our only options are to try to reason with him, or…

I didn't want to think about it, but I didn't really have a choice.

I felt around in my bag until my fingers felt cool metal.

A gun is too loud.

My fingers wrapping around the metal, I slid my dagger out of my bag. This dagger has served me well and saved my skin multiple times since Zane gave it to me after finding it in some ruins shortly after we escaped Avid in the first place. *Hopefully I don't need it to save me today.*

There was a crushing *thunk* as the door crashed open, breaking my thoughts. I caught a glimpse of Jackson's ratty ginger-brown hair and scarred face as he came toppling into the room and crashing onto the floor, Luka barreling on top of him.

Jackson released a horrendous screech as Luka pinned his scrawny neck to the ground. Jackson reached out, clawing and snarling at Luka like some kind of rabid animal.

"What are you doing?" Skylar hollered at Luka over the chaos. "Someone's going to hear!"

"I think we're way beyond that!" Braylin replied, peering out of the doorframe before turning his attention back to Luka. "You're killing him!"

"That's the point!" Luka grumbled, swatting Jackson's flailing arms away and throwing his own wide hands back down on Jackson's neck. "I'm sick of how he treats us! Like trash! As if he's any better!"

"Don't kill him!" I growled, trying to pull Luka off of him.

Luka kicked at me, narrowly missing my knee.

"We'll tie him up! Just don't kill him!"

After a few weak attempts to fight back, Jackson's head eventually sunk and his arms went limp with a soft pat as they hit the floor.

Luka pulled his hands back from Jackson's neck and shook them as if he had touched something nasty. He turned to us, his eyes wide and his lips slightly parted as if he had something to say.

"Is he dead?" I asked awkwardly, my eyes bouncing between him and Jackson.

Luka stood shakily to his feet. He ran the back of his hand under his nose with a loud sniff before grunting, "I'm good. He's fine. He's just unconscious. I'll get something to tie him up—just stay here."

He disappeared behind the door and returned a moment later with some thin, stained rope.

"What's that from?" Braylin asked, eyeing the filthy rope.

"We collect trash here," Luka answered as if it were a common-sense question.

Luka used some of the rope to tie Jackson's hands and feet together just as he was beginning to stir.

"What am I supposed to do now?" Luka asked, his eyes red. "Keep him locked in here forever? As soon as he gets out, he's going to kill me or have me dragged off to Ironwood or—"

Luka began to hyperventilate.

"You can come with us, or you can stay. Your options haven't changed. If you stay, you'll just have to keep him locked up for a while. If our plan works, the exile towns will be done and you'll be safe."

"Who knows how long that'll be," Luka said breathlessly.

"When I was in Delaisse, we lost two town reps in a month because one of the druggies was absolutely psychotic. Officials never did anything about it except pick a new representative. If he stays locked up in here for a while, no one will question where he went," Skylar said.

"What happened to the guy who did it?" Luka asked.

Skylar shrugged. "My uncle told me he overdosed on whatever he was on. Point is—you're still safe here. Officials don't even care if criminals are killing criminals. That's one less person to send rations for, in their eyes. I wouldn't go drawing attention to yourself for tying him up and keeping him prisoner, but you're safe if you decide to stay. Once one of the officials notices that Jackson isn't around anymore to answer their questions, they'll probably move on and pick a new rep. Honestly, the new rep is who you should be careful of—they might be worse, especially if they have to be paranoid that someone is going to kidnap or kill them. Just don't let people know. Give him food and water, and keep him locked up. No one has to know."

Luka looked lost in the room as he processed.

"The three of us need to leave as soon as possible. Officials are already looking for us. Are you coming with or staying here?" I asked.

"Remember, if you come with us, there's no turning back. As soon as even the first official sees you with us, you'll be associated with us from then out. There's no going back. You'll have a target on you just like we do. Stay here, and nothing has to change for you. You'll still be alone here, but you've already helped make a stand with how much you've helped us. It's up to you if you want to do more and risk everything, or stay here," Skylar said. "And there are risks involved with that too—it just depends what level of risk you're up for. Here, the worst that could happen would be Jackson escaping—by the sounds of it, no one else would care that he's missing."

"I—" Luka gaped back at me. "I can't do it. I'm sorry. I'm so sorry. I can't go with."

"It's okay, Luka!" I said. "Honestly, I don't blame you. It sucks out there—"

"It sucks in here," he said gruffly. "I just can't bring myself to leave."

"I understand," I said. "You've helped so much already—thank you."

"Of course," he said, his head hung low. "Let me know if I can ever help in any way. I'd have no problem making Raine look like that." He pointed to Jackson, who was beginning to blink back the light groggily. "Or worse."

"I can think of something," Skylar said. "More paper. And food. Your rep is tied up—now would be a *great* time to snag some for us."

"No problem—that's something I can do," Luka smiled. "If two of you want to grab more paper, the third can come with me to get food. Just be quick and be careful—people have already noticed that there are 'new people' here."

"I'll come with," Skylar's hand shot in the air.

"Perfect. We'll be back in a few minutes."

Braylin and I filled our bags with the completed letters and as much paper as we could, as well as a few pens—including the marbled pen from Mr. Montgomery. We reorganized our bags to make space for food, and before we knew it, Skylar and Luka had returned with a couple bags full of food and water. We crammed our backpacks as full as we could but still had an extra bag full of rations.

"Keep it," Luka said. "I get hot meals every day. You'll need that way more than I will. You guys should probably get going pretty soon. It's still early, so officials won't be here for a while, but best to get a head start."

"Thanks again for everything," I said, feeling genuinely grateful for Luka. Every petty thing he had done to me when I was living in Avid seemed like it was all just a make-believe story. When I looked at him now, he looked like nothing more than a nervous kid who lost his only friends.

"Thank you," Skylar and Braylin repeated.

"Stay safe," Luka said.

"We will," I reached out and hugged him. Clearly catching him off-guard, he let his hands hang at his sides for a second before throwing them around me and squeezing me back.

"Oh!" Braylin exclaimed as Luka and I separated. "I almost forgot."

He fished around in his bag and pulled out one of the letters, holding it out to Luka.

"In case you decide to write more. But we understand if you don't. We also don't know when or *if* we will be coming to Avid again anytime soon, especially after—"

"Got it," Luka said with an awkward half-smile and a nod.

"In case we can't make it back," I said. "Thank you again. Really."

"Shall we?" Skylar asked, cutting me off.

Braylin and I exchanged glances before nodding at Skylar.

Outside the gates of Avid, Skylar, Braylin, and I began our trek back toward Fallmont. The walk took less than a day to make, but the sun was out. We had to wait until night to deliver the letters. We reached some ruins a relatively safe distance from Fallmont before stopping for the day in an old brick house.

"I'm going to try to knock out some more letters before tonight if anyone wants to join," Braylin offered, taking a seat in a faded wood chair in the kitchen.

"I've got nothing better to do," I said, joining him at the kitchen table.

"Except watch paint dry, eat dirt, and jump off a cliff," Skylar muttered, receiving confused stares from Braylin and me. "Kidding! Sheesh. I *love* writing the same letter over and over! Could do it for days!"

"That's good!" I joked back. "Maybe Braylin and I ought to leave you here to write while we deliver the first batch."

"Ha!" Skylar smirked. "And let you two get caught so soon? You don't stand a chance without me!"

By the time the sun was beginning to set, we had 106 Dawn Letters. We divvied the letters up—35 each, with one extra so we could copy the original again later.

"When we get there," I started as we made our way to Fallmont. "I think we should stick together. I know we could cover a greater area faster if we split up, but we need to watch out for each other. Let's stick close together and keep making our way down each street until we all run out of letters. It'll be plenty dark when we get there, so we have that going for us."

"Good plan," Braylin said.

"If we do get separated, meet back at last night's ruins, if you can," Skylar suggested.

"Perfect," I said, thumbing through my stack of letters. "Well, we've got our plan. What could possibly go wrong?"

SIX

The walls of Fallmont towered ahead of us. We crouched in the sand dunes, illuminated only by the moonlight, expecting to see guards looking out at every angle. It was always alarming seeing guards in our path, but this time, there were none. Something about it felt ominous.

"Where are they all?" Braylin asked what we were each wondering.

"I don't know, but I don't trust it," Skylar replied.

"Is it possible all the officials are spread throughout the New Territory searching for us and there aren't enough left to guard the gates? Or is that blind optimism?" I asked.

"That's just stupidity," Skylar said. "It's a trap. We're still going to deliver the letters, but we definitely have to watch our backs more than we already thought."

"Let's make a run for it. Stay low. Keep your gun where it's easy to reach, but only use it in emergencies. I've also got my dagger if we need, but hopefully we won't. Once we get to the gate, I'll open it with the Key," I said, clutching the Key in my right hand. "From there, we hit the closest houses we can find."

Skylar and Braylin didn't argue.

"Alright. Let's go!"

We took off in a careful but uncomfortable run as we tried to stay crouched down until we reached the walls of Fallmont. Once we reached the gate, I motioned with my finger for the other two to stay put as I crept around the corner, peering through the gate. No one. *This doesn't look right.*

I waved Braylin and Skylar toward me as I began to unlock the gate with the Skeleton Key.

"Hey!" someone hissed.

"What?" I whispered back at my friends.

"That wasn't us," Skylar replied.

I peered through the gate again, trying to search for the mysterious figure.

"Get back!" the voice warned. It seemed louder. Closer.

"Where is it coming from?" I panicked, my head spinning, now scanning the sand scape for the source.

"Up here!"

Reluctantly, I looked up at the top of the wall.

There Fabian sat, straddling the wall with his stomach and chest pressed flat against the top as he looked down at us.

"Oh, hell no," I grit my teeth.

"Watch out," Fabian warned, sitting up rapidly. He reached on the side of the wall opposite us and, with a deep grunt, pulled a wooden ladder over the top of the wall. He plopped the end of the ladder into the sand on our side with a quiet *psssbttt* before quickly scurrying down.

Before he reached the halfway point, I threw myself at the ladder, knocking it and him to the side and into the sand. Fabian groaned as he sat up and rolled his shoulders.

"I probably deserved that," he grumbled, fumbling in the sand for his large-rimmed glasses.

"Damn right you deserve that, you traitor!" I growled, pulling out my dagger.

"What's going on?" Braylin asked, his eyes darting between Fabian and me. "Do I shoot him?"

"*You* don't shoot anybody," Skylar said, her hand hovering over her gun at her waist.

"Nobody shoot anybody!" Fabian exclaimed. "I'm here to help. Whatever you need. I don't care why you're trying to get back into Fallmont, but I'll do whatever you need!"

"Liar!" I spat. "He's a traitor! He turned Zane and me in when we were in Fallmont searching for the Key, and then they tortured him! They made Zane drink acid! And it's all *his* fault!"

"I know I don't deserve forgiveness. I know I can't make it up to you. I know you hate me, and frankly, I don't blame you," Fabian said, his tight strawberry blonde curls bouncing on top of his head as he lowered his head in shame.

I spun the hilt of the dagger in my hand, training it on him from a distance.

"Woah," he said calmly, holding his empty palms outward. "How can I prove it to you?"

"You can't!"

"Just let me explain myself," he said with a shaky exhale.

"You have one minute," I narrowed my eyes, never lowering my weapon.

"I'll take it," he forced a relieved smile, reminiscent of his familiar dorky grin I was once so used to.

"59… 58," I began to count.

"Okay, okay! After you two were arrested, I went back home. I was disgusted with myself—you were my best friend ever since I could remember, and I betrayed you."

"50… 49," I spoked up again.

"Uhm—" Fabian contemplated a summary. "I sat in their rooms! When people were exiled and put in the holding cells in Fallmont—I'd request guard duty and I'd spend some time in the rooms with the exiles. I wanted to hear their stories. I figured if my best friend was an exile, not all exiles could be bad like I thought. They're still people with stories and friends and families. I tried to let one go—I did. They caught me just before I had a chance. The other officials didn't know that I was going to let her go, but they found out I had been sitting in the holding rooms, and they didn't like that, so they let me go. I'm not an official anymore. I hate that I ever reported you—and I have to live with knowing I hurt my best friend. But now I understand—this system is corrupt. Some exiles truly are dangerous, but some of them were exiled for horrible reasons! When I betrayed you…I didn't understand at the time that our world has a pretty skewed view of right and wrong, and words can't express how sorry I am. I'll always be sorry. I don't know why in the world you would come back to Fallmont after that, but I'll do whatever you want to make it up to you."

I stood for a moment, still in a defensive pose, wielding my dagger.

"I don't believe you," I shrugged, cocking my head to the side before creeping closer to Fabian.

"Please!" he wailed, dropping to his knees, palms still displayed. His small hazel eyes grew red as they welled up with tears. "I don't know how else to prove it to you. I'll do anything!"

"It doesn't matter!"

"Please!"

"There's nothing you can—"

"They took mom!" he howled. "One day I told mom about the girl I was going to set free—Maddie—and after they fired me, my mom snuck in and freed her. Maddie was a single mom. She was only twenty years old and she had an infant. She stole money to buy diapers when they arrested her. My mom cried through the whole story and couldn't stand knowing that Maddie and her baby would be separated. One of my friends—an official—told me what happened when they exiled my mom. They didn't even let me say goodbye, and nobody told me where they sent her."

My eyes began to sting as I watched my old best friend melt in front of me.

"I had no idea," I sighed, letting my arm fall to my side. "I'm so sorry, Fabian. Your mother was like family to me." I let the dagger fall into the sand, where it sunk blade-first with a soft thump.

He nodded rapidly, sniffling as he removed his glasses to wipe his eyes.

"I really do want to help," he said, looking up at me, still on his knees as I approached him to help him up.

"I want to trust you, Fabian, I do," I said. "I'm going to let you in on part of what we're doing, but if I find out you've betrayed us at any point, I will make sure I'm the one to kill you. Please don't put me in that position."

"I won't. I promise!"

Skylar and Braylin stood on the side, staring back at Fabian and me.

"Before I tell you anything, answer something for me," I started.

"What's that?"

"Where is everyone?"

"Raine set up a curfew in Fallmont. Everyone's at home right now. I heard from some of my friends about how you broke out of Ironwood. It isn't public knowledge, but Raine told all the officials. Raine won't tell the citizens exactly why she's enforcing a curfew, just that there's a need for 'reinforced security.' As for the officials… there are a few roaming the streets in case anyone breaks curfew, but most them are in City Hall. Raine is afraid you're going to attack her. I mean, I can't say I'd blame you for wanting to. I heard what happened to your boyfriend—I'm so sorry, E."

"It's fine," I said sharply. "Anyways, it's good to know most of the officials are off the streets. We could use your help with these."

I held up my share of the Dawn Letters.

"Paper?" he asked.

"Letters. We call them Dawn Letters. We're delivering them under the doors of every house that we can. That's all you need to know for now. How about you take Skylar's share, and she can watch our backs?"

Skylar handed over her stack of letters with a relieved smile as I handed her my dagger from the sand.

"Couldn't trust anyone more than me to be look-out," she grinned smugly.

We filled Fabian in on the plan to stick together, and as soon as we were ready, I used the Key to unlock the gate. According to Fabian, the gate required a key to open it from either side, which is why he used a ladder to get out. I ushered everyone in through the entrance before closing it behind myself. The city was eerily dead compared to my previous visits. Typically, the walls of the skyscrapers were covered in colorful screens with flashy displays, the streets were full of lively people and the smell of fried food, and there were lights everywhere. Now, Fallmont was dark. The skyscrapers loomed overhead, glassy and lifeless. The only light came from emergency streetlights spread sparingly through the streets. I couldn't smell anything fragrant—instead, I caught a whiff of old trash from a nearby dumpster. Looking down the road, there were houses near us that looked as though no one had inhabited them in years. I felt like the city was nothing more than some ruins.

"Why's it so dark if everyone's home?" I whispered to Fabian, stunned for a moment in the middle of the street.

"It's late," he said with a playful scoff. "Most people sleep, ya' know."

"Oh," I replied, my face growing warm. "Alright, let's start here."

We raced to the nearest houses. Braylin, Fabian, and I each spread out just enough to deliver to different doors. We stayed in Skylar's range as she followed us, keeping watch. She stayed low, clutching the dagger at her side as her head swiveled around, constantly checking all directions as the rest of us slid letters underneath each door we passed. At one point, we heard footsteps approaching from around a corner, and we all ducked behind one of the pungent dumpsters that was wedged between two empty shops as we waited for the officials to pass. When we were sure they had moved on to another street, we resumed our deliveries.

"Guys," I called in a hushed voice, hiding behind a small fence between two brick buildings. "Can we make a quick detour?"

"*Now*?" Skylar hissed, her and the boys hurrying to join me.

I flattened my lips and stared back at her.

"Fine—what is it?" she asked.

"Do you remember Legend?" I asked. "I think we could use his brother's help."

With Legend's help, my friends and I were able to adjust well to Fortitude. His brother, Zaire, brought Zane and me to Fallmont when we decided to propose the reinstatement of the prison system to Raine. The two brothers ran a business out of Fallmont where they worked to develop improvements on government vehicles until Legend was exiled for funneling money from peoples' bank accounts into his business. From there, Legend ended up in Fortitude, and his brother continued the business, making occasional trips between exiles towns and Fortitude.

Fabian agreed to lead us to Zaire's business, being sure to take us down alleys with more coverage and fewer officials patrolling. We neared a large garage with an attached office space. Along the front wall of the office side of the building, there was a door with a small window at eye-level. I snuck up to the door and peered in the window, seeing nothing but an empty receptionist's desk. Waving the others over, I pulled out the Key and unlocked the door. I stepped inside first with the others close behind.

"I'll be quick," I told them, hurrying down a short hallway behind the front desk. There were two doors on either side of the hallway, each with a metal sign affixed to the front. *Zaire Lomax* was engraved in bold font on the face of the metal plate.

I had no idea his last name is Lomax.

I tried the door, but it was locked. Once again, I pulled out the Key. Opening the door, an automatic light turned on above me, illuminating a simple office. On the far end was a basic wooden desk stained a dark brown, almost black. There was a red padded swivel chair, a few file cabinets, and some awards in a glass cabinet. Upon closer inspection of his desk, I spotted a single picture of Zaire and his brother, beaming widely. My friends now stood in the doorway at this point, curiously observing me as I pulled out a pencil and paper.

Zaire,

It didn't work.

We could use your help.

Find me outside Fallmont.

E

I reread my letter a few times, hoping it was obscure enough not to be dangerous in the wrong hands, but clear enough that Zaire would know who I was and what I generally needed his help with. Having a connection with a vehicle and city access could prove incredibly useful for supplies, preventing us from having to continually risk our lives to bring food back to our ruins.

I folded the letter and placed it carefully underneath the picture frame stand, leaving the room and relocking the door behind me.

We ensured everything in the office was as we had left it—including locking the front door again.

After leaving the office, we resumed our letter delivery from that side of the city.

We were almost out of letters when we heard a voice in the distance.

"Stop right there!" the voice boomed, seeming to bounce off the surrounding buildings.

We were between houses, with none of us at any doors at the moment when we spotted two officials pointing their guns at us.

"What now?" I hissed under my breath to Fabian.

"Don't move," he whispered back, raising his hands. "Put the dagger away, Skylar. Before they're close enough to see that it's a weapon."

Skylar let out an audible grumble as she tucked the dagger into the waist of her pants and covered it with her shirt.

When the officials came closer, I was able to see their faces. One was a curvy woman with what appeared to be a permanent snarl on her lip. The other, a younger looking man, had longer hair pulled back in a shaggy bun. His face looked inquisitive, but not threatening.

"Fabian?" the young man asked, his tone gentle.

"Hey, Jason," Fabian replied, sounding casual, but his posture slumped in embarrassment.

"What are you and your cousins doing out past dark?" Jason asked.

"My co—"

"—I'll take them home," Jason hurried, leaving the woman's side, his arms held out at his sides as he ushered us the opposite direction.

"Make it fast," the woman complained, resuming her patrol.

"Come on," Jason said calmly.

I shot a look at Fabian, trying to figure out what was going on. He shrugged and continued to walk as Jason guided us. He led us down a couple blocks and around a few turns before stopping at a smaller house with chipping paint along the sides.

"The gate is one more block away and to the right. Make it fast. If you get caught, you're out of luck. You never saw me. We never spoke. Go," Jason said, his voice urgent and his once friendly expression now looking dire.

"Thank you, Jase," Fabian said, reaching out to shake Jason's hand.

"Now!" Jason warned.

Fabian, Braylin, Skylar, and I took off down the street, hooking a right as soon as we came to an inter-section. The gate was straight ahead. When we reached it, we flew through it, having left it unlocked from earlier.

Once out of Fallmont, I turned and locked the gate behind us to remove any unnecessary suspicions of our presence. We started to run back toward the ruins we had stayed at when Fabian stopped in his tracks.

"Come on," I said, waving him onward. "Let's keep it moving."

"I can't," he said. "The ladder is outside the walls. Plus, I could be more help inside Fallmont. People don't know I'm helping you, so I can still live peacefully there and just work as an inside man. We can set up a meeting place, and I can bring supplies when you need them, or whatever else you need help with."

Honestly, that would probably work better than bringing him to the ruins with us anyways.

"Alright. There are some ruins that way," I pointed. "That's where we'll be. When you come, come alone. Make sure no one is following you—best to keep it to night visits."

Fabian nodded before taking off back to Fallmont.

We reached the ruins a short time later, claiming our space in the same dilapidated building as before. When we had finally settled down for the night, the persistent silence between us broke as Braylin spoke.

"We did it," he said, sounding tired. "I didn't even process the fact that we were successful until now. Tonight might have been the start of something big." He smiled triumphantly.

"Don't get ahead of yourself," Skylar said, getting cozy on the couch.

"He's right." I felt a strange sense of joy for the first time in what felt like a long time. "The most we can do now is lay low for a while and write more letters while we hope some of the ones we delivered tonight will make a difference."

Braylin smiled confidently. "They will."

SEVEN

We were no longer in the ruins, but instead surrounded by desert in all directions. I was on my knees in the hot sand with Skylar and Braylin sitting on their knees beside me. In front of us stood Raine and Zane.

"Why would you do this to us, Eos?" Braylin asked me, tears in his eyes.

"She never really cared about us," Skylar answered gravely.

The two turned to face Raine and Zane. Raine was holding a pistol at her side, her face void of all emotion. Zane's expression matched hers as he guided her arm up, steadying the gun at Skylar, who was the furthest to my left. Zane's eyes moved slowly until they met mine. With a twitch of a smirk, he called off, "One!"

Boom.

Skylar fell with a puff of sand around her. I opened my mouth to scream, to yell, to beg them to stop, but nothing came out.

The pistol was now aimed at Braylin, immediately to my left.

"Two!"

Boom.

Thick red oozed from the wound in Braylin's head as he fell, droplets of blood leaking into the surrounding sand, dyeing it crimson.

"Three!"

I woke with an icy chill racing through my veins. I was still in the ruins, and Skylar and Braylin were sleeping peacefully in the living room. My chest was visibly thumping with my heartbeat as I sat up and rubbed the sweat from my face. Before getting up from my makeshift bed, I stared at Braylin and Skylar for a moment, watching their breathing.

They're okay. They're safe. You're safe.

With a shaky breath, I stood. Involuntarily, my body lurched with a single sob before I could control it. *One and done. Stop that. It was a dream.* I reminded myself over and over that we were safe. I stood in silence for a few minutes before deciding to wake Skylar with a gentle touch of the shoulder.

"Mmmgh," she muttered sleepily as her eyes fluttered open.

"Shh," I urged. "Don't wake Braylin. Come outside as soon as you're up. Please."

I stepped out into the warmth of the late morning. Heat radiated off the dark ruins, creating a haze around them, but the sun felt comforting. A few minutes later, Skylar stepped outside, her hair in a loose and tangled bun. She crossed her arms and looked at me with a raised eyebrow.

"I had another dream," I said softly.

"Did you sprout wings and fly?" she teased.

"Not funny. It was horrible, and they keep happening."

"Well, what was it about?"

I sighed, hesitant to share that I dreamt about her getting shot in the face. Not exactly the kind of thing one wants to hear.

I told her about the dream, and the details of the other nightmares I have had recently.

"That's messed up," she said with a huff, her eyes wide. "Why'd you wake me up to tell me? I don't really think there's anything I can do to help with that. I hate to sound like a jerk, but this kind of sounds like a you problem."

"I know. I guess I was hoping you'd have some kind of advice. I didn't want to tell Braylin because I figured he'd sugar coat things and tell me nothing is my fault and 'things will get better' and all of that. That's great and all, but I don't need that right now. I need someone who will tell me if I'm being irrational."

"I don't think you're being irrational. You want my honest opinion though?"

"That's what I said," I urged.

"I think it *was* your fault."

My heart dropped, and I was filled with heaviness. "Excuse me?"

"Zane died because you insisted that Raine would understand if you just confronted her with your ideas. He would still be in Fortitude if it weren't for your plan – you would be too. But you know what? It's done. Stop killing yourself over the past and just use what you're feeling to drive you."

"I am—"

"No, you aren't. You're pretending. We see right through you, E. Braylin and I have talked about it before. We think you're in complete denial about the whole situation."

"I'm not in denial!"

"Literally in denial about denial... *Tsk tsk*. I have an idea," she said. "Say it. Take ownership of what happened and feel what you've gotta' feel when you do."

"Say what?"

"'Zane died and it's my fault' might be a good starting place."

"Seriously, Sky? This isn't some kind of joke!"

"Do you hear me laughing? Now say it."

"Why?"

"Stop stalling."

"I'm not stalling."

"If you weren't stalling, you'd have said it by now."

"Zane died and it's my fault," I said. "Happy?"

She stood there completely silent, her expression softening as she observed me.

The weight of the words sunk in as I stood in the quiet of the moment. The pain first seemed to plunge like a dagger into my chest before flooding outwards, filling me with energy.

"You okay?" Skylar eventually asked.

I nodded, my eyes trained on a random spot on the horizon as I focused on the adrenaline surging through my veins.

"Now think about how you're feeling. You've got to process your emotions better if you're ever going to heal from this. What are you feeling right now?"

"Pissed off."

"Well," she chuckled. "That's something! I can work with that. Mad at Raine? At yourself? At Zane?"

"Just… mad."

"Alright. We'll give it some time. Let's go back inside for a bit."

"I'm going on a walk," I said, taking off at a brisk pace toward the spot on the horizon.

"I don't want Braylin to wake up in the ruins by himself and get lost trying to find us. If you're not back in a few minutes, we're going to hunt you down, okay?" Skylar said playfully but her eyes squinted, watching me for a moment before reentering the ruined house.

My steps quickened until they turned into a sprint as I headed toward nothing in particular. I just wanted to move. The ruins seemed liked a black blur beside me as I focused on the horizon. I couldn't hear anything but a persistent ring in my ears. The sun seemed unbearably hot, but I continued pushing without looking back. All of a sudden, everything went blindly white as I felt myself fall forward for what felt like infinity.

Everything was black and all I could hear was what sounded like shoes scraping on sandy ground.

How long was I out?

I tried to open my eyes, but I couldn't tell if they were even closed—I couldn't feel anything, I couldn't see anything, I could only hear.

What's going on? Where am I? Why can't I see? Or move?

The scraping turned to a grunt, followed by louder footsteps on a harder surface. My hands and feet began to tingle as the feeling came back. As it did, my vision began to return slowly—it was dark and fuzzy at first, but when it fully returned, I could see a man standing in front of me. I tried to move, but I could hear the clank of handcuffs bound around a metal pipe behind me.

"You're not an official," my voice slow, each word taking considerable effort to form. I looked up at the man. He must have been in his forties or fifties. His clothes were dark and ragged, and his long, wiry hair clung to his sweaty cheeks.

"Clearly," he scoffed, setting down some kind of strange rifle.

"What's with the weird gun?" I asked, stretching my legs in front of me as the feeling returned. "I've never seen one quite like that."

"Tranquilizer. How'd you think you wound up here?"

I shrugged. "At first I thought I just passed out from the heat or something."

"It's not that hot outside," he said. His eyes shifted around the room and his hands trembled as he paced side to side in front of me.

"Nervous about something, friend?" I looked at him with a closed-lip smile. "First time kidnapping someone?"

"Shut up!" he growled.

I looked around, taking in my new environment. It looked like a cellar. The walls were made of large stones. There was a flight of stairs to the far left, and a couple dim lightbulbs dangling from wires strung through the ceiling.

"You do know who I am, don't you?" I asked. "Of course you do. You wouldn't have bothered otherwise."

"I'm not stupid!" His nervous eyes trained on me as he stopped in his tracks.

"Could've had me fooled."

"Shut up!" he snarled again. "You better watch what you say!"

"Why? You plan on turning me in, don't you? Raine would want me alive, I'm assuming. I doubt there's a reward for turning me in dead. Raine would rather make an example of me."

"Doesn't mean I can't make this a lot worse for you."

"I wouldn't, if I were you."

"Why's that? You've got nothing to stop me!" He grinned confidently. "I took your stuff. A dagger… a gun."

"Yeah," I said, dragging out the word mockingly. "I'm not going to need those."

He stopped talking and simply looked at me before rolling his eyes.

"So, are we going to get a move on? What's the next step? I'm bored."

"Just sit there and shut up. Someone is coming for you. They'll be here in a while—it's not a long drive."

"A drive, huh?" I nodded. "So, you contacted an official? Too scared to deliver me yourself?"

"Not scared—smart. My wife is running to Fallmont as we speak. She's getting an official so we don't have to put up with you any longer than necessary. I've already had to more than I care to. You're obnoxious, you know that, kid?"

I shrugged. "At least I'm not a weirdo who kidnaps girls."

"You're not a 'girl,' you're a criminal worth a lot of money. Turning you in would earn my wife and I enough money to move back into the city and retire from hunting runaways. They tell you it's a rewarding career, but they don't warn you about the living conditions when you're forced to live outside the city. Turning you in is all I need to move back. Worth it, if you ask me."

"I didn't ask you."

The man grumbled and rolled his eyes again.

"That eyeroll makes you look like a teenage girl."

The man picked up the tranquilizer gun and aimed it at me.

"Don't you ever shut up?" he complained, his voice gravelly.

I shrugged. "Making conversation. I know you said it wouldn't be long, but I'm getting impatient. I thought you wanted to make things worse for me? Putting me to sleep would be doing me a favor. Why don't you take that dagger out of my bag? Oughta' be more fun for you."

He looked back at me, confused as he lowered the gun and retrieved the dagger from my bag. "You sadistic or something?"

"Actually, if I enjoyed *being* in pain, that'd make me a masochist."

He clearly had to restrain himself from rolling his eyes again.

I chuckled.

"Something funny?" he hissed, staring at me and then admiring the glimmer from the lightbulb overhead reflecting off the dagger. "You need to learn when to shut up."

"I'm enjoying myself immensely. This is exactly how I wanted to spend my day. What about you?" I stared back at him, batting my eyes.

When he didn't reply, I spoke up again. "So, what's that wi—"

"I've told you multiple times now to shut up," he growled, getting up in my face as he squatted in front of me with the dagger. "I'm starting to think that I'd be better off cutting out your tongue."

I grinned and proceeded to stick my tongue out. As he reared back ever so slightly with the dagger, I threw my foot upward, sending it crashing into his crotch. With a wail, he fell completely forward, sending the dagger skidding across the dirty floor. He rolled away and to the side, holding himself and groaning. While he was down, I sent the toe of my boot sailing into his jaw. He let out a pained cry, reaching for his face. His eyes looked up at me and he began to angrily scurry toward me, reaching out for my foot, which I pulled back away from him. Just as he got closer, I rammed upward with my foot again, narrowly missing him. He grinned, but not for long as I began frantically kicking outward, a few of my kicks landing against his shoulders and chest.

"Let me go!" I squealed, feeling my heart racing.

"Fat chance!" he replied, spitting some blood onto the floor with a splatter.

"Aren't you tired of getting beat up by a girl?"

At this, the man was practically snarling as he lunged at me, fist-first. Just before his fist would have made contact with my face, I moved, his fist colliding with the pipe behind me with a rattle instead. He fell curled up on his side howling and holding his fist in his other hand. At this, I pressed my boot down on the side of his neck, pushing down with a strained groan.

"You're going to unlock my cuffs now," I told him.

"I don't—have—key," he sputtered, trying to catch his breath.

"Um, yeah. You do. That's a nice keyring you've got hanging from your belt, buddy. Unlock my cuffs. *Now.*"

He reluctantly removed his keyring with his good hand and took off a tiny silver key.

"Can't—reach."

"Slide it toward my hands, I'll do it myself," I grumbled.

He did as I instructed, and the key stopped near the pipe. I twisted my wrists around, stretching my fingers unnaturally as I made contact with the tiny key. Once I was able to pick it up, I inserted it in the lock and undid the cuffs. When my wrists were free, I shook my hands to get the feeling back in them, all the while keeping the man's neck fixed under my foot. I stood slowly, pushing a bit more weight onto his neck as I gained full control.

"Let—me go. Please," he struggled to breathe.

"First, I'm going to help you with that eye rolling problem of yours," I scooped up some of the sand from the floor, pinching some off in between my fingers.

The man writhed as I pried his eye open with one hand and sprinkled a little sand above him. As soon as I had, I released my grip on him and bolted for my dagger and bag. I continued up the stairs without looking back.

I could hear his delayed footsteps behind me, followed by a crash as he ran into something within the house. I continued running, his footsteps and yelling growing faint as I bolted out the front door of a little cottage.

I stopped instantly as soon as I was out in the desert again.

I don't know where I am.

EIGHT

That man tranquilized me, and I have no idea how long I was out. I don't even know what direction he took me, or how far.

I decided any direction was better than no direction, so I went around to the back of the house and started sprinting. I figured, just in case the man tried to come back out and shoot me with the tranquilizer gun again, it'd buy me a little time if I wasn't running straight from his front door.

When the lone cottage was far enough out of view that I was confident the man would neither see me, nor be able to catch up, I slowed to a walk. There was nothing around me to suggest where I might be. I dug in my bag and pulled out a water bottle, taking a desperate swig as I kept moving.

A while later, I came across tire tracks worn into tightly-packed sand, almost as hard as rock. *A path for the officials' trucks. Best to stay away.*

I changed my course of direction to move perpendicular to the makeshift road, but just as I did, I could hear a truck in the distance.

My head swiveled around, looking for the incoming truck. As soon as I spotted it, I ran the opposite way, kicking up clouds of sand behind me. The driver had obviously spotted me and decided to come speeding after me, getting as close as they could without leaving the tracks. I was still sprinting away when the truck stopped along the edge of the tracks and I could hear the truck door open.

"Eos!" the driver yelled after me.

I didn't turn to look, I just kept running.

"Eos! It's okay! It's me!" the voice insisted.

Curiosity got the best of me, and I glanced over my shoulder while running, tripping over a small dip in the sand and landing face-first with a *thump*.

"Zaire?" I managed to mutter, standing to my feet and sweeping the sand off myself.

I could hear him as he trotted toward me.

"What are you doing here?" I asked him.

"What do you mean?" he asked, his smile fading into confusion. "I got your letter."

"Good—I'm glad it made sense. Hey, look, I have an important question," I said, hurrying through the chit-chat. "Where am I?"

"What? Are you okay?" Zaire's brow crinkled on his ebony forehead, which was dotted with even darker freckles and beads of sweat.

"A guy shot me with a tranq, I got away, I'm here, I have no clue where I am. Skylar and Braylin are in some ruins near Fallmont waiting on me."

"I appreciate the quick summary, but that still doesn't answer my question," he chuckled nervously. "Are you okay?"

"Peachy."

"Come on, I'll give you a ride. We aren't far from Fallmont, which is why I figured I'd drive around this way looking for you, so your ruins must not be far either."

I nodded sleepily, trudging after him back to the truck. After I tripped, I had become aware of just how exhausted I was.

Zaire opened the passenger door for me and held out a hand to help me in, which I accepted. I flopped into the seat and, when he closed the door, I rested my head against it. Before Zaire had even taken his seat, I was asleep.

"Eos," I heard Zaire call softly. "Hey, wake up."

I grumbled groggily and sat up in my seat.

"We're getting closer to Fallmont and I need you to keep an eye out for the ruins you were talking about. The roads don't go through all the ruins, so I might not be able to drop you off directly in them, but I'll get you as close as I can. The ruins have roads, but they're usually a mess, and most of them aren't connected to the main roads."

"I've noticed. That's fine anyways," I said, rubbing a little sand from under my eyes, shuttering as I thought of the kidnapper writhing in his basement.

We drove for a few minutes longer before I was fairly confident that I could see the ruins.

"There," I pointed.

"Alright. I should be able to get to that road pretty easily," he said. "That guy didn't take you too far off, I guess."

I didn't say anything.

"I brought a bag of supplies in case I found you. Figured you could use some stuff. Food, water, bandages… the usual exciting stuff."

"Thanks," I said softly, gazing out the windows.

We were both silent for a minute while he drove.

"Do you mind me asking what happened?" Zaire started. "And I don't mean today. I mean after I left you and Zane in Fallmont. Obviously, I know your plan didn't work—the exile towns are still here, and I know you said in your letter on my desk that it didn't work. I can't imagine Raine just let you guys mosey out of the city though."

"She shot Zane. Sent me to Ironwood. Braylin was there too—he's the brother of one of the girls that came to Fortitude with me. Skylar caught word and eventually broke us out."

Zaire whistled in shock. "That's crazy. Zane didn't make it?"

"No."

"I'm so sorry to hear that. He seemed like a great guy."

"He was."

"I don't blame you if you decide to stay away from all of that now, but do you still plan on changing Raine's mind somehow?"

"Something like that."

He gave an awkward little nod, his eyes shifting away. "This is about as close as I should get to the ruins unless I want to risk getting my tires stuck. Are you going to be okay or do you want me to walk with you?" Zaire parked the truck on the road; the ruins were only a short walk away.

"I'll be alright. Thank you."

"Are you sure? I can at least wait here for a while until I can tell you aren't coming back out to tell me these are the wrong ruins."

"They're the right ones. I can tell now," I said confidently. "Can I ask you something before I leave?"

"Sure," Zaire shrugged.

"Can you help us?" I asked. "Just... sometimes. With supplies, maybe?"

He thought about it for a moment. "I think I can manage that. I'll bring stuff back from my runs to Fortitude and I'll just swing by over here to drop it off. I just dropped some exiles off at Fortitude earlier, actually. I figured it would be a good time to look for you, but I didn't have much time to collect supplies—hence why there's just a little bag. Your friends are all doing well, by the way.

Last I heard from Legend, Yulie and her baby are still healthy. I guess the baby was sitting just right, and the stab wound didn't even touch him."

"Him?" I asked. "They found out it's a boy?"

Zaire's mouth stretched into a wide smile, his teeth shockingly white.

"Yeah! They haven't come up with a name yet, but Legend told me they recently found out the baby's a boy. One of your friends apparently was able to fix the ultrasound equipment in Fortitude."

"That's fantastic! Who fixed it?"

"I have no clue how to pronounce her name." Zaire chuckled. "Legend told me who, but I don't remember."

"Does Astraea sound familiar?"

"Yeah! That's it. Az-tray-uh?" he sounded out.

I nodded with a giggle. "You've got it. Most people just resort to calling her Trae."

"Got it. I'll keep that in mind." His eyes sparkled as he smiled. "Do you plan on staying in these ruins long?"

"As long as we safely can, I presume."

"I'll come check on you the next time I'm out making a run, and I'll be sure to bring some supplies. I've made great progress revamping the trucks, so the officials have been letting me out more often than before to 'get extra parts' and 'test the new equipment.' Little do they know, I've got all the parts I need stockpiled in Fortitude, so I just pick some up every time I drop exiles off. I'll swing by the next time I'm on a run. If you aren't here, I won't take it personally." He laughed.

I hopped out of the truck, grabbed the supply bag from the trunk, and waved goodbye as I set off toward the ruins. When I reentered the crumbling mess we called 'home,' I was greeted by a frantic Braylin.

"Where were you all day?" he asked in a frenzy, rushing over to the door. "We were worried sick!"

"Speak for yourself," Skylar said, her arms crossed as she leaned against the far wall. "The poor girl just needed a break from you."

Skylar laughed as Braylin shot her a stern look over his shoulder. "You look exhausted, E. What happened?"

"Just got caught up," I answered.

Braylin looked at me, clearly unsatisfied with my answer.

"I'm fine," I said with a weak chuckle.

"You sure?" Braylin asked, crossing his arms.

I nodded, working my way through an unsatisfying yawn.

"Does running away make you sleepy or something?" Skylar dug. "We checked around the ruins and couldn't find you. If it had gotten any later, we would've left the ruins to go search the damn desert for you. Don't do that again because I won't go looking next time."

"Has anything happened since I left?" I asked, ignoring the threat.

"Not a thing," Skylar answered. "We wrote some more letters and were going to deliver them tonight. We can go without you. You won't be much good to us if you're sleepy and careless. I'll give you the Key when we get back."

"I'll come with," I said, curling up on the couch under my blanket.

"Look at yourself, E. You're not going anywhere," Skylar argued.

"It's still pretty bright out, so I know you aren't going anytime soon. Let me just get some sleep and I'll be ready to go."

"Sure. Whatever," Skylar said, her voice seeming to trail off as I fell asleep.

When I woke up, the room was dark and I was alone. Confused, I hurried to the door and stepped out, looking up and down the broken street. Skylar and Braylin were walking toward me from Fallmont, which looked eerily dead with only the moonlight illuminating the skyscrapers that once shown bright with flashy lights. When Skylar and Braylin grew close, I could see them more clearly. They both held something concealed by cloth in their hands as they walked toward me with a strange look of peace on their faces. Once they reached me, they simultaneously dropped the cloths, revealing Raine's severed head in Braylin's hands, and Zane's in Skylar's.

"This is what you wanted," Skylar said warmly. "Isn't it?"

"We took care of it for you," Braylin smiled, his look sinister. "That's what friends are for."

Just then, I jolted awake, the familiar cold panic surging through my body. Just like my dream, the room was dark and I was alone. I hesitated for a moment, trying to ignore the sensation in my chest as if someone had their fingers prying into my heart. I stood and eased myself to the door. With a deep breath, I opened it and peered out. Skylar and Braylin were on their way back from Fallmont, which was glowing from the moon, identical to my dream.

Please don't be carrying heads. Please don't be creepy. Please be normal.

I tried to steady my breathing, tightening the muscles in my legs to stop my shaking as I watched the two come closer.

Their hands were empty.

I breathed a sigh of relief, though my legs never got the memo that the coast was clear as they continued to tremble.

"E? You're awake?" Braylin asked as he came closer, spotting me peeking out of the door. "Are you okay?"

"I'm fine," I lied.

"Sorry we went without you. Like I said, you needed rest," Skylar said.

"How'd it go?"

"Great! No problems. We hit a different street this time—one on the other side of the city. We were careful," Braylin tacked on the last statement upon noticing my concern.

"Here's your key back," Skylar handed me the Skeleton Key.

"I think we should take a break from the letters for a bit," I suggested.

"What? Why?" Braylin asked as everyone reentered the house. "We won't know yet if they're working—don't give up already!"

"I'm not, but I think we should lay low for a bit. What if one of the houses we delivered a letter to was an official's house, and they show Raine the letter? Everyone in Fallmont will be on high alert. I say we hang back and have Fabian give us an all-clear in a few days, maybe even a week, to see if anything has been said about us to the officials."

Just then, the door burst open and there Fabian was, hands on his knees, panting.

"Speak of the devil," Skylar said.

"You good?" Braylin asked, approaching Fabian tentatively.

"Yeah," Fabian huffed. "Just need to catch my breath. Ran as fast as I could. I've been waiting all day to tell you!"

"Tell us what?" I asked.

"I'm getting to it," he laughed breathily.

"Is it about the letters?" Braylin asked with a nervous smile. "Are they already making a difference?"

"Technically yes, but it's complicated," Fabian said, stretching as he straightened up. "But I think you'll consider this good news nonetheless."

Skylar, Braylin, and I watched him impatiently.

"Raine arrested a minor," he said, a delighted grin on his face.

The three of us stared, speechless.

"Are you joking?" I asked, breaking the silence. "What kind of monsters do you think we are if you think that we'd find that to be *good* news?"

"No! I don't mean it like that," he corrected, his grin melting into a look of panic. "It isn't directly good news—"

"It isn't good news at all!" I objected. "Some poor kid has to grow up and grow old in an exile town!"

"He hasn't had his trial yet, so it's not for sure. And he won't have to grow up in an exile town if your plan works. But the point I'm trying to make is that this really ticked off the citizens in Fallmont. The kid was the son of a well-known businessman back home, and I think the kid might have read a copy of the letter because, apparently, he was causing some commotion on the street. He was speaking out against Raine. I don't know if the kid has his own reasons or if it was your letter, or both. But Raine sent some officials to exile him. He's only sixteen, so the citizens are furious. Everyone knows the kid's dad—he's a really influential and respectable guy, so the news travelled fast. Right now, it's all just chatter about Raine, but it's a start."

"He wouldn't be the first minor to be exiled," I said, feeling a burning in my stomach. "One of my friends was exiled as a minor."

"Not to undermine your friend's experience," Fabian started, a nervous look on his face as he chose his words carefully. "But there are so many people that know this kid and his family. This is big news, and if he's exiled, it could get even bigger. And it doesn't look good for Raine."

"That poor kid," I sighed. "I hate that some innocent kid could be exiled, even if it helps us."

"Think about it this way," Fabian said. "If your plan works, he wouldn't be exiled for long. He'd be one more person you're fighting for."

"He's right," Skylar said. "If exiling this kid starts to help people see how corrupt Raine is and how ridiculous the exile town system is, it's worth it even if he has to spend a little while in one of the towns. He'd probably be sent to Clamorite because he was protesting and causing a commotion, so it could definitely be worse, from my understanding."

I nodded reluctantly.

"What now?" Braylin asked. "It sounds like Eos was right to think we should back off delivering letters for a little while. Maybe see if anything comes of this boy's case before we write more?"

"I agree," Skylar said confidently.

"Do you guys need any supplies in the meantime?" Fabian asked. "I brought a little food and some water bottles."

He unloaded his backpack on an empty table, vegetables, bread, and water bottles tumbling out.

"I also grabbed these, in case you get bored," he said, holding up a pack of cards.

NINE

Fabian left before the sun rose, taking nothing with him except his empty backpack and our empty water bottles. Once the slightest hint of sunlight crept through the cracked windows, Skylar, Braylin, and I opened the deck of cards. All the cards were there, but the corners were bent on most cards, torn completely off on others.

"You cheated!" Braylin accused Skylar as she grinned, revealing her cards at the end of a game.

"Oh yeah?" she snickered. "Prove it."

"Playing cards with criminals is a horrible idea," I suggested with a lighthearted laugh.

"You're not wrong," Skylar said, dealing another hand of cards.

"I'm going to get some fresh air for a few minutes before the next round," I said as I stood and stretched with a dramatic groan. "I'm taking my cards with me, though. I don't trust either of you!"

"We don't need your cards to cheat," Skylar teased.

"Do you need supervision, E?" Braylin asked mockingly, his hands on his hips. "Wouldn't want you disappearing again."

"I'll be fine. I'm only stepping outside this time, so I'll just be a minute."

Outside, the air felt refreshing compared to the staleness of the ruined house. My skin began to feel warm as I stretched my arms out with a deep breath. Remembering the cards in my hand, I turned them over to peek.

Three queens, a three of clubs, and a nine of hearts.

Not bad.

I involuntarily smiled, knowing Braylin and Skylar were likely manipulating the deck of cards while they waited for me.

Just then, I saw a large figure bolt into one of the buildings along the far edge of the ruins, slipping inside the door in one swift movement. I felt every ounce of the peace from the moment drain out of my body, as if the sweat beading on my forehead and chest carried it away. I let the cards fall from my hand, scattering across the ground as I shoved my way back through the door and into our ruined house. I skittered toward my bag, pulling out my dagger and ignoring the concerned slew of questions from my friends. I crouched by the front door, peering around it down the street.

"Weapons!" I hissed to my friends. "Let's go!"

I raced back out the door, my dagger tucked into the waist of my pants. Braylin and Skylar followed me through the door with their guns drawn.

Confused, the two slowly followed after me as they watched me creep toward the house at the end of the ruins. I pulled the dagger from my waist before turning the doorknob slowly, carefully pushing the ragged door open. Before moving forward, I threw another look over my shoulder, checking for my backup.

The inside of this house was a similar layout to ours, but in worse condition. A large glass light fixture had fallen from the ceiling, leaving behind a bunch of frayed wires and shattered glass littered on the floor. Most of the windows had been reduced to glass shards, affixed menacingly in the window frames around the living space. Chunks of the ceiling had crumbled down, and the rugs were stained charcoal.

I crouched low as I scurried behind the dusty couch, the glittering glass on the floor crunching underneath my combat boots. After a moment of squatting in silence, I pulled myself up enough to peer over the top of the couch. My eyes were met by those of a familiar face.

"Eos?" his deep, hoarse voice called to me.

"Cromwell?" I answered the man as I cautiously rose. "What are you doing here?"

The last time I saw the Bellicose representative was when he helped Zane, Lamb, and I escape his exile town after he encouraged me to learn how to properly fight and defend myself without a weapon.

"There was a huge breakout at Bellicose. A newer exile went into a frenzy at the gate during ration delivery. They shot him, but not before he took out a tire on their truck. There was some kind of issue with the gate during the whole commotion—a lot of us managed to get out. Another truck of officials caught a few of us a day later trying to find food. Brought us to Fallmont and put us in holding cells. The next morning, we were supposed to get shipped off to Ironwood, but I managed to escape when they were trying to transfer me from my cell to the truck."

He held up his cuffed hands, the metal quietly jangling as he began to speak again.

"You're a thief. Can you pick these?" he asked, his muscular and once-intimidating stance now seemed scaled-down. He seemed weak, but still full of confidence all at once.

"Yeah," I said. "No problem. I've got something that'll help."

I motioned for him to follow me. As we turned to the door, we nearly rammed into Skylar and Braylin, who stood frozen and stunned at the doorway.

"Who—" Skylar started.

"This is Cromwell," I cut her off. "He is—was—the representative of Bellicose. He's a friend."

"How—" Braylin's eyes bugged out of his head.

"Long story," I said. "Excuse us."

The three followed me back into the ruined house, where I pulled the Key from my bag and slipped it into Cromwell's cuffs. With a careful twist, I adjusted the Key to fit the lock in the cuffs. The lock made a soft click and the cuffs pulled open.

Cromwell nodded.

"How many escaped?" I asked.

"Escaped?" Braylin chimed.

"There was a breakout at Bellicose," I answered.

"I don't know," Cromwell said, rubbing his thick nose ring with a freed hand. "Maybe five or six. Paren was one of them, but he was also one of the ones to get caught with me. They were planning on transporting each of us separately—too much "of a risk to have a bunch of us in one vehicle, I imagine. They kept saying I had the 'honor' of being first—they said they've never had a representative try to escape."

"Paren is still in Fallmont?" I asked, feeling my heart thumping in my chest.

Cromwell grunted. "I'm guessing. They might be moving him today since they didn't have much luck with me. Or they're looking for me first. No telling what those pricks are doing."

"I'll be back as quick as I can," I said, pocketing the Key and tucking both my dagger and my gun into the waist of my black jeans.

"Is this *the* Paren? The one from the Dawn Letters?" Skylar asked.

"Yup," I said, reaching for the door.

"What? You can't be serious!" Braylin called after me as I bolted out the door.

The morning was quiet without my friends alongside me. Running toward Fallmont, the only sounds were those of my boots grinding against the sand with each step. I was sprinting at this point, and Fallmont was growing closer by the second.

I didn't think this through.

I stopped in my tracks.

It's daytime. There's no way I'm going to blend in with everyone in broad daylight and casually walk out with an escaped criminal.

I sunk into the sand, resting my head in my hands as I thought.

There's nothing I can do except wait until night, but it might be too late by then.

Just then, I heard the scuffing sound of someone running through the sand behind me. I looked up, scrambling to stand.

The sound came from Skylar as she trotted up to me, her gun bouncing on her hip.

"You followed me?" I asked.

"You think I trusted you to get far on your own?" She snickered, her petite nose crinkling as she did.

"I have before," I said with a loud sniff as I crossed my arms.

"You're the most wanted criminal in the New Territory." She stared at me, eyes narrowed. "And you almost waltzed into the same building that the leader—the same leader you practically threatened not that long ago—works in… to free a criminal… who escaped from a town of violent criminals… in the middle of the day."

Ouch. It sounds even worse when she puts it that way.

"Okay. What do you suggest then? And don't just tell me to go back to the house and forget about it."

"I'm not. Clearly this Paren person means something to you—so *I'm* going to get him."

"How is that really any better?"

"They know you're traveling with a group, I'm sure. But they don't really know my face, and they expect me to be with you, if anything. An average-height, average-looking brunette doesn't really scream 'criminal,' does it?"

"You don't even know him," I said. "You're insane. I'm going—I'll just wait until dark."

"You're literally a walking target! It's one thing when you go with some backup, but you're not going by yourself."

"I don't need you there—you'll just slow me down."

Skylar scoffed, crossing her arms and staring back at me with wide eyes.

"I don't mean it like that."

"How do you mean it?" she asked, tilting her head to the side.

"I just mean…" I sighed. "I just want to get in, find him, and get out, and I know what he looks like."

"But I know where to look, and I know his name. I'm also assuming you can give me a general idea of what he looks like, unless I'm wrong?"

"Don't worry about it!" I argued. "I'll be fine!"

"No one knows who I am, no one knows they should be targeting me too. This'll go a lot smoother if you just let me get him."

"No!"

"Give me one good reason why not."

"Because."

"That's not a reason," she said, her arms dropping to her sides as she huffed.

"You don't need to get hurt—or worse—by looking for *my* friend."

"A friend of yours is an ally of ours," she said. "And let me remind you—I broke you out of Ironwood. I think I deserve a bit of credit. I can handle this."

I lowered my eyes, exhaling and running my hands through my hair.

"What does he look like?" she asked.

"He's fairly tall, kind of muscular, blond, blue eyes. He has dimples. I don't really know how else to describe how he looks. Handsome, I guess," I said with an awkward smile. "He's just a really good person, and I'd hate for him to go to Ironwood."

"Don't worry—I'll find him," she nodded, her serious expression unfaltering.

"You're going to need this," I said, offering her the Key. "You want my dagger?"

Back at the house, I filled Cromwell in on our work with the Dawn Letters and what our end goal was. I told him about Zane, my face growing more flushed with every word of the story.

Cromwell's expression was stiff the entire time. The only moments I could even guess that he was paying attention was when he'd let out a loud huff through his nose as if to say "wow."

"Care to join our efforts?" I offered, smirking to myself at the thought of Cromwell responding with another nose-huff.

"How can I help?" he asked gruffly. "I'll wring Raine's neck myself if you need."

I would've thought he was joking if it weren't for the fact that Cromwell was a massive and intimidating man who looked like a live brick wall as he stared back at me, arms crossed. Knowing he was representative over a bunch of violent criminals also contributed to how daunting he appeared.

"For now, we're just lying low. Then, we'll write more letters. Hopefully, at some point, it will start to degrade the public's opinion of Raine Velora."

"That's it?"

"For now," I said, pulling my shoulders back to stand tall, but still he towered over me.

"Alright," he conceded, taking a seat on the couch. "What now?"

"Now, we wait. If you get bored, here's the original letter." I dug out the letter and handed it to him. "You can make copies if you want something to do."

The day crept by achingly slow, with no sign of Skylar and Paren. The sun disappeared over the horizon and left Cromwell, Braylin, and me in the dark ruins. At this point, we decided to keep the front door open because the constant open-close every time I went to see if they were here was beginning to drive the other two insane.

"I'm going to sleep," Cromwell said plainly. "Wake me up when they're back."

I stood in the open doorway and nodded without turning to face him.

"I think I might try to get some sleep too," Braylin said, putting a hand tentatively on my shoulder. "E? I think you might want to get some rest. Time will go quicker if you're asleep, and I'm sure they'll be back when you wake up."

"It's okay," I said. "I'm just going to wait up a bit longer."

Without another word, Braylin turned and left to arrange his makeshift bed for the night.

It didn't seem to take long for the two to fall asleep, but once I was confident they wouldn't notice my absence, I tucked my gun into my waistband and slipped out the open door and into the moonlit desert. With the gritty scrape of every step, I took off running toward the subtle glow of Fallmont. It was a bit windier than I was used to, and sand was whipping around me as I sprinted. Suddenly, sand flew into my eye. I stopped in my tracks and shielded my face with my hands, blinking rapidly in a futile attempt to rid my eye of the sand.

I groaned. Every blink felt like I was grinding my cornea down with sandpaper. I continued to shield my face with both hands as I tried to force myself to cry in a desperate attempt to wash out the sand. As I did, the wind roared even more violently, and I could feel sand pelting my jacket sleeves. I narrowed my hands around my eyes even more to block out the continuing flurry of sand, but the light of Fallmont vanished in the distance.

My eyes still stinging, I uncovered my face and squinted. As the storm continued to pick up, it became impossible to see which direction I was going. Determined to find my friends, I closed my eyes to block out the sand since I couldn't see far anyways, and I pushed onwards.

A few steps later, as I went to put my foot down, I was caught off-guard by a dip in the sand beneath me. I stumbled, falling forward blindly and colliding with the rolling sand. With a frustrated pout, I squeezed my eyes shut tighter and frantically peeled off my long jacket. My face near the ground, I covered myself completely with the jacket, tucking it under my arms and legs to form a sort of shell over my body. I hunched over, the side of my gun pressed tight against my hip. The sand beneath my shell was still, but around me, the wind and sand howled hatefully at me.

Just then, there was a sharp jabbing on my back that felt like someone was poking me. I attempted to ignore the sensation for a minute, but eventually, I felt a tugging.

Someone was trying to pull off my jacket.

TEN

I reared back out of my jacket-shell, throwing myself to my feet as quickly as I could to face the aggressor. With one eye squished shut and the other barely peering open enough to see, I stared back at a masked Fabian.

"What are you doing out here?" I cried at him over the sound of the ferocious winds.

His eyes were protected behind what looked like science goggles, and his mouth and nose were shielded by a blue medical mask. He reached into a bag, pulling out identical goggles and a mask, handing them to me.

Without question, I pulled the mask and goggles on, blinking my eyes rapidly again to wash away the sand and dryness.

He pointed behind me, toward the ruins, and waved for me to follow him.

I shook my head and pointed toward Fallmont, its few emergency streetlights glowing subtly in the distance, to which Fabian responded by cocking his head to the side.

I put my jacket back on and continued on my path to Fallmont. After a moment, I stopped to see if Fabian was following me. Sure enough, there he was. I half expected him to try to stop me, but instead, he stood just a few feet behind me, patiently waiting for me to continue.

We walked briskly the rest of the way to Fallmont, pausing periodically when the sandstorm became too much to walk through or too intense to see through.

When we finally reached the gates of Fallmont, I could see Fabian's ladder on the ground, halfway buried because of the wind.

Fabian propped the ladder up against the brick wall. I pointed at him and then dramatically gripped the sides of the ladder and displayed a wide stance. As I turned back to him, he nodded and took his place holding the ladder, clearly understanding my message. I stepped over his arm and positioned myself on the ladder, looking back at Fabian for confirmation. His eyes were focused as they stared back at me past his goggles. I turned back toward the ladder and began my ascent.

Nearly two-thirds of the way up, the wind gushed past me. I dug my fingers into the sides of the ladder, pressing my body as close as I could to the rungs. I felt like I could hear my heart thumping in my chest as I held on, waiting to see who would win—me or the wind. I took a deep breath and moved my right hand to the next rung, keeping my body as flat as possible as I pulled myself up, rung by rung until I felt the top of the walls of Fallmont. I peered over, checking for officials, but there wasn't a soul in the dark streets.

Cautiously, I pulled myself on top of the wall, straddling it and pressing my stomach down flat. My cheek pressed into the sandy cement of the wall as I faced outward so I could see Fabian. I reached for the top of the ladder and pushed down on the sides to steady it. Briefly, I released the ladder with one hand to signal to Fabian, who responded with a confident step up.

The ladder swayed and shook with every step Fabian took and with every gush of wind, but I continued to steady it, despite the awkward angle I created by trying to stay as flat to the top of the wall as possible.

When Fabian had just crossed the halfway point on the ladder, a blast of wind rammed into him without warning, ripping the ladder from my grip. I let out a brief squeak of surprise before clamping my mouth shut to stay silent as I watched Fabian tumble into the sand with the ladder. A cloud of sand puffed up around him. I stared in silence, waiting for it to clear. Out of the cloud, I saw a shaky thumbs-up and felt my body relax.

He's okay.

After a few moments, I could see Fabian lying there, his chest heaving. Then, he used the wall to help himself to his feet. He was a bit unsteady at first, as he lifted one of his feet from the ground and rolled his foot and ankle around. He placed it back on the ground and repeated the exercise with his other side before raising up another thumb to me.

Fabian picked up the ladder and leaned it against the wall again. He watched me, waiting to be sure I had a good grip on it. This time, he scurried up with alarming speed, as if trying to outrun the wind. When he was able to reach the top of the wall, I scooted back to give him room. From there, he began to lift the ladder and move it down into Fallmont until the rubber feet on the bottom contacted the ground below. I locked eyes with Fabian, and he motioned for me to go first.

I sat up and situated myself to begin climbing down. Firmly gripping the top of the wall, I tested out the ladder by slowly letting my weight down on it. After watching Fabian practically fly off moments before and knowing this side of the wall didn't have a bed of sand to land in if I did fall, I was a bit uneasy climbing down. The ladder shifted slightly, but it seemed stable. I took one step, and then another, my legs wobbling with each move.

As I reached the bottom, I heard some voices from around the corner. I froze in place for a moment, trying to pinpoint the distance and direction they were coming from. Fabian climbed down after me, and seeing the panicked look in my eyes, he pulled the ladder down and placed it carefully on its side behind some bushes a few feet away—just enough to make it less noticeable.

"Stay in the bushes," I said softly to Fabian before running on my toes toward a nearby house.

The voices seemed closer, and the storm seemed much quieter from inside the city walls. I began to hear the voices well enough to make out what they were saying.

"I don't know when they're doing that though," one of the voices said.

"I'm guessing at night, like she said. When else would they be able to without one of us seeing? Or without someone else seeing and telling us?" the second replied.

"I guess. Not really worth it no matter when they're finding time to do that. What good does it do?"

The second grumbled. "Who knows. Didn't you say your sister and her husband got one of those letters?"

"Yeah, and they threw it away. That's what everyone should do, but some idiots just have to feel rebellious or something. I mean, seriously? You get a letter from some bored kid looking to cause trouble, so you risk getting shipped off to Delaisse over a prank. Kids can't be exiled—though I'd be in full support of it—but if adults are tagging buildings because they let this kid influence them? I just don't get it."

Letters? Could they be talking about the Dawn Letters? What do they mean tagging?

I listened intently to the voices as I clung to the edge of the nearest house, shadowed by a large, tacky lawn ornament composed of colorful bottles melted together. From behind the display, the moon light shown through, decorating my skin in deep reds, blues, and greens.

The wind howled, echoing down alleyways, sending sand rolling across the city streets.

"Getting tired of this damn storm," the first official grumbled.

"Hey," the second one said. "It could be worse. I heard they sent Henry driving through it tonight."

"Pity. It was nice knowing him." The first chuckled darkly.

There was a smack followed by joint laughter.

Their voices began to fade over the growing wind. As it died back down momentarily, I began to make out their voices again.

"Look, all I'm saying is that the problem would be solved if we could find and exile the little brat who started this," the first voice said in response to something the second must have muttered.

"I disagree," the second argued. He sounded tired. "Think about it—if you have some people who are easily manipulated and you give them some kind of leader, even if it's just some kid, and then you arrest their leader… Won't that make the kid some kind of martyr? These people are clearly reckless—what makes you think they wouldn't act out if we arrested the kid?"

"Arrest all of them," the first said. They sounded like they were rounding the corner nearest to my hiding place, but I continued to squat behind the bottle display as still as I could. "I can't imagine there are that many to begin with. They might *all* be kids even. If it's bad enough, I bet we'd have a case for exiling them all."

"Geez, Rod, why do you hate kids so much? Doesn't your sister have a kid?"

"Yeah. Saunders, my nephew. He's four, so he's too young to do anything worse than color on the walls."

"It's not that different than what these people are doing."

The next statement was drowned out by the sounds of the sandstorm whipping around outside the city. As the storm forced some of the wind and sand into the streets, I felt a twinge of guilt for leaving Fabian in the bushes, likely unable to hear anything but the wind surrounding the city.

At this point, I could see the two of them through the glass display. One of them was lankier. He walked with a drowsy slouch, his empty hands swaying low at his sides. The other was shorter and stockier and carried his gun aimed forward as if actively searching for a target.

I eased my hand over to my gun, pulling it slowly from my waist. Squatting and holding as still as possible, I watched the two of them continue down the street, their words growing muted.

I should get Fabian before I look for Paren, but he'll only slow me down. I'll get him on our way out.

I waited a few more minutes before easing out of my hiding place, keeping as concealed as possible by nearby walls and yard decorations as I started toward City Hall.

The streets were as empty and silent as could be expected with the new curfew in place. At one point, I heard another pair of officials nearing me, but their voices faded as they turned down a different street.

When I reached City Hall, it felt like a boulder fell on my chest and crushed it. I stood there, staring at the lifeless building in front of me as I remembered the last time I stood in that place. For a moment, I almost felt Zane's touch on my shoulder again. I almost heard his warm voice reminding me that I was doing the "right thing," or so we thought. I almost saw his soft eyes with their usual glimmer of excitement. Everything came plummeting back down to reality when the front doors of City Hall crashed open and a pair of officials exited.

I decided to creep up as close as I could while hiding behind a short, decorative brick wall not far from the side of the building. I hunched down, concealing my head and my entire body behind the wall as I waited, listening.

"Put your hands in the air!" yelled a familiar voice.

My veins turned to ice as I stayed frozen beneath the wall. The voice sounded like the official from earlier, Rod.

Just then, I heard a hollow clatter.

"Please, man!" a new voice cried. "I was trying to help, I was—"

"Save it," Rod barked. "You're done here."

I listened intently, hearing the familiar click of handcuffs. The officials and the criminal began to walk toward the door, their steps growing louder. Almost as soon as the commotion had started, it was over, leaving me to the silence of the empty city center.

Cautiously, I peered over the side of the wall. As I suspected, they were all back inside City Hall. Something to my right caught my eye. The walls of the buildings in the city center were all white or various shades of grey, but there was one noticeable difference on an otherwise plain wall directly across from City Hall. On the wall, there was a large blue water drop spray painted over what appeared to be a yellow sun. On the ground in front of it was a can of blue spray paint.

I guess they really are developing a graffiti problem here. This is nothing like Delaisse, though. And why a water drop? The officials were talking about the letters inciting graffiti artists to tag buildings – perhaps the sun is representative of the Dawn Letters. Why was that guy covering it up with a water drop?

After refocusing myself, I pulled my shoes off, keeping them hidden behind the wall. I'd have a better chance of sneaking in and out if I can stay quiet, and even though my socks were worn thin, they would help muffle the sound of boots or bare feet against tile. Before I stepped away from my hiding place, there was a loud crashing sound at the front door, followed by yelling.

I peered around from my spot, trying to get a look at the source.

"FREEZE!" an official bellowed, pointing his gun at someone as they ran full-speed down the street away from City Hall. Several officials took off after him, and I was fairly certain the target was the graffiti artist from moments ago.

He must have broken their grip and decided to make a run for it. That's gutsy. Good for him though.

The official who was aiming down the street lost his target and sprinted after the rest of them, keeping his gun in hand.

Now's my chance.

I left the gun at my waist, keeping a hand trained over it. With a deep inhale, I pulled the City Hall door open gently—just enough to peek inside. Much to my surprise, the door was unlocked. *I suppose they assume the curfew will actually keep people in their homes.* With a brief surge of relief, I realized the main room was empty, likely because the officials had to chase down the graffiti artist who made a break for it. The relief subsided when I realized I didn't know how to get to the holding cells. Nibbling on my lip as I moved, I slipped inside the crack in the doorway, easing the door shut behind me.

Weighing my options, I scanned the room. The huge chandelier loomed over me, each of its faux diamonds reflecting little glimmers of artificial light. The slick white marble of the walls and floor mirrored the already excessive light of the room. For a building with a lot of foot traffic during the day, the floors still appeared perfectly polished. It felt as if there was a spotlight and a huge "LOOK! Here she is!" sign flashing above me as I stood there in my dusty black jacket and worn out socks.

Ahead of me, I saw the counter that was usually surrounded by bankers and visitors, but was now completely empty. There was a door straight ahead of me—just to the left of the counter, and one on either far side of the large room.

Three options. My eyes shifted between the doors. *I know it isn't the door closest to the counter—that's for the stairs. That's how Zane and I got to Raine's office. As much as I want to go up there and put a bullet in her brain myself, I know she probably either isn't there at night or has a plethora of officials guarding her door.*

It was a 50/50 shot that I would pick the correct door, so I turned right and hurried over, balancing my weight on the balls of my feet. As I neared the door, I heard voices echoing around the monstrous, empty room. Instantly, I turned to run for the bank tellers' counter to hide. As I reached the counter, I tried to slow to a stop, but my socks were too slippery. My feet gave out from under me as I grabbed the counter to catch myself. With a loud *crack*, my jaw hit the edge of the counter on my way down to the floor. Holding back a pained cry, I waited, crouched behind the counter, clutching my jaw.

I heard the door open and the voices immediately grew louder, seeming to boom from within the open room. The two spoke of dropping off a "thug" to the holding ward officer.

That must be where Paren is.

Without thinking, I pushed myself up enough to peer over the edge of the counter to see exactly where the officials came from. When I was able to see, I could tell they came from the opposite door that I had been about to walk through. *Good to know.*

I watched as the two left the building. When the door shut fully behind them, I stood to my feet and rushed toward the correct door. Pressing my ear to it, everything seemed silent on the other side. I turned the knob little by little and eased the door open. In front of me, there was a concrete winding staircase that looked far less glamorous than the main room. The door closed quietly behind me as I tiptoed down the stairs, but as the door shut, a majority of the light seemed to disappear from the stairwell. The only thing keeping me from tumbling down the stairs blindly was the presence of sparsely placed little amber lights along the edges of the stairs. Every step that I took, I worried more and more about how the guard watching over the holding cells could spot me before I would see him. Hesitantly, with my legs shaking in the eerie silence, I reached for my gun. With the gun out of my waistband and pointed at the floor, I continued down the seemingly endless stairs.

When I reached the bottom, there was a long, wide hallway set before me with hardly more lighting than the staircase. There were rooms with ID scanners above each door's handle on either side of the hallway. Two officials sat at the end of the path. One official slouched over in a chair asleep in front of a single door on the far end. His arms seemed as big around as my waist. The other guard, about half the size of the sleeping guard but equally intimidating, sat in a chair against one of the walls. He was completely unaware of my presence as he focused on frantically scribbling in a tattered notebook in his lap.

I gnawed furiously on the inside of my cheek as I tried to calm my nerves. With a deep breath, I raised the gun in front of me. *Don't shoot, just scare,* I reminded myself. My stance wide and my stare unwavering, I clicked the safety off, waiting for the guard to notice me. When he seemed oblivious to the click, I ground my heel into the gritty concrete, making an obvious scraping sound. This seemed to get his attention, as he turned to face me.

"Woah," he said, his eyes wide. He lifted his hands, letting his pencil fall to the floor with a clatter.

I held one finger up to my lips, motioning for him to stay quiet. I wrapped my hand back around the base of the gun, trying to keep it steady so he wouldn't realize how shaky my hands were.

"What do you want?" he asked, his hands still up in surrender. "I don't get paid enough for this anyways. Seriously, just don't hurt me, okay? I have three kids and a wife, I wanted to be a writer, but we need the money. I don't care about this job, I just—"

I narrowed my eyes at him and tilted my head, trying to hint that he needed to stop talking.

"Right," he said, understanding the message.

"Paren," I whispered raspily. "Prisoner. Escaped from Bellicose. Blond, tall, blue eyes."

"There," the official whispered back, pointing at a door on my right.

"ID."

He nodded, unclipping his ID slowly, holding it up to display it to me before tossing it gently at my feet.

Keeping the gun trained on him, I squatted down and picked up the ID tag.

Gunnar Blevins, the tag read. The man pictured on it had a dopey, lopsided smile and dark acne scars. The man in front of me had the same complexion, but the dorky smile was replaced by fear as he stared back at me, his eyes continually shifting to the gun.

"Thank you." I nodded as I turned to scan the ID against the scanner. As soon as I had turned, I heard rapid scraping sounds. Before I could see what the sound was, the huge sleeping guard pounced on me, knocking the air from my lungs as I collided with concrete. I involuntarily screeched, sending the bottom of the gun colliding down with the top of his skull. Gunnar began to run for the stairs as the other guard tried to wrestle the gun from my hands. The guard had my hands above my head on the ground as he battled me for the weapon. The gun was nearly yanked from my hands, but I managed to loop my fingers around it tightly, lifting my arms from the ground. As I tried to pull the gun from his grip, there was a sharp bang.

He stopped fighting me as he stared up at something just long enough for me to wriggle out from under him, scanning the ID as I stood in one swift motion. The scanner beeped and I pulled the door open as the guard began to push himself up. Inside, Paren sat in a corner, his clothes tattered and eyes bloodshot.

"Run, *now*!" I bellowed at him.

His eyes flickered up to meet mine and the look of despair melted from his face. Without a word, he scrambled to his feet and darted out the door. As I stepped back out of the cell, I turned to see Gunnar, his hand on his stomach.

"Don't look at it, buddy," the bigger guard assured him, now standing at his side and supporting Gunnar as he began to slump.

"What do I do?" Gunnar panicked, his bottom lip quivering and his eyes full of tears as he crumpled to his knees.

The other guard turned to face us, a look of burning hatred in his eyes. He turned back to Gunnar, stopping briefly to think.

"I've got you," he said calmly. "I'm going to get you help."

He scooped his friend up in his arms and turned to the stairs, pausing. His focus shifted to us just long enough to speak directly to me.

"Burn in hell."

Before I could respond, he disappeared up the stairs.

ELEVEN

"What happened?" Paren asked.

"Later. We have to go—someone was bound to have heard all of this, even if we are underground. Let's get out of here."

Paren and I raced up the spiraling stairs. He tripped twice on the way up, urging me to keep going both times. When we reached the top, we barged through the side door and flew full-speed toward the exit. Just as my hands connected with the front door to open it, I heard voices from behind us, commanding us to stop. I hesitated for a split second before throwing the door open, allowing us both to fly out. Outside, the air felt warm and the sky was still dark. As we ran, I glanced at the wall concealing my shoes. *No time,* I thought as we hurtled down the street, officials charging after us.

"Turn!" I changed direction, skidding around a tall building with black glass windows covering the walls.

Paren stayed close behind me as we ran, and I made as many turns as possible to lose the officials. I was out of breath, my lungs were searing, but I kept pushing. I patted my pockets as the gate came into view before remembering that Skylar had the Skeleton Key. I remembered Fabian was hiding with the ladder, and as we reached the gate, I tucked my gun back into my waistband.

"Fabian!" I called to the bush. "Ladder! Now!"

Fabian scampered out from the bush, leaves stuck to his hair and clothes. He reached behind him quickly and pulled the ladder out, propping it up against the wall.

"Why the ladder?" Paren asked, nearly wheezing.

"Gate's locked," I said as Fabian began to climb.

"Let's just unlock the gate!" Paren argued.

"You need a key for either side; let's just go! I'll hold it—hurry up!"

"Go ahead," Paren said, reaching for the ladder.

He used his feet to steady the rubber ends of the ladder as he held out a hand to help me onto the ladder. I scurried up the rungs and clung to the top of the brick wall as I straddled it, keeping out of the way as Fabian steadied the ladder for Paren from our perch.

As Paren began to climb, I could see a cluster of officials in the distance running toward us. Now that we were elevated and in plain sight, it was as if all officials on patrol that night were now headed straight for us.

"Hurry!" I commanded Paren. "They're coming!"

"What's going on? What did you do?" Fabian asked, his eyes wide as he realized how many people were after us.

"Officials—a lot of them. Broke a friend out of a holding cell," I said as Paren reached the top. "Get it over the wall!"

With the ladder on the outside of Fallmont, Fabian began to climb down.

"Sorry! Just want to be able to steady it for you!" he called up.

"It's fine, but we're running out of time!" My heart was pounding in my chest in rhythm with the footsteps of the officials storming toward the wall.

"Hold it!" I ordered Fabian as I steadied the ladder over the other side of the wall.

I began to scurry down the ladder with Paren immediately after me. Gunshots and shouts were ringing out on the other side of the wall, growing closer to the gate.

"Jump!" I ordered as Paren reached the halfway point on the ladder.

I launched myself off the ladder clumsily, knocking it to the side as Paren and I tumbled into the sand. Sharp grains tore across my cheeks as I fell, landing with a force that felt like the wall itself had collapsed on my ribcage.

My vision went black momentarily, but when it came back, I gasped for air, sucking back the dusty oxygen. With a sputtering cough, I hurried to my feet, turning to check on Paren. Curled up in the sand, Paren was clutching his ankle.

"Paren!" I called.

"Guys, they're almost at the gate!" Fabian urged.

"I'm okay." Paren groaned, standing carefully. When he put his weight on his right leg, he let out a cry of pain.

"Come on!" Fabian yelled, supporting Paren as he stood. "Grab his other side and let's go!"

"That way!" I pointed along the wall.

The three of us moved as fast as we could, hoping to turn the corner before the officials could start shooting. Before we reached the corner of the walls, a brawny figure came hurtling from our destination, nearly tackling me as he barreled toward the officials who had begun to push open the gate.

"Cromwell!" I screamed after the figure. "What are you doing?"

He snatched up the ladder and slammed his massive body into the gate with an echoing clang, knocking several of the officials backwards. Before they could react, Cromwell slid the top of the ladder beneath the handles, the bottom of it wedged into the ground. When the officials tried to push on the gate, the ladder dug deeper into the sand.

"I'm coming!" a voice shouted desperately from behind me.

Shots fired off from the inside of the gate, and before Cromwell could move from their line of sight, he was hit. With a rumbling yell, he darted to the side, away from the gate.

Braylin trotted up from behind, passing me and moving straight for Cromwell.

"Stay away from the gate!" I warned him.

Braylin sprinted past the gate, narrowly avoiding being shot by an ornery official with a snarled lip. Squatting down, he rolled up Cromwell's short sleeve, exposing the gunshot wound.

"It grazed him," Braylin sighed shakily. "I'll help you clean that back in the ruins."

Cromwell and Braylin carefully rushed back across the sight of the officials, most of whom were gone—likely in search of something to help remove the ladder from the bottom of the gate.

Seeming unphased by his bloody gash, Cromwell scooped up Paren, tossing him like a limp doll over his good shoulder. Without a word, he marched off to the right, away from Fallmont.

"Where are you going?" Braylin called after him. "Wrong way!"

"Don't want them to see where we're hiding," Cromwell grunted. "Just a detour."

After a roundabout way of reaching our ruins, Cromwell practically threw Paren onto the couch, launching a cloud of dust around him.

"Geez!" Paren managed through sputters. "Glad to see you, too!"

"Where's Skylar?" I asked.

"I wanted to ask you the same thing," Braylin said, his voice somber.

"She hasn't come back yet?"

He shook his head.

"She wasn't in Fallmont?" Cromwell asked.

"Not that I saw." I ran my fingers through my hair, tugging on a knot to break it loose.

"We'll find her." Braylin smiled weakly. "She can't have gone far, right?"

"Right," I sighed. *But she might have been taken far.*

"It's too bright out now to go looking, but if she's not back by night, we'll go look for her," Fabian suggested.

"Can I help somehow?" Paren asked from the couch.

"You can sit there and look pretty," Cromwell smirked.

"Funny!" Paren said, his voice almost squeaky.

"In all seriousness, though," I said. "You'll be more help to us if your ankle properly heals. Get some rest."

"Here," Braylin tucked a small stack of pillows under Paren's ankle. "I'll find something to use as crutches in case you need to get up."

Braylin disappeared into one of the other rooms.

"I'll help him," I offered, rushing to follow him.

In the other room, there was a shattered television hanging from the wall, and two tattered armchairs. Braylin was rummaging through a closet with a splintering door on the far side of the room when I closed the door of the room quietly behind me, blocking out the sounds of Cromwell helping get Paren up to speed on our plans.

"Braylin," I started.

"Do you think this could work as a crutch?" he asked, holding out a golf club.

"Braylin," I repeated. "It's ab—"

"I think he's too tall for this, but it might work." He set the golf club aside.

"Braylin!" I growled. "It's about Skylar."

"What about her?" he asked, pausing.

"She has the Key."

"You gave her the Key?" Braylin gaped back at me. "What were you thinking!"

"I was thinking she wouldn't disappear!"

"Do you think she ran away on purpose?"

"I don't kn—"

"Gave up on the plan and ran away with the Key?"

"I d—"

"What if officials took her, found the Key, and are torturing her for information?" His eyes grew wide and his face turned pale.

"Look, Braylin! I don't know! I know as much as you do!"

"Sorry," he grimaced, color creeping back into his cheeks.

"We'll find her," I promised.

That night, we agreed to get a bit more rest before going in search of Skylar. Paren, unable to sleep, eased himself to his feet with the help of his golf club cane.

"I'm going to step outside and get some air," he managed with a yawn.

"Don't go far," I advised. "In case you can't walk well enough to get back here."

"I do what I want, *mom*," he said with a chuckle, reaching for the door. "I'm not leaving the front of the house anyways—I'll be fine."

I rolled back over under my blanket on the floor with a groan, when I heard Paren again.

"Guys?"

Reluctantly, I pushed myself up to look at Paren with a sleep-deprived, "What?"

In the doorway, Skylar stood and stared blankly into the house, her clothes shredded and tattered, her hair a tangled mess.

"Skylar!" Braylin yipped, running over to hug her.

Frozen, she kept standing there. Her eyes glazed over as she stared into the room, not looking at anyone or anything in particular. Braylin wrapped his arms around her with a toothy grin that quickly subsided when Skylar's arms continued to dangle at her sides.

"Why are you wet?" he asked, slowly pulling away from the hug and looking at his arms and shirt.

Silent, he stepped into the moonlight, twisting his arm to catch the light. Braylin's arms and shirt were entirely covered in blood.

Before he could utter a word, Skylar collapsed on the floor.

"Skylar!" I hurried to her side, rolling her onto her back. "Get her to the couch!"

Cromwell stooped down and carefully lifted Skylar, carrying her over to the dusty couch.

"What happened to her?" Fabian asked, his eyes bulging behind his glasses.

I gingerly shifted the shreds of her shirt to get a better look at her abdomen. Her skin was nearly unscathed, except for a few minor cuts and scrapes.

"I don't think this is her blood."

TWELVE

"Wake up!" Braylin shook Skylar, his hands visibly shaking during every pause.

"Calm down!" I urged. "She's probably just exhausted and dehydrated. Go get her some water and stop shaking her."

Braylin sniveled, nodding weakly before retrieving one of the water bottles. When he returned, he also brought a rag he had found in the kitchen. He unscrewed the cap and poured some of the water on the rag.

"Can you please try to wash some of the blood off?" he asked, his eyes red. "I wouldn't feel right doing it."

I nodded, accepting the rag. Hesitantly, I lifted the bottom of her shirt, fully exposing her stained abdomen. When she didn't move, I took the rag to her skin and began to gently scrub up the thick blood. As I began to reach around her side to continue cleaning her, she sat up with a jolt.

"Get off of me!" she yelped.

When she tried to slide herself off the couch, she let out a pained scream.

"What did you do to her?" Braylin panicked.

"Nothing!"

"It burns!" she screamed, falling off the couch and onto her knees. She pawed helplessly at her back; her hands covered in shiny red.

My heart thumping in my throat, I scampered behind her to look at her back.

"Skylar, take off your shirt," I asked.

"It hurts!" she wailed.

"Get her shirt off!" I yelled to all the bystanders.

Paren squatted in front of her and tugged her shirt over her head as she flailed, leaving streaks of blood across his face and arms.

I swore under my breath.

"What is it?" Paren asked.

"It's a water drop," I sighed, looking at the large carving on Skylar's back. It looked as if someone drew on her back with a knife or a razor. "It says 'Raine' underneath it."

The boys all crowded around behind Skylar, craning to get a better look.

"Why a water drop?" Braylin asked.

"It's a Raine drop," Fabian said, his voice hushed.

Skylar broke into exhausted sobs on her knees, letting her face sink to the floor.

"But who would do that to her?" Braylin asked.

"It could have been anyone," Fabian answered. "There are a lot of people in Fallmont who adore Raine and aren't taking kindly to the letters."

"Could it have been an official?" Paren asked.

Skylar shook her head, letting out a particularly loud sniffle.

"Who did this to you?" Cromwell asked. "I'll kill them myself!"

"I already did," she replied feebly.

A chilling silence fell over the room as we all stared down at Skylar, her back arched and her face in her palms on the floor, blood oozing along the Raine drop with every deep shuttering breath she took.

"From now on, let's try to avoid going into the cities alone." My suggestion was answered with unanimous nods.

Just then, there was a clatter as Skylar threw something weakly across the floor without lifting her head.

The Skeleton Key.

Later into the night, Skylar eventually let me clean her back and bandage her up. When she was in a fresh, albeit dusty, shirt from one of the closets, she sat in the corner of the couch with her knees up and her arms around her legs.

"Do you want to talk about it?" I whispered, carefully sitting beside her.

She stared forward, unblinking as she nibbled on the inside of her cheek.

"That's fine. I don't bl—"

"I didn't even get close to City Hall," she murmured.

"What?"

"They must have seen me from the window. I was walking down the street, I heard something behind me and turned around. Nothing. When I turned back, there were three of them."

"You don't have to talk about it if you don't want to," I said.

She continued, as if I never said anything. "Two men and one woman. They were in their pajamas. The two men picked me up and held my arms and legs together, and the woman was just smiling at me. They took me into one of the houses. I didn't scream because I didn't want to be caught by officials.

The guys kept holding me down and she started… carving." At this, Skylar started shaking, her face still blank.

I reached for my bag, rifling through it and pulling out a packaged brownie. "Here," I said, holding it out to her. "I think you should eat something."

"I asked them why they were doing that," she continued, ignoring me. "The girl just said they saw me sneak in and they knew who I must be. They called me 'Dawn' and said that I should never forget who is really in charge. I tried to fight them. Eventually one of the guys messed up—he let one of his arms get too close to my face and I bit down as hard as I could. I could taste the blood, but I kept biting until the other let me go in order to help his friend. As soon as they released me, I reached for the dagger and immediately lunged."

I stared back at her, stunned. I know she's killed before, but she seemed genuinely traumatized. *I guess torture will do that to you.*

"I killed the girl first," she said with a shaky exhale. "I'm sorry I gave up on looking for your friend, but I had to get out of there. I'm glad you found him anyways."

"Don't worry about it," I said. "I wouldn't have wanted you running around in your condition anyways! You need food, water, and some rest."

"This isn't working, E," Skylar sighed, easing herself onto her side on the couch with a pained grumble. "The letters, I mean."

"But they are," I said, moving to make room as she stretched her legs across my lap.

"I don't know how you can be so confident."

"When I was looking for Paren," I started, "I saw some graffiti near Town Hall. It was a big sun. I wouldn't have understood at first it I hadn't overheard some officials. It's Dawn graffiti. Someone is doing it because of our letters. Even if only one person believes us, it's a start!"

"It's not enough," she said with a quick shiver.

I moved her legs onto the couch as I stood, carefully placing my blanket over her as she closed her eyes. Across the room, Braylin and

Cromwell slept soundly, completely still through the course of our entire conversation. Paren and Fabian, however, were nowhere to be seen. Curious, I decided to search the house for them, but they still weren't there.

"Paren?" I called quietly, peeking my head out the front door. "Fabian?" I squinted in the dim light, my eyes met by Paren's concerned gaze from across the street. "What are you doing?"

Paren leaned heavily on the golf club cane, which scraped against the sandy pavement.

My eyes continued to focus, eventually making out Fabian's figure beside him.

I stepped out into the street, closing the door gingerly behind me. My arms crossed, bracing against the surprisingly nippy wind, I made my way over to the two boys just as Fabian shoved Paren. Paren's golf club cane gave out and he stumbled, groaning in pain.

"What's your problem?" I shot Fabian a nasty look before running to Paren, steadying him and handing him the golf club.

"You didn't tell me he's Bellicose *trash*!" Fabian spat, his lip curled in a snarling rage.

"So what?" I stood tall, getting in Fabian's face.

"He's a *murderer*—he hurts people for *fun*!"

"Who told you that load of crap?" Paren scoffed.

"You're from Bellicose—once you told me that, that was all I needed to know!"

"Not all Bellicose are serial killers, Fabian!" I said.

He scoffed, crossing his arms.

"Let me ask you something," I said, lowering myself as I thought. "I just want to know what you think."

Fabian rolled his eyes.

"Give her a chance, douchebag," Paren said flatly.

"Take Paren, Braylin, Skylar, and me. You know what? You met Zane, too. Go ahead and add him to the list. Knowing what you know about us—who is the best person and who is the worst? Actually, rank us. In order. Worst person to the best person."

"What kind of question is that?" Fabian said with a condescending snort.

"One that I want answered. Go ahead."

"Well, what exile towns are Braylin and Skylar from?"

"Nope. No questions from you until you answer mine."

"That's not fair."

"How not?" I asked. "How is it any more fair of you to judge them by what town they're from?"

"Because it tells me what kind of person they are—it tells me what they've done wrong."

"Sucks. Knowing what you know—how would you rank us?"

"Well, the first one is easy. Paren is the worst because he's violent." Fabian paused, looking over at Paren behind me, as if expecting retaliation. When nothing happened, he proceeded. "I guess I would say that Skylar is probably the second worst—there's something about her. She's alright, I guess. Braylin seems harmless, but I bet he's hiding something. Is he from Equivox? He seems like the lying sort. If you approved of Zane, I can't imagine he was that bad. Plus, he was just a thief. Petty greed and status got the best of him. Then you, but that's just because I know you're not a bad person."

I stared at him for a moment to make sure he was done rationalizing.

"Come with me," I said, beckoning him into the house, with Paren following after.

Inside, Skylar had woken up again and was lightly sipping on a water bottle in the kitchen.

"Hey!" I exclaimed, loud enough to wake the others.

My friends grumbled sleepily, eventually waking enough to look me in the eyes.

"Braylin," I started. "Please tell Fabian where you were exiled and why."

Braylin shrugged. "I was exiled to Clamorite with my sister for protesting with some other locals. Our parents work for the same company, and they both suffered huge pay cuts when the boss's son started working for the company. Their boss paid his own son a fortune for doing absolutely nothing, and our mom even had to sell her engagement ring to pay the bills. Cindee and I were furious, so we joined some of the others who were affected, and we protested."

"Sky," I called. "How about you?"

She yawned, her eyes so bloodshot I could see them from across the room.

"I escaped Delaisse," she said, her voice sleepy and raspy. "Graffiti artist." She shrugged. "No just cause. I enjoyed it—it was freeing. Four years of it and I never got caught… until I did."

I looked at Fabian, who was silent as he processed.

"Zane stole for his family," I said. "He didn't steal for self-gain, he didn't steal for status or money or fun. His brother was sick and his family couldn't afford food because of the medication. He stole to provide."

"What about you?" he asked, his eyes hopeful.

"I was stealing expensive rum," I said bluntly. "I wanted to keep some for myself, and I wanted to become a messenger, travel to another city, and sell it for a lot of money."

Fabian's face melted into sheer disappointment. His eyes seemed to sink back into their sockets, his smile lines faded into smooth skin, and his gaze sunk low.

"And Paren," I said.

"I beat up a man for harassing a woman at a bar," he said, his voice and posture appearing humble, as if he didn't see his actions as valiant or selfless.

"I've killed someone," I admitted. "An official. After I escaped Avid. I was trying to get away, and I stabbed him. They even sent me to Bellicose and I escaped."

Fabian's eyes began to turn red, and the redness traveled across the rest of his face quickly. When he tried to look at me, he turned his gaze and quickly hid his face. After a loud sniffle, he turned on his heel and rushed out the door.

Braylin tried to hurry after him, but I held my arm out. "Let him go."

"What was that all about?" Cromwell asked.

A day and a half later, Fabian returned, his bag full of supplies.

"Thank you for not abandoning us," I said with a soft smile.

"You aren't who I thought you were," he said, residual disgust lingering in his words. He refused to meet my eyes as he pushed past me and into the house.

"I'm sorry," I said, my tone insincere as I trailed after him into the kitchen.

"It's only slaughter, right?" he said, his voice squeaking at the last word. "Definitely nothing you should have told me, right?"

"It was self-defense."

"It was only someone's life," he said mockingly as he overturned his bag, sending supplies tumbling across the counter.

"Is that the part of this that bothers you most?"

"Yes! Sorry if finding out my childhood best friend is a murderer should have been easy to accept, but it isn't!" At this, his head shot around and he stared at me with bloodshot eyes. "You sure proved me wrong, Eos. The people in Bellicose aren't the worst criminals. Neither are the people in Avid, Clamorite, or Delaisse. Not even Equivox. *You*. You are the worst criminal. You're a liar, a thief, a murderer, a rebel. You belong in almost every exile town. You've never vandalized anything or done drugs, have you? Would hate for you to be so close to being this well-rounded!"

"Actually," I murmured as he glowered at me.

"What?" he spat.

"I tried drugs. Just once."

"Are you joking right now?" He laughed manically. "Such a *great* sense of humor! Truly stellar, Eos Dawn!"

"I'm just trying to be honest with you," I said calmly. "But I need you to believe me—I'm not a murderer. Most of us have killed people in self-defense—it's part of the territory of being on the run. I hate it as much as you do. Worse. I have to live with it."

The two of us stood there in silence for a moment, awkwardly pretending to read the labels on cans of corn and packets of oats. The rest of our friends stood across the room, staring back at us as if they were watching a boxing match and were waiting to see if one of us really had knocked the other out.

"What can I do to make things right?" I asked softly, not looking up from the can of corn in my hand.

"Just give me some time," he said, sliding a cup of chocolate pudding across the counter before heading to the door.

I swallowed a lump in my throat before looking up to face my friends, who immediately pretended to have been tidying up the room instead of eavesdropping on the entire conversation.

That night, no one spoke to me before bed. I understood that no one was upset with me, but I don't think they knew what to say. It's hard to say the wrong thing when you don't say anything at all.

After a vivid dream where I relived the moment when I stabbed the official who cornered me in Equivox back when I was still searching for the Skeleton Key, I woke up soaked by my own sweat. My sweaty and sticky limbs collected the dirt and grime on the floor, making me feel filthier than I did to begin with.

What I wouldn't give for a shower.

I splashed a conservative amount of water on a towel from the kitchen, using it to scrub at my dirty skin. The rag hardly made a difference, but I managed to wipe clean a small patch on my arm, revealing the pasty skin beneath the filth. Frustrated and still sweaty from my nightmare, I decided to step outside. The night air felt extra cool on the clean patch on my arm. The sky was speckled with stars, and the moonlight silhouetted wispy clouds above. I sucked back some of the cool air, crossing my arms and looking up and down the street. A few houses down, I spotted two figures. One was leaning on a makeshift cane.

"Paren?" I called sleepily, making my way toward him. As I grew near, I could make out the other figure—Fabian.

"Is everything okay, guys?" I asked, worried the two were fighting again.

"Fabian was just telling me an interesting piece of news," Paren said, his eyes twitching up with his playful smile. "I'll let him share."

"Raine messed up," Fabian grinned. "Big time."

"How?"

"She exiled that kid."

I felt my eyes involuntarily widen. "The boy who protested? Why? She's not supposed to ex—"

"I know," he continued. "Everyone in Fallmont knows this kid, too, which makes it even better."

"*Better*?" I gaped. "That poor kid! What was she thinking exiling a child? I didn't think she'd actually do it!"

"I've got more details than the last time I heard about him. From what I heard, the boy read one of those 'pesky Dawn Letters' and he was outraged. He's only 13, but he helps a lot with his dad's business. They're the most established financial advisory company in the New Territory.

They've helped just about every local businessperson in Fallmont get started. The boy, Derek, found the letter before his parents. The next morning, he was telling everyone he came across about how messed up the exile town system is. I guess it was a bit of a sensitive topic for him anyways—his father was framed not long ago when a local company went under. The guy in charge of the business claimed his financial advisor had been stealing from his account and lying about where funds were going. I still remember that day—I was an official at the time—a bunch of us were called to escort the man to City Hall for the hearing, and Raine was quick to decide his sentence. We hadn't even started toward City Hall before she sent someone to tell us to just take him straight to Equivox instead. Some of my buddies on the force with me said they heard Raine accepted a bribe from the guy's competitor, but I was never able to confirm that."

"That's ridiculous!" I said, uncrossing my arms and running my fingers through my tangled hair. "But you said the kid was exiled. When? Was his dad actually exiled?"

"No. Since so many people knew and trusted the man, they demanded a fair hearing, and they ended up providing enough evidence that he was innocent. The kid was shipped off just the other day though. Clamorite. Raine caught word that the boy was speaking out against her, and she tried to squash the rumors while she still had a chance. I think the only reason she even gave him a hearing was because people threw such a big fit. But she ended up having him exiled because he was 'too big of a threat.' If you ask me, she just made things worse. Everyone knows and loves Derek, and now that word is getting out that he was exiled—especially as a minor—people are paying a bit more attention to your letters. I think it might be time that you write another one."

"And we've got the perfect story," Paren said with a hopeful smile.

THIRTEEN

It took us two days to write enough copies of the second letter. This time, we were able to produce far more letters than the first, now that we had a team of six working together. We didn't do much talking during these couple days, but we learned that Cromwell has stunningly clean penmanship and that Paren is an excellent storyteller. The second letter was almost completely written by Paren, with some tidbits about Derek's story as told by Fabian. When the letter was complete, we each passed it around to read it.

"It's missing something," Braylin said, cocking his head to the side as he scanned over it again. He grabbed a pen and made a quick adjustment, holding the paper up for us to all see. At the bottom of the page, beside our *Dawn* signature, he sketched a simple picture of a shining sun.

"Since it seems to be the unofficial symbol for us, I figure we should start making it a household icon."

"I love it." I smiled, knowing my happiness was genuine for the first time in a while.

"Oh!" Fabian chimed. "You know what rain does right?"

He stood, grinning at us all as he waited for an answer that never came.

"It falls," he said, his smile flattening. "What if we put that as some kind of slogan or something? 'Raine will fall' or something like that?"

He raised his eyebrows impatiently. "Oh, come on! It isn't that bad!"

"It's kind of cheesy," Cromwell said.

Everyone nodded in agreement.

Dejected, Fabian grunted. "Fine."

"It's alright," I said. "We can go ahead and add it. Why not, right? It's cheesy, but it's catchy."

With a grateful but smug grin, Fabian snatched up a stack of letters and began scrawling the new phrase on each one.

That night when the letters were finished, everyone agreed to help deliver them. Paren's ankle was improving, but he knew he would slow us down, so he decided it would be best to stay back in the ruins. Skylar's back had scabbed over and mostly healed, leaving behind a Rainedrop scar, and the seemingly endless days spent in the ruins had made her even more angry and restless than usual. Braylin, Skylar, and I were armed with our guns, and Skylar had returned my dagger to me. Cromwell found a piece of bent pipe in some of the rubble around our makeshift house, and Fabian filled his pockets with chunks of broken brick.

"What exactly do you plan on doing with pockets full of rocks?" Skylar scoffed.

"What else do you recommend?" Fabian shot defensively.

"Are you planning on stoning someone to death?" she asked.

"If I have to. I'd rather not have to."

"That'll work *great*," she mocked.

"Take it," I said, handing Fabian my dagger. "I've got a gun."

Fabian looked uncomfortable, pausing before taking the dagger.

"Better keep those rocks," Skylar said. "We might have time to skip stones across the lake at Equivox after a nice moonlit stroll through Fallmont."

Fabian's forehead creased as he glared at Skylar, his eyes never blinking and his stare never faltering as he turned out his pockets, letting the pieces of rubble clatter to the pavement. He bent down and picked up one of the rocks, holding it out to Skylar.

"In case there's an emergency," he sneered.

Skylar chuckled, pocketing the rock.

Just then, we heard a low rumbling in the distance.

"Do you guys hear that?" I asked, my voice hushed.

My question was answered by silent nods and wide eyes.

The rumbling grew louder and closer.

"Inside! Now!" I commanded, ushering everyone back in through the door, shutting and locking it behind us.

"Hide!" Skylar hissed, as we all scurried into the various rooms, fitting ourselves into closets and behind furniture.

The sound was now directly outside the front door. It sounded like the engine of one of the official's trucks.

My heart rattled my chest with every beat, and I was convinced it would expose my hiding place inside the cobwebbed kitchen cabinets below the sink.

The rumbling continued to hum, muffled by the walls of the house. Time crept by painfully, the muscles in my back and shoulders screaming at me, begging me to crawl out of the cabinet and stretch them. Suddenly, there was a furious pounding on the door. My chest lurched with each landed knock.

"Eos!" a deep voice called, stifled by the locked door. "Are you in there?"

My legs began to cramp.

"It's Zaire! Are you in there? It's safe— open up!"

"Don't open it!" I heard Skylar warn me from another cabinet.

"Zaire's a good guy," I whispered back. "I trust him."

"What if he's not alone? And are you sure it's him?"

"I've got my gun. You have yours? Follow me to the door."

I heard Skylar's cabinet open as she toppled out with a thud, followed by pained groans.

As I stepped out and stretched, my muscles seemed to tense up even more, as if saying, "Screw you— you had your chance to stretch."

The knocking had stopped, presumably because Zaire had moved onto the next house. Skylar and I reached the door and I tentatively unlocked it, holding my gun in front of me as I eased the door open.

There was no one in the doorway. I took a couple slow steps outside of the house, aiming my gun as I scanned the street, first spotting the truck in the distance, its headlights illuminating the street, then spotting Zaire next door. He was alone.

"Zaire!" I called to him, lowering my weapon.

"There you are!" He turned with a smile. "I was worried you weren't here anymore!"

"How did he know where to find you?" Skylar asked through gritted teeth, obvious spite in her voice.

I brushed off Skylar's question, running to greet Zaire, whose arms were held open.

"What brings you out this way?" I asked, accepting his hug.

"Still plan on changing Raine's mind about the exile town system somehow?"

"Not exactly *her* mind, but yes. Why?"

"Wanted to make sure you hadn't changed your plans and decided to just live out your days in the ruins," he said with a light chuckle.

"Nope. Still sticking with the plan."

Without another word, Zaire smirked and trotted off to his truck down the street.

"Am I supposed to follow?" I called after him, deciding I probably should come with.

When we reached his truck, he opened one of the rear doors as a set of feet hopped onto the dusty road.

"Hey, stranger!" The tattooed, piercing-covered girl grinned at me, waiting for me to process her arrival.

"Bexa!" I stared. "What's going on?"

"I told my brother about what happened to Zane," Zaire said solemnly. "He passed the word on to your friends back at Fortitude, and the other night, Bexa came to him and demanded to be taken to you. So, here she is."

"I'm sorry for what happened to Zane, but I'm sure you've heard that plenty. I'm here to help do whatever you need to do to get to Raine." She adjusted her frizzy brown hair in its messy bun and widened her stance. "I'm in favor of killing her, but I'll leave that up to you."

"Check the trunk," Zaire said, suppressing a smile.

By now, Fabian, Cromwell, Paren, and Braylin had stepped outside and made their way to me, but Skylar was still observing from a distance. I stepped toward the back of the truck as Zaire pulled it open, the trunk door making a horrendous squeak.

I gasped and let out an airy laugh. "Is this for us?"

"Everything in the trunk." Zaire clarified with a nod.

Skylar approached as the others peered around the back of the truck, taking in the bounty that Zaire gifted us. In the trunk were bags full of food, water, medical supplies, clothes, and even alcohol.

"Thank you!" shouted Braylin, tears collecting in the corners of his eyes as he beamed at Zaire. "This is incredible!"

"What's in it for you?" Skylar asked, arms crossed and glare unwavering.

"Lighten up, sweetheart," Paren handed a bottle of whiskey to Skylar, who took it with a grimace.

Without repeating her question, Skylar focused back on Zaire, cocking her head to the side.

Zaire rolled his eyes with a sigh. "Can't I just be helpful?"

"No."

"Damn, girl," Zaire said, his pitch squeaky. "E and I are friends, and I support the cause. I shuttle criminals to a free city—what more do you want from me? I even helped get you to Ironwood in the first place to find E—or did you forget?"

"Stop giving him a hard time, Sky," Bexa said.

"Welcome back," Skylar said plainly.

"Back? You're the ones who went missing," Bexa scoffed with a playful smile.

"How are the others? How's Cindee? Why aren't they with you?" Braylin began babbling.

"They're fine. I didn't tell them where I was going. I wasn't sure how dangerous things would be, so I decided not to."

"Does Cindee know I'm here? Does she know I'm okay?"

"*I* didn't know you were here, so no," Bexa said gruffly, following her response with a hurried "sorry" when she processed Braylin's gloomy demeanor.

I spent a while filling Bexa in while we all migrated the supplies from the truck to the ruined house. We filled the cabinets, shook out the towels and blankets, and even managed to find an old broom to attempt to sweep some of the ever-present sand out the door. By the end of it all, the place was actually beginning to look like a home.

"When are you sneaking in those letters?" Bexa asked me as I folded my blanket and draped it over the back of the couch.

"We were going to do it tonight before you guys showed up," I answered.

"Sorry to inconvenience you," she sneered. "It's not that late—what if Zaire could drop us off inside?"

"Hah!" I heard Zaire reply from his perch on the countertop, where he sat and aggressively gnawed on a lollipop. "Fat chance!"

"Seriously?" Bexa whined. "Why not?"

Zaire furrowed his brow and looked at me as if to ask if Bexa was crazy.

I shrugged.

"No way!" he insisted.

"I have an idea," Skylar said confidently.

Bexa, Cromwell, and I crammed into the backseat of Zaire's truck, with Cromwell awkwardly overflowing from his seat in the middle. In the front, Skylar stretched out comfortably with a smug grin.

"It's a short drive," Zaire grumbled. "Don't get comfortable."

Skylar reached into her bag full of letters and pulled out the bottle of whiskey from earlier, taking a swig with a wince.

"Relax!" She smiled.

Zaire sped up, the truck bouncing every time it hit a slight dip in the desert road. On one particularly abrupt bump, Zaire floored the gas, sloshing Skylar's whiskey all over her face as she reached for another taste.

"Ugh!"

"*Oops.*" He chuckled, a satisfied smile growing across his face.

When we could spot the gate, Zaire began to slow down.

"Get ready," he said. "You only have a few seconds once I reach the gate."

He crept closer, braking when he was a few feet away. Instantly, Bexa, Cromwell, Skylar, and I rapidly exited the vehicle, ducking behind it just as Zaire hit the button in his truck to open the front gates. The gates slowly began to open, and Zaire eased forward with us crouching and trailing behind it. When we cleared the gate, the four of us darted to the side, taking off down an alley as Zaire continued straight down the street to go about his usual business without us. Each of us had a bag full of letters, and our goal was to deliver them as quickly as possible without splitting up too much. We hurried down the street, keeping low as we ran doorstep to doorstep to leave behind letters.

As we made our way through several streets, we came across a familiar house—the same one with the stained-glass art that I saw during my last visit. As I approached the front door with a letter ready in my hand, I heard voices from down the street. I threw myself behind the stained-glass decoration, peering around the side of it to check that my friends had heard the voices and found cover as well. They were nowhere to be seen, so I had to hope for the best.

"Rod!" called one of the voices, echoing down the street. "You better come look at this!"

Rod—he's one of the officials from the last time I was here. He must just be a night watchman or something. What did they find? Or who?

"Is that one of those letters?" I heard Rod ask, his voice gravely.

"Looks like," his partner replied. There was a pause. "I guess they heard about that kid that was exiled. Read the letter."

Another long pause.

"Damn." Rod growled. "Raine's not going to like this. But we lapped this street already tonight not long ago and these definitely weren't here before. The scumbag leaving these can't be far."

At this, the officials' voices grew hushed and I could no longer make out what they were saying. I stayed crouched in my position, hearing the occasional grinding of a footstep against pavement, revealing that at least one of the officials was growing nearer.

"Let go!" I heard Bexa yelp.

"I got her!" Rod's partner called triumphantly as Rod whooped from across the street.

Nearby bushes rustled violently as I heard Bexa protest.

Just then, through the stained glass, I saw Cromwell appear out from the side of a house as he came barreling toward the officials with metal pipe held high.

Crack.

Cromwell's pipe made contact with Rod's head as Rod let out a string of profanity from the ground. As Cromwell made his way toward the other official, who I could now see holding Bexa, Skylar appeared beside me, crouching behind the glass structure.

I pulled out my gun, stood from my squat just a little as I peered around the side of the stained glass, and aimed at the official holding Bexa. The official had his gun out and began to raise it at Cromwell.

"Don't!" Skylar warned me.

I flicked off the safety and began to squeeze the trigger just as Skylar pulled on my legs, sending the two of us tumbling to the ground, the bullet shattering the stained glass and sending shards of glittering color in a spray around us.

I pushed myself up, my heart racing.

Was I too late? Did he shoot Cromwell? Is Bexa okay?

"Get in!" hissed a man, peering through the front door of the house. His eyes looked familiar, but the voice didn't belong to anyone I knew. "*Now!*"

Skylar and I scrambled to our feet and flew into the house as the man opened the door for us.

"Hide," he directed plainly, closing the front door with him outside.

I exchanged confused and panicked glances with Skylar before we picked a closet packed full of sweaters and cleaning supplies to hide behind.

"Is everything okay, officers?" I heard the man call from outside. "I heard a gunshot!"

"Get back in the house!" Rod boomed. "It's not safe for citizens outside right now!"

"Yes, sir," the man replied, his voice louder as he approached the house.

The front doored opened and then shut again. There was the deep *thunk* of a deadbolt.

"You can come out," the man said calmly.

Skylar and I eased our way out of the closet. In the living room, a young man and woman with gentle smiles greeted us.

"Why did you save us?" Skylar asked gruffly.

"You're the ones who write the Dawn Letters, aren't you?" the woman asked, her voice sweet and her honey blonde hair woven into a long, complex braid. My eyes trailed along her braid, stopping at her protruding belly.

"Yes," I replied.

"We want to help," the man started. "Your cause is very close to us, and we'd love to do whatever we can."

"How can we trust you?" Skylar asked.

"You're the ones with guns," the man answered. "How can *we* trust *you*?"

I looked at Skylar and shrugged. "He has a point."

"I'm Gavin," the man replied, his soft brown eyes squinting cheerily as he reached out a hand.

I shook his hand awkwardly.

"This is my wife, Mallory," Gavin said.

"Is the baby a boy or girl?" I asked, thinking of Yulie.

"We're waiting until we have the baby." She smiled, hugging her belly. "I think it's a boy, but Gav thinks it's a girl."

I smiled half-heartedly. "Did you happen to see if our friends were okay while you were out there?"

"The only people I saw were two officials in the street. There was no one with them, but they both looked badly hurt. How many people were with you?" Gavin asked.

"Two others."

"I'm guessing they got away. Did you guys plan a meeting place or anything in case of emergencies? We could look for them, if you'd like."

"It's okay," I replied. *Knowing Bexa and Cromwell, they're probably looking for us right now.*

"You're welcome to stay here as long as you'd like," Mallory offered. "We have a guest bedroom. I made potato soup, if you're hungry. It's still on the stove."

I looked at Skylar and back at Mallory, giving her an energetic nod.

I expected Skylar to protest, but she seemed just as eager as me for a warm meal.

We sat crowded around a tiny dinner table in a tight kitchen, devouring Mallory's potato soup, which was full of glorious stringy cheese.

"This is incredible, thank you!" I said mid-bite.

The freckles on her face rose with her cheeks in a grateful smile as her husband draped an arm around her shoulder and rubbed it lovingly.

"Are you a chef or something?" I asked, trying to be friendly and conversational. *I feel a bit out of practice. When was the last time I talked just to make conversation?*

Mallory giggled playfully. "No. I'm a nurse."

"Oh!" I said, trying desperately to think of something to say. *Please don't say something awkward.* "That's useful!" *Dammit.*

She laughed again. "Sometimes. It'll be helpful when the baby is old enough to start running around."

I smiled before taking another bite of soup. The conversation had died off and left the air with nothing but the clinking of spoons against bowls.

"Can I ask for something?" I started, scraping the sides of the bowl clean and licking the spoon. "I really don't want to seem greedy, but it would mean the world to me right now."

"What's that?" Gavin asked, his face growing serious.

"Can I use your shower?"

He laughed warmly. "Of course!"

FOURTEEN

I never wanted the shower to end. When I eventually convinced myself to step out and get dressed, I found that my clothes had been replaced by some clean pajamas folded on the sink. I dried my hair, which now smelled of lavender and honey. The pajamas were silky and cool to the touch. I held the collar of the shirt to my cheek, feeling the smooth texture against my clean skin, letting out a content chuckle. Back in the living room, Skylar was sitting with Gavin on the couches, sipping out of a petite porcelain cup. Mallory reentered the room and handed me a floral teacup with a sweet smile.

"Let me know if you'd like more sugar. I already put a little in there."

"Thank you," I said, accepting the cup. "For everything, I mean. This is incredible."

"Of course." She smiled. "This is just as amazing for Gavin. I haven't seen him this thrilled in a long time. It's good." She looked over at her husband lovingly.

"Are you finally done in there?" Skylar called to me. "I feel bad even being in their house with how gross I am… Dying to take a shower."

"Sorry about that," I said with a lighthearted laugh. "It just felt really nice to shower and I didn't want to get out."

Skylar rushed to the bathroom, abandoning her empty teacup on a faded coaster.

"Go ahead and get comfortable!" Gavin called. "If you're cold, feel free to grab a blanket from the basket."

I reached into a large wicker basket on my way to the couch, pulling out a grey fleece blanket, wrapping myself up as I sat with the tea.

I feel like I'm visiting family right now.

The sound of the shower started up, and I could hear Skylar call out a satisfied, "Oh my God!"

The three of us sat in the living room and laughed.

"So, Skylar was telling us that you guys have been holed up in some ruins for a while. That must be rough. How have you guys managed to get food and water?" Gavin asked.

"We have a couple connections that have helped us out a lot. Fortunately."

"That's good. I can't imagine what living out there must be like. You guys are welcome to stay here as long as you need or like. It's just the two of us, and we never really have guests over, so you'll be safe here."

I stared back into Gavin's soft brown eyes, trying to shake the strange familiarity of them.

"Do you know how many people may have been impacted by our letters? I know some people out there are really angry about them, but I have no idea how many people are on our side."

"More than I think you realize," Gavin said. "I just think people are afraid to outwardly agree with you guys. Raine has her officials wrapped around her little finger, as well as a lot of other people. One wrong move, and you might find yourself framed for something and exiled."

"Or just straight up missing." Mallory chimed in. "There have been some rumors about people going missing recently. No one seems to know what's going on in the city right now."

"Missing?" I asked.

She nodded. "One of the ladies from my book club lost her sister. She said her sister got one of your letters and was really touched by it and tried to question an official. The next day, when my friend went to visit her sister, she said she was missing. No one had heard from her or seen her, and that was about a week ago. People don't just go missing in the city. Something's up."

"I'm so sorry to hear that," I said, my throat feeling tight. *People are going missing because of me.*

Just then, there was a large cracking knock at the door.

"Open up!" a voice boomed.

"Hide!" Gavin hissed under his breath. "Go in our bedroom closet—move the safe and hide!"

I scrambled toward the bathroom, throwing open the door.

"Officials!" I warned Skylar. "We need to hide— now!"

Skylar shut the water off without question, yanking a white towel down from the hook and throwing it around herself as she scurried after me, sliding across the ground with her wet feet.

"*Bedroom*!" Mallory whispered as we passed her. "Under the bed—quick!"

We burst into Gavin and Mallory's bedroom just as the front door opened.

"Hello, officer," Mallory greeted calmly and sweetly. "Is everything okay?"

"What about the closet?" I asked Skylar as she began to crouch to crawl under the bed.

I threw open the doors, spotting a waist-height, glossy black safe that took up a large portion of the closet.

"Help me move it," I asked, grunting as I tried to wiggle the safe out of the closet.

We pulled the safe forward, revealing a hole in the wall. Skylar crawled through it, with me behind her, shutting the closet and pulling the safe just close enough to the opening to keep it out of view.

I could hear the sounds of the official interrogating Gavin and Mallory from the other side of the house.

"It was my understanding that you stepped out of the house during the incident earlier tonight," the official stated. "I've been sent to search your house for the criminals who escaped the scene. If you're aware of any criminals and their whereabouts, should you choose to disclose this information to me, you and your wife will be granted immunity. I will simply take the criminals and leave you be. Should I find any criminals in your house and you have not revealed this information to me, I will be forced to bring you to trial at the court's nearest convenience for pending exile to Equivox. Are you aware of any criminals on your property?"

"No, sir," Gavin answered.

"Do you accept the terms of this search?"

"Yes."

Skylar and I tried to quickly situate ourselves in the deep, dark hole in the wall. The ground felt like compacted dirt, but the walls felt wooden. The hole was just tall enough for us to sit upright, but the space was narrow enough that Skylar and I were squished together, shoulder to shoulder. A hard briefcase and a plastic bucket sat pushed against the wall toward our feet.

We sat in the darkness, smelling the cool earth beneath us as we tried to breathe as slowly and silently as possible. Every now and then, we could hear the official throwing open another door or sliding furniture away from the walls. Eventually, we heard him pull open the closet door, letting a sliver of light in through the edges of the safe. The sliver of light illuminated the briefcase and the bucket, which I could now see was full of something. I leaned forward to get a closer look into the bucket. It was full of empty syringes.

I sat back against the wall quickly, hearing the squeak of metal hangers against the rod in the closet. There was a painstakingly long silence before I could hear his footsteps retreat.

"Is there anything else we can help with, officer?" Mallory asked from the front of the house. "My husband said some officials were badly hurt. Are they okay? Perhaps I could deliver a casserole to their families while they heal."

"They'll be okay, thank you."

"Well, let us know if we can be of any assistance," Gavin offered. "I didn't see anyone else in the streets except two officials when I stepped out, but I'll keep an ear out in case any of the neighbors saw anything."

I heard the front door open, but there was a pause.

"Why are there four cups?" the official asked.

"Oh," Gavin sighed.

"That would be my husband, sir," Mallory chimed instantly with an airy giggle. "He never picks up his dishes, and he always gets a new cup instead of reusing the same one. I told him he needs to stop that silly habit before the baby comes—I don't want anything fragile lying out when we have a baby around."

Another long pause.

"You folks have a good night, okay?" the official said after a while, and I could hear the door close behind him.

After a few minutes, I could hear footsteps in the bedroom, and then the opening of the closet doors.

"Guys?" Gavin asked, pausing for a moment.

He then moved the safe from the opening of the hole with a grinding scrape.

"You guys okay?" he asked, offering a hand.

"Well enough," I answered as we crawled through the hole, our palms and knees covered in dirt. The towel around Skylar was brown with filth.

"Sorry about your towel," she said, trying to pat some of the dirt off in futility.

"No worries." He smiled. His voice quiet, he clasped his hands in front of him. "Please, don't tell Mallory about the hiding place."

"Why do you have a bucket full of syringes?" I asked outwardly, keeping my voice low.

Skylar's eyes grew wide. "Wait, what?"

"Gav?" Mallory called from the other room.

"Later, please," Gavin pleaded. "I promise, I'll explain. Just don't say anything to Mallory."

I nodded solemnly as he moved the safe to cover the hole back up.

After Skylar finished her shower, Mallory and Gavin showed us to the guest bedroom.

"I feel like we should go back to the ruins," I said with a yawn. "The others are probably worried, and I want to know that Bexa and Cromwell made it back safe."

"Let's get some rest," Skylar said. "It's been a long night, and I'm not even sure how much time we'd even have left before the sun comes up. Bexa and Cromwell are two of the toughest people we know—I'm sure they're fine. And sure, the others may be worried, but they're smart enough not to start looking for us yet."

I nodded sleepily, not admitting that I was grateful for a reason to stay and get some sleep.

The bed was fairly large, so Skylar and I decided to share. I felt like it had been days since I last slept, so I was asleep shortly after the lights were cut.

Raine was bound to a chair in front of me, her wrists and ankles shackled to its legs. Tears and mascara streamed down her cheeks as she scowled at me in a bitter rage.

"So, tell me again," I started. "Why?"

"Why aren't you going to win?" She gleamed. "Because you're weak. You're nothing without him."

My face grew instantly hot and my vision turned white as I sent my fist soaring into Raine's nose with a thick crunch. Warm blood covered my knuckle. Shaking my sore hand, I flicked blood across the cement floor.

Where am I?

"Or perhaps, do you want to know why you're still trying?" she asked, blood trickling to her lips and sputtering as she spoke. "It's because you don't have him to talk some sense into you."

Crack. Another punch. More blood.

"Or would you rather know why I shot your little boyfriend in the face?" She grinned, her teeth thick with crimson blood. "*Because it was fun.*"

Crack.

"What the hell?" Skylar shrieked, clutching her nose as she stood over me from the side of the bed. "What was that for?"

"I'm so sorry!" I cried, hurriedly sitting up.

"Why bib you bunch me, you *freak*?"

"I thought you were Raine, I'm so sorry!"

"I'b obviously nob Raine!"

"I must have been dreaming—I'm sorry!"

"Girls!" Mallory gasped as she entered the bedroom. "What happened?"

She darted away and returned with a rag, holding it out to Skylar.

"She bunched me because she thob I was Raine," Skylar grumbled through the rag.

"I didn't mean to! I was having a dream. What were you doing over me anyways?" I said, realizing that Skylar must have been craning over me before I punched her.

"You were makink weirb noises anb I wanbeb to bake sure you weren't dyink or sombtink!"

I looked guiltily between Skylar and Mallory, unsure of what to do next.

"Come sit down," Mallory said, guiding Skylar to the living room and getting her some ice.

"What happened?" I heard Gavin ask groggily as he trudged into the living room.

Mallory filled him in while Skylar sat, pinching her nose with the rag. When it stopped bleeding, her nose began to swell.

"*Great*," she said when she checked it in the mirror.

"It makes you look tough," Gavin teased with a half-hearted smile.

Skylar glared at him.

When Gavin and Mallory retreated to their bedroom to get ready for the day, Skylar pulled me back into the bedroom.

"I thought you were done having nightmares?"

"I guess not." I stared at her.

"Clearly." She rolled her eyes.

"I already said I'm sorry about a dozen times, what more do you want from me?"

"Why are you still having nightmares?"

"No clue."

"What happened in this one?" she asked.

"Raine was tied up, and I punched her," I said, looking at her blackened nose, feeling guilty. "Repeatedly."

"Did she say anything?"

"A little."

I recounted the conversation to her while she stared at the ceiling pensively.

"This dream seems a lot angrier than the other ones. I mean, sure, the one where you saw me getting shot in the head was violent, but you weren't the attacker. In this one, you seemed more in control than you did before. I guess that's a step? I'm not really sure what to tell you this time."

I groaned. "I just want the nightmares to stop."

"I know," she looked at me, her gaze full of genuine sympathy, despite the dark bruise reminding us both that I punched her in the face. "Enough of that though. What are we going to do next?"

"We need to find Bexa and Cromwell."

"I figured that much," she glared and batted her eyelashes. "I meant *how* are we going to do that?"

"I assumed you meant that. I was just trying to stall because I have no idea how we're going to find them in the largest city, especially now that it's daytime. We can't even get back to the ruins right now, so at least we have all day to come up with something."

Mallory made us a generous hot breakfast of bacon and eggs as the four of us ate in the living room.

"Have you been delivering new letters?" she asked as she collected our empty plates. "Something different than the first one?"

"Yes," I replied. "A second version with different stories on it. We talk about that young boy that was recently exiled from here."

"Derek?" Gavin asked.

I nodded.

"It's a shame what happened, but a fantastic idea to include him in the letter. A lot of people were close to his family and have seen the boy grow up. He's such a well-behaved kid—a lot of people are outraged about what happened. I think people are going to be more receptive to the letters than they were the first time around."

I gave an unconvincing smile.

"Are you okay?" Mallory asked, stopping on her way to the kitchen, her arms carefully balancing the stack of dishes.

"Okay enough, I suppose," I said lazily. "I'm just not sure what else we can do besides pass out these letters."

"What were you hoping the letters would do?" Gavin asked.

"What do you mean? I wanted them to turn people against Raine. I wanted to expose her for the monster that she is."

"That's a good start, but what were you hoping people would do if they saw what you wanted them to see?"

"I don't know." I sighed. "I guess rise against her? Protest? Overthrow the government?" I said, half-jokingly.

"Have faith in your plan and have patience then. Your plan is to change peoples' hearts and minds, therefore leaving it up to them to act upon their newfound knowledge. You can't force people to act—you have to inspire them."

That day was the first time in a long time that I truly felt safe. When night finally fell, I felt reluctant to ever leave our new friends' cozy home, but I knew we needed to find Bexa and Cromwell. Skylar and I discussed our plans to go back to our base to see if our friends made it back, and they encouraged us to come back if we ever needed a place to stay.

"Just slip in through the side window. We'll leave it unlocked. Knocking is too loud, and if we have to leave something unlocked, we'd rather it not be the front door," Gavin informed us as we hoisted our bags over our shoulders. We were wearing our old clothes again, but they were freshly washed and smelled of oranges.

"You're welcome back whenever," Mallory reminded us. "I mean it."

"Thank you," Skylar and I repeated in unison.

"Take these to your friends," Mallory said with a wide smile, handing us each a wrapped loaf of fresh cinnamon bread.

"You didn't have to go through all of this for us!" I said, gaping at the bread, which was still slightly warm in my hands. I took a deep breath and breathed in the sweet cinnamon aroma.

"As we've said, this cause is very important to us—especially to Gavin. We really appreciate everything you guys are doing and the risks that you're taking."

I set the loaf on an end table and hugged her and Gavin.

I wanted to ask Gavin about the hiding spot and the needles, but I didn't want to betray his trust by asking in front of his wife.

Picking the bread back up, I stepped out into the city streets. The light from their house cast a bright line across their front lawn, illuminating the colorful shards of the shattered glass lawn ornament like thick glitter. The door closed behind us, leaving us in the darkness of the street.

FIFTEEN

We immediately clung to the wall of their small house, staying low. Skylar followed close behind me as we made our way down the streets and back in the direction of the city gate. At one point, I was so on edge that I nearly drew my dagger on Skylar when her foot ground against a rock.

"Seriously?" She glowered at me, backing up. "Cool it! You punched me already—if you try to kill me, I'll kill you first."

"Sorry," I sighed, lowering the dagger. "The sound seemed more distant—I thought maybe someone was following us."

"Who do we have here!" crowed a young voice in a menacing singsong.

I turned to face the source of the voice—a teenage boy with spiked blond hair, followed by three others who all looked closer to our age. The boy rattled a can of blue spray paint as he approached us, leaving behind an unfinished Rainedrop painting.

"You do realize the irony of painting that, don't you?" Skylar said, straightening up and crossing her arms confidently. "You're painting a symbol to support someone who exiles people—*for life*— who tag buildings… like you just did."

"We aren't some thugs though," one of the others, a pale girl with a long face, replied. "We support her because she keeps murderers, thieves, and real criminals off the street."

"What've you got in those bags?" the blond asked, coming close and reaching for my bag. Instinctively, I lashed out and shoved him, the hilt of my dagger hitting him with the swift reflex. He stumbled backwards, tugging my bag and nearly pulling me over as he tried to correct his balance. When he stood, he pressed a hand to his brow and removed it, revealing blood on his hand and a gash on his face. His forehead began to scrunch up as he quickly raised his can of paint to my face and pushed the trigger, sending a stream of blue into my eyes and mouth.

I let out a brief scream, trying to stifle it so as to not wake the citizens in the houses around us.

"What's your problem, kid?" Skylar growled. I could hear the scuffling and grinding of shoes on pavement as an obvious fight broke out. My eyes were shut as tightly as I could close them, but I knew I needed to get the paint out and help Skylar.

Blindly, I pawed at my bag and felt for a bottle. When my fingers touched the familiar plastic, I pulled it out and clumsily unscrewed the cap.

Get it over with.

I took a sharp breath and pried my right eye open first with one hand, pouring water into it with the other. The stinging seemed to hit all at once and I let out a gravelly groan as I bit my lip, forcing myself to rinse out the other eye. I blinked away the excess water, wiping my face on my shirt. When my eyes were clear, I looked up and spotted Skylar pinned up by the largest of the group against the wet paint of the Rainedrop, her feet thrashing in the air as she clawed at her neck.

Dagger in hand, my eyes still burning, I charged toward the group. The others began to reach out toward me to stop me, but I flailed around with the dagger, aiming for every piece of flesh I could see in my fury. A few times, my strikes landed—confirmed by the shrieks and colorful language of our attackers. When I got close enough to the larger one, I threw my arm forward from my side, sinking the dagger into his muscular back. He immediately dropped Skylar, who collapsed on the ground like a ragdoll. I ripped my dagger away and stepped back as he processed, trying to paw at his wound to get a look at it. Pulling my gun from my waistband, I aimed it from person to person within the group and stared each one down individually.

"Try me," I grinned, my teeth undoubtedly painted blue like the rest of my face. Bloody dagger in one hand, aimed gun in the other, the group began to back away slowly.

"You're sick," sneered the blond.

I shook my head twitchily. "There's no cure for me." I lurched forward as if about to attack, and the boy ran the other way, one of his friends following. The other looked from me to the large man with his bloody wound.

"Please, let me help my friend," she asked. It was the first time this girl had spoken, and her voice was soft. Her hair was in tight blonde curls that sat fluffed in a frame around her face.

My stomach began to burn like fire, and I dropped to my knees.

"Are you—" she began to ask before cutting herself off and racing to her friend, helping him down the street after the rest of their long-gone group.

When the burning subsided, I crawled a couple feet over to Skylar, who was conscious but slumped against the cement wall. Hair disheveled, face sweaty, and her entire backside covered in blue, she rolled her head to the side to look at me. I leaned back on the ground against the wall with her. She let her head exhaustedly flop onto my shoulder.

"This sucks."

I scoffed.

We sat for a moment, catching our breath before we rose and readied our weapons again. As we left the smudged Rainedrop behind, Skylar flung an indignant middle finger at it before turning on her heel to trot after me.

When we had safely made our way out of Fallmont and back to our base, we were surrounded by the familiar faces of Braylin, Paren, Fabian, Bexa, Cromwell, Zaire, and his brother, Legend. Two girls I didn't recognize were talking to Paren, who had recently started walking without support from a golf club.

"Bexa, Cromwell!" I called, jogging over to greet them. "I'm so glad you're safe! Are you okay?"

"You have no faith in us, do you!" Bexa laughed. "We're totally fine! You think a couple officials are a match for us? You're the weakling here—the only reason we weren't panicking was because Skylar was with you."

Skylar grinned and flipped her hair.

"You think she's really any tougher than I am?" I asked with a playful scoff.

"Yup," Bexa and Cromwell answered together plainly.

"I'm just as capable as she is!"

"You're capable, but Skylar can be terrifying," Bexa said. "If you wouldn't have come back when you did, we probably would have started looking, but we were confident you'd be fine. Skylar would slaughter a path back if she had to."

At this, Skylar looked unamused.

The playful bickered continued until, out of nowhere, Legend swooped me into an unexpected hug with a kiss on the cheek. "Hello, gorgeous!" he cooed.

"Uh, hey," I muttered, mildly uncomfortable. "When did you get here?"

"Not long before you," he replied, releasing me. "Why so blue?"

"I'm just tired, that's all." I sighed.

"No." He let out a light but awkward chuckle. "I mean… literally. Why are you *literally* so blue?"

"Wh—" I reached for my cheek, feeling the crusty paint on my skin. "Oh. Long story."

"What are you doing here?" I asked him, pouring some water on a rag and scrubbing aggressively at my face.

"Let me," he offered, taking the rag and retrieving some soap from a box of new supplies. "I figured I'd come for a visit, but Zaire and I also had an idea we'd like to propose."

"Oh?"

Legend washed blue paint from my forehead. "Man, this stuff is really on you, isn't it? Well," he started, a sly glimmer in his eye. "How do you feel about going home?"

"I don't have a home."

"Your *old* home."

"Avid? No thanks."

"*Older.*"

"No!" I exclaimed, backing away. "Why would I want to go back? They all turned their backs on me—even my own parents!"

"There's a party—"

"A party? Legend, you have ten seconds to tell me why I should ever even *consider* going back to Rockhallow!"

"I'm trying!" He chuckled warmly, his voice patient.

I stared back at him expectantly. He set the rag down and his smile faded.

"There's a party—well, more of a gala—of government staff and city representatives. This year it's being hosted in Rockhallow. Zaire has become well-known and highly-regarded over the years for his work with the trucks—they've even tasked him with some technological advancements within the cities, but I can tell you more about that later." He scanned my impatient face as he sped up his speech. "Anyways, Zaire has been invited to this gala, and we thought it would be wise to send you as his date."

"Excuse me?" I sputtered and laughed. "His date? To a government event? How many of your little red pills did you take, Ledge? That's ridiculous."

"I know, I know." He smiled uneasily, his patience slowly waning. "But there are a lot of people with a lot of influence, and I thought, if you could plant some seeds about how corrupt the exile town system is… those are the people you want to plant seeds with. Some of them may already have doubts, from what I've heard. You could be the one to topple those dominos."

"Great idea, in theory," I said. "But you forget that I'm probably the most recognized and wanted criminal in the New Territory. I don't think they'll let me casually waltz into their government gala."

"It's a masquerade."

"So, I'd wear a mask and hope that no one recognizes me still?"

"Zaire and I have something else in mind. We'll give you details later—we're still working on the logistics. The gala is in two days—we'll keep you posted."

"You do that," I jeered. *Fat chance. I'm not going to that gala.*

Legend began to walk toward his brother when I called him back to me.

"Who are those two?" I whispered to him, pointing to the girls near Paren.

He smiled. "Arke and Iris. Twin sisters. Iris is from Equivox and joined Fortitude about a year ago. She and I are good friends. I think Arke is from Delaisse. I don't know her well—we found her wandering the desert outside Fallmont and Iris made me pull over."

"Ark-y? What kind of name is that?"

"What kind of name is Eos?"

"Touché. Anyways—what are they doing here?"

"I told Iris about your operation here and she absolutely loved the idea. Her and her sister are incredibly close, so when we picked her sister up, she told Arke, and both wanted to come help in any way they could."

I nodded pensively, eyeing them from across the room. "When they're done with Paren, I'd like to meet them."

"That can be arranged!" Legend smiled, his stunning teeth gleaming against his dark skin.

I continued scrubbing at my blue face when, moments later, Legend returned with the twin sisters. Both of the girls had silky chestnut hair, caramel skin, and galaxies of freckles on their cheeks and noses. The only differences between the two girls were their noses and the length of their hair—the girl to my right had long, thick curls. Her sister had a pixie cut and a noticeably more bulbous nose.

"Iris, Arke, this is Eos," Legend gestured and the girls smiled in unison.

I put a hand up as an awkward hello.

"I love what you're doing," the girl with the pixie cut beamed. "Enough's enough with this system—it's time to tear it down!"

Her sister nodded enthusiastically, her curls bobbing.

"I'm sorry," I started. "Who is who?"

"Oops!" Pixie cut said. "I'm Iris. That's Arke. Sorry- I've just been excited to meet you!"

"Well," I said uncomfortably. "I'm not really sure what I'm doing most of the time, but if you're on board with that, we'd be happy to have as much help as we can get."

Arke and Iris nodded.

"How much has Legend told you?" I asked them, dreading giving them the get-up-to-speed speech.

"A lot. And your handsome friend over there told us the rest," Arke smiled, her eyes flicking toward Paren.

"We don't really have anything going on right now, so there's a lot of waiting involved. We have more letters to deliver, but we had some issues with the last delivery, so we might want to wait a bit."

"We can handle it!" Arke said energetically.

"Have you ever been to Fallmont?" I asked skeptically.

"That's where we were from before we were exiled," Iris said confidently. "We can handle it."

"If you're sure," I said, handing them each a hefty stack of letters. "Just be careful. This is from some of the locals," I drew a circle in the air around my blue face. "And one of my friends was carved up by some psychos. They definitely don't play nice there."

"We'll be safe," Arke said. "We'll wait until tonight to leave."

"Do you have anything to protect yourselves?"

They both pulled out taser flashlights, clicking them on and letting the electricity buzz.

"Fair enough," I said, my eyes wide. I turned to Legend, who met my gaze with a shrug. "Good luck."

The girls smiled and trotted back to Paren, proudly showing him the letters.

"They can be trusted?" I asked Legend for assurance.

"They hate Raine almost as much as you do." His eyes locked onto mine.

"That's impossible."

Later that afternoon, Legend and Zaire returned to Fortitude, leaving us behind with all of the supplies. Our little group of three had turned into a team of nine.

"I'm afraid to go home," Fabian told me as he approached me. He handed me a sandwich as he bit into his own.

"What?"

"I'm afraid to go back to Fallmont," he said. "It's become incredibly hostile there—it's like everyone is watching over everyone else, waiting for signs of treason. I have to watch my every word, my every step, my every thought. That's why I haven't gone back. Who would've thought I'd feel safer in the ruins with a merry band of criminals?"

I rolled my eyes and laughed before taking a bite of the sandwich.

"I know it's important for me to go back though, isn't it?" he asked gravely. "I'm more useful as an informant than I am sitting around here—" he took another bite. "—eating up your supplies."

"If you can manage, it really would be helpful. If it weren't for you, we wouldn't know about Raine exiling a child, and we wouldn't have such a compelling story for the second letter. Any other dirt you can get us brings us one step closer."

"I figured." A piece of lunchmeat fell into his lap. "I heard the twins are headed to Fallmont with Paren tonight—I'll go back with them." He picked up the meat scrap, checked it for dirt, and popped it in his mouth.

"Take this," I handed him the Skeleton Key. "Easier than using a ladder to get in—if the ladder is even there. But please send it back with Paren."

He nodded, pocketing the Key.

As he walked off, Cromwell and Bexa came over and immediately started talking.

"Cromwell and I have an idea," Bexa said. "You know how more and more people have been joining the team?"

"Yeah?" I pressed.

"This house is pretty small. It was already a bit of a tight fit with all of us here, but now there are a couple more people, and hopefully even more will join. Cromwell and I were thinking of scoping out the other buildings in these ruins to see if any other ones are livable—either to house more people in one, or to just split people between two. What do you think?"

"I think that's a great idea!"

Bexa smiled and elbowed Cromwell. "Ready, bud?"

"Don't call me that," he said with faux gruffness. "How about waiting until tonight?"

"No one is ever in the ruins during the day, right?" Bexa turned to me for confirmation.

I shrugged. "Doesn't hurt to be extra careful." *Plus, with so many people all gone tonight, I can enjoy a little extra peace.*

A few hours of resting after the twins, Paren, Fabian, Cromwell, and Bexa all left the house, Braylin, Skylar, and I all worked together to tidy things up. The house grew messier faster with every person that joined our team, but the three of us managed to get things looking acceptable in no time. As I was putting the finishing touches on the living room, Bexa burst through the front door.

"You guys all need to get out of here—now!"

"What's going on?" Braylin asked.

"Officials are checking every house. There are at least a dozen of them! Cromwell is headed toward Fallmont to warn the others when they head back." Bexa hunched over, out of breath. "Let's *go*!"

"Where?" Braylin began to panic.

"Anywhere!" I answered, pushing him and Skylar out the door ahead of me.

I looked up and down the street, but there wasn't an official in sight.

"Where are they?" I asked.

"They haven't reached this street yet, but I can only assume they will soon. They're a couple blocks that way," Bexa pointed toward the left as we ran.

The four of us sprinted toward the right of the house, making our way to the edge of the ruins. With every step we took, my bag bounced against my hip.

"Let's just steer clear of the ruins until the coast is clear," Skylar advised as we reached the last house, running past it.

We continued running until the ruins grew small in the distance. Out of breath, I stumbled and fell on my knees into the sand.

"I'm sorry," I huffed to the others. "I'm exhausted."

"It's fine," Bexa said, sitting in place. "We should be fine here for a while."

"Thanks for warning us," Braylin said, nodding at Bexa.

"I wasn't just going to leave you guys there, stupid," Bexa said, staring at Braylin. I couldn't tell if she was being playful or was genuinely offended that he insinuated that she might have left us there.

Hours went by with us sitting in high alert, constantly scanning the dark horizon for movement. When the sun finally began to rise, the sky ignited in a fiery red-orange that caught on the edge of every cloud in the sky.

"Do you think it's safe to go back?" Braylin asked. "It's been hours."

"Guys," Skylar said softly.

"I'm assuming it's fine now," I said, standing and dusting the sand from my pants.

"Hey," Skylar said.

"Where do you think the others are right now?" Braylin asked.

"Cromwell said he'd just make sure they stayed off somewhere kind of like we did. They might be back for all I—"

"Guys!" Skylar interjected impatiently.

"What?" Braylin asked, turning to her. She wasn't looking at him, or any of us. Instead, she was staring off at the ruins.

"Do you see that?"

In the distance, a thick cloud of black smoke billowed out from the ruins.

"Is that coming from our house?" Braylin asked, scrambling to stand for a better look. "What's going on?"

"Officials," I said coolly.

"Let's go!" he said, snatching up his bag.

"No!" Bexa stopped him. "We need to wait a bit. There's nothing we can do now anyways, and we need to be sure they've left."

"But we could put it out—"

"With what?" Skylar asked, her voice breaking. She cleared her throat. "There's nothing we can do."

Braylin stared at me, speechless, and I looked back apologetically, agreeing with the girls. "I'm sorry, Braylin."

"Look!" he said, pointing at the ruins. "I think they're leaving. See?"

I squinted, trying to make out the shapes of the cluster of trucks exiting the ruins at once.

"Please," he urged. "Let's go back."

"Alright," I said, following him as he started the trek back, with Bexa and Skylar following behind us.

The closer to the ruins we got, the thicker the air felt. Along the outskirts, the air was heavy with smoke, filling our noses and throats. Once in the ruins, we split up, checking each street for officials before returning home.

As we all reconvened, we made our way to the house, which once we reached it, we were able to confirm that it was the sole source of the smoke. The officials must have found our supplies while searching the ruins, assumed it was our hideout, and burnt it all.

"How did they know where to even look for us?" Skylar asked me, her voice hushed as we stared from down the street at the wreckage of what used to be an already charred building. All that was left was an empty shell of a house. The roof had completely collapsed and burned, everything inside had been turned to ash, and the windows were busted in.

I carefully stepped closer to the house, pulling the top of my shirt over my mouth and nose to block out some of the smoke. Once in front of the house, I spotted a huge black gift bag with a card taped to the front.

"What is that?" Bexa asked, coming to my side.

Without an answer, I tentatively approached the bag, tearing the card from its front.

E,

Got here too late. Will bring more supplies. You know what to do with this. Be ready tomorrow before sunset.

-L & Z

I set the note down and reached into the giant bag, pulling out a black and crimson ball gown.

"Woah," Braylin breathed, staring at the dress.

"Who left that? The officials? What's it for? Is this some kind of sick joke?" Skylar asked.

"It's from Legend and Zaire," I said. "I'm going to a government gala tomorrow night."

"Glad you have time for parties while the rest of us are trying to take down the entire exile town system," Skylar teased.

"Zaire has a plan," I said.

"Oh yeah?" Skylar mocked. "Does his plan include putting a bag over your head so no one recognizes you?"

"Not quite," I said, digging in the bag and pulling out an elegant black masquerade mask.

"Watch out, everyone," Skylar said. "It's our masked hero. No one will ever know who she is behind that mask! Black and blonde hair? Oh! It could be anybody!"

"I think Zaire had something else in mind, too," I said, my voice grave as I pulled out a couple gallons of water, a pair of scissors, and box of black hair dye.

SIXTEEN

"Oh man!" Skylar burst out laughing. "This is going to be great!"

"It's not funny," I glared at her. "I happen to like my hair how it is."

"Whatever will we do without the heroic Skunk?" she said in a singsong.

I sighed, throwing everything back in the bag.

"Hey," she said, her laughter dying down. "I'm only picking. This is temporary anyways, right? It'll grow back."

"Yeah," I sighed.

"I can help you cut and dye it if you want," she offered.

"Heck no."

"What's going on?" I heard Paren call from down the street as he sprinted toward us with the twins and Cromwell following.

Bexa filled them in as they all stared in horror at the smoky house.

"We found some other ruins not too far from here," Cromwell offered.

"I can't yet," I said, thinking of the gala. Zaire wouldn't be able to find me if I were hidden in some other ruins. "You guys go ahead, just give me directions."

"I know where they are," Paren said. "I'll stay behind with Eos and we can join up when she's ready."

Cromwell nodded, turning on his heel and shepherding the group out of the ruins.

"How long do we need to stay here?" Paren asked. "What's the bag for?"

I told him in detail about how Zaire planned to bring me to Rockhallow for a government gala to "plant seeds" in the minds of doubtful government workers and influencers. Paren seemed more confident in the idea than I had anticipated—I half expected him to try to convince me not to go.

"I think that's smart," he said. "I'll help with your hair. Do you have enough water left to help with the dye?"

"How do you know how to dye hair?" I asked.

"I used to work in the salon when I was younger. Mostly just swept hair, helped shampoo customers, things like that. But I picked up a few things while I was there." He smiled proudly.

Paren and I scoped out a few of the houses nearby and found one suitable enough to stay in for the day. I set my stuff down and dug out the dye, scissors, and the gallons of water that Legend and Zaire had left in the bottom of the bag.

"Let's get to work," Paren said, making a snipping motion with the scissors as he walked to the bathroom, pulling a kitchen chair with him.

I grumbled nervously and followed him.

"Have a seat in my salon, darling." He smiled, sticking the chair in the bathtub.

I stepped into the tub and sat awkwardly on the chair.

"Can I borrow your blanket?"

"Sure," I said hesitantly. "It's in my bag." I pointed toward the living room.

He returned with my blanket, giving it a shake and wrapping it over my shoulders, pulling my hair out over it. I laughed nervously.

"Ready?" he asked, and I heard a gritty snip as a tuft of my hair floated toward the ground.

"What?" I shrieked. "What kind of warning is that? 'Ready?' SNIP!"

"If I were to wait until you were actually ready, we'd be here all day." He chuckled, continuing to cut, combing my hair out gently as he went.

"We *are* going to be here all day," I reminded him.

"I'd rather not spend it standing in a bathroom," he laughed warmly and I felt the corners of my lips turn up in a smile.

"Are you giving me bangs?" I gasped as he clamped the scissors over some of the hair at the front of my head.

"Did you not want bangs?"

"No!"

"Oops."

A short time later, Paren announced that step one was done.

"Go ahead," he said confidently. "Go check it out in the mirror! It's a bit dirty, but you can still see yourself in it."

"I don't want to," I said. "I'll look when it's completely done."

"Your choice," he said, setting down the scissors and unboxing the dye. "I recommend you get out of the chair for this part."

I stepped out of the tub and he removed the chair for me. On the floor, I leaned my head back over the wide tub, the cool ledge touching my bare neck as I flopped my shortened hair over it and into the tub.

"It feels short, how short is it?" I asked. "I feel naked. Is it cold in here?"

Paren chuckled. "It's not that short. I mean," he looked at the pile of hair in the tub, "I did cut a lot off, but you had a lot of hair to begin with."

I whimpered and it turned into a laugh.

"Atta' girl!"

When Paren had finished dyeing and rinsing my hair with the jugs of water, he found a raggedy old towel from a closet and used it to dry me off as best he could.

"My masterpiece!" he said proudly, puffing out his chest and grinning cheesily.

"Is it that bad?" I joked.

"No! It looks good! Go look!"

"I'm too scared!"

"After all you've been through, you're too afraid of a haircut and a dye job? Come on! Please look at it," he said with a whine, taking my shoulders and migrating me toward the mirror above the sink, but I pressed my eyes shut. "Open your eyes!"

"No!" I said, shaking my head dramatically.

"Okay, how about this… There's a bit of dye left. If you don't like how your hair looks, I'll let you dye my hair—and black is *not* my color. Deal?"

I snickered. "Alright, fine."

I opened my eyes. Staring back at me in the mirror was a total stranger. I have always had the same hair style—I've never strayed from my usual. But now, my hair was short, but not incredibly so—it just barely graced the tops of my shoulders. Paren had managed to give me fringy bangs across my forehead, and my hair was now entirely coal black.

"Well?" he asked impatiently as I ran my fingers through it. It felt strange how short it was.

I kept staring back at myself in shock.

"Oh no," he sighed. "I'm so sorry. It'll grow back! I'll never touch your hair again! I swear!"

"I love it," I breathed.

"What?"

"I love it," I repeated, a smile creeping on my face.

Paren let out a breathy, relieved laugh. "Thank goodness!"

I turned and hugged him.

"Oh—" he said, caught off-guard. "You're welcome, I suppose."

"Let's have something for lunch," I suggested. "I've got some stuff in my bag. Speaking of—can you hang onto my bag for me while I'm at the gala?"

"Do you think it's about time to get ready?" Paren asked after we spent the day sharing stories about our families. "Sun should be going down pretty soon."

I agreed, taking the ballgown out of the bag and into the bathroom. I shut the door behind me and undressed. Intimidated, I stared at the stunning dress with its elegant lacework. Carefully, I stepped into the dress and hoisted it up. The fabric was thick and heavy, but the dress wasn't overly poofy. I attempted to lace up the back myself but couldn't quite tighten it. Frustrated, I spun around backward in the dress and attempted to lace it up part of the way with a better view instead but found that I couldn't manage that either. I grumbled and shuffled out of the bathroom.

"I need help," I said pathetically as I stepped into the living room.

Paren looked over at me from the tattered and stained couch. "Woah," he said, eyes wide. "You look beautiful."

I scoffed. "I can't lace it up. It's too heavy, and no matter how I try to lace it up, I can't hold it in place at the same time."

Paren stood and wove the corset back ribbon through each loop as I held the dress in place. When he finally tied the ribbon off, I released.

"How's that?" he asked as I turned to face him.

I gave a little wiggle. "I can still move. It isn't exactly comfortable, but it'll do. Thank you."

"Did they include shoes or anything?"

I disappeared into the bathroom and returned with a pair of short black heels, the mask, and some glittery jewelry.

"Fancy!" Paren raised a pinky finger to the air as if holding a teacup. "Is that them I hear?"

Hushed, I listened and heard the sound of an approaching truck.

"Let's hope."

Paren stepped outside and I waited until he was out of sight before I reached into my bag, retrieving an old shirt. With my dagger, I sliced off a couple strips of fabric. I sheathed my dagger and tied it securely to my leg with the strips of fabric before joining Paren outside, where Zaire was there to greet me with the passenger door open.

"Where are your gloves?" Zaire asked, looking at my dirt-stained hands.

"Hello to you too," I said, holding the gloves up, along with the mask.

"You look great," he said with a sweet smile, closing the door behind me once I managed to pull the full dress into the passenger seat.

Paren waved to me from the doorway as I pulled on my gloves and gave him a dainty wave in return.

Voices muffled by the car, I could hear Paren and Zaire exchange a few words before Zaire hopped into the driver's seat and shut the door.

"Go ahead and put your mask on," he suggested, backing the truck up. "These ruined roads are such a pain. Sorry about the bumpiness while we're getting out of here."

"It's fine," I said. "But why put the mask on so early? Rockhallow is far from here, isn't it?"

"Fairly," he said. "But just in case anyone sees us or stops us along the way. A lot of people will be wearing them, including me. We don't want anyone recognizing you in any way. I have to say, by the way, your hair looks great."

"Thanks," I said, holding the black masquerade mask to my face and carefully tying the ribbon at the back of my head.

"Can you hand me mine? It's in the glovebox."

I reached into the glovebox, spotting a basic silver mask with an elastic band around the back. I handed it to him and he used one hand to slip it over his head.

"Get cozy," he said. "It'll be a while."

"Are we going to be late?"

"It doesn't start until late. We'll be on time, trust me."

The drive was mostly silent except for a few occasional tips from Zaire to prepare me for the gala. According to him, most of the guests would be older gentlemen, but there were going to be a handful of younger guests. The younger guests, he said, were most of the ones who already doubted Raine. Zaire advised me to be subtle about my phrasing so I wouldn't raise suspicions. We worked on our backstory and a fake identity for me in case anyone asked. My name would be Everly Newton. I was a student in Fallmont—Zaire thought that a student would be vague enough that no one from Fallmont would question it if they didn't recognize me from town. If anyone asked, Zaire and I had been dating for 6 months.

"You're studying…" he hesitated, trying to think. "What's something you know a lot about?"

I shrugged. "Do I know a lot about anything?"

"Criminology?"

"Not nice!" I laughed.

"It could work. It lends credibility to the fact that you'll be talking about the way crime is handled in the New Territory. You could say you want to get into the justice system but haven't made up your mind exactly what you want to do yet."

"Fine," I said. "Are we almost there? Will there be alcohol?"

Zaire chuckled. "Yes, there will be alcohol. I don't know much more than that—this is the first time I've been to this thing too. I know generally who is going, I know where to go, I know there will be food, and I know Raine will be there—so be careful."

My face grew hot and my hands began to shake.

"Can you roll the windows down?" I asked shakily. "It's a bit hot in here."

"You okay?" he asked, turning to me as he rolled the windows down.

"Yeah," I managed through thick gasps, my eyes beginning to burn.

"Hey—" he stopped the truck and put it in park. "It's okay. She won't recognize you—we made sure of that."

I shook my head frantically, my eyes squeezed shut. "It's not that."

"What is it then? She won't hurt you. She has no idea who you are—she won't hurt you. You're going to be completely safe."

I continued shaking my head, my eyes shut tight.

"Is it because of Zane?"

I felt my body lurch as a single sob escaped my throat. My legs began shaking furiously beneath the layers of the ballgown.

"Eos," he pleaded. "I know it hurts. But we're doing this for him. We're doing this for everyone who has ever been screwed over by Raine. I'll be with you the whole time. As soon as you need to go—you just give me the word. I'll tell people you aren't feeling well, and we will head back without question, okay?"

I nodded, sniffing and blinking back tears before they could spill over.

"Are you going to be okay to do this?"

"Yes," I sniffled once more, clearing my throat before repeating myself. "Yes."

Zaire continued driving, and eventually, we made it to the front gates of Rockhallow. He dug into his pocket, retrieving two paper tickets and waving them outside his window. The gates began to creak as they opened.

"Couldn't you have just used a button on your console?" I asked, looking at a row of buttons in the truck.

"In theory, yes," he said. "But for the gala, it's courtesy to ask for entrance with the tickets. Or, at least, that's what a friend of mine told me. She's been to a couple of these galas."

"Will she be there tonight?" I asked.

Zaire nodded. "She's trustworthy, too. She knows I'm bringing you, and she knows who you are. We can trust her."

We drove down several streets before reaching the city center. I eyed the courthouse where they brought me for my trial, sitting tall on one end of the city center. Beside it, there was an old government building I had never been in or given so much as a thought to. Zaire drove past the city center, pulling to a stop along the side of a nearby street. He climbed out of the truck and walked around to my side, opening the door for me and offering a hand.

I took his warm hand, stepping carefully onto the sidewalk. He closed the door for me as I situated my dress around me and made sure my mask was secure. With a polite smile, he held out his arm, which I willingly took as he guided me back toward the unfamiliar government building.

"Names?" asked a suited man, stationed near the front of the building. He tapped his clipboard with a pen impatiently.

"Zaire and Everly."

The man's eyes scanned rapidly over his chart before pausing. "Ah," he said, flicking his pen in a 'check' motion. "Enjoy the gala."

Zaire nodded once, escorting me past the suited man. At the door, Zaire's fingers clasped around the dingy brass handle. Giving me a final, cautious nod, he pulled. A wave of cigar smoke and stale perfume washed over me as I stepped into the room.

There were at least five, maybe six dozen people in the room, each one of them adorning glittery masks and expensive-looking formalwear. I tried to gather my thoughts, but they were rapidly being drowned out by the chorus of clinking glasses, bellowing laughter, and a band consisting of only a pianist and two women with stringed instruments.

"Keep moving," Zaire urged me, his callused hand settling on my shoulder as he guided me forward, my heels clicking against the sand-colored tile, almost catching in the tulle under my gown every few steps.

Zaire plucked a glass of champagne from a server's tray as we walked. He took a dainty sip with a toothy grin and handed the glass to me. I put the crystal glass to my lips, staring at Zaire over the brim of it as I drank. With a sharp choke, I managed to swallow the bitter bubbles.

I pulled Zaire in close as if trying to dance. Beside his ear, I whispered, "Where do I even start? Do I just pick someone at random and ask, 'Do you have a moment to talk about our corrupt leader and how we could improve our government?'"

"I wouldn't go about it quite like that." Zaire smiled, giving me a quick twirl before pulling me back in. "Just do what feels right."

"May I cut in?" An older man stood beside us, his bald head so immensely covered in wrinkles and liver spots that it resembled rotting fruit. He wore a thin, metallic gold mask that matched his gaudy golden tie. His lips curled over his stained teeth in a questionable smile as he eyed me up and down.

Zaire looked at me, hesitant, his eyebrows both raised high.

"Why not," I said, snatching another passing flute of champagne and tossing the liquid back like a shot. I handed the glass to Zaire as my new dance partner put his hands low on my hips.

"What's your name?" He continued smiling, his buggish eyes looking like they might roll right out of their sockets and fall through the holes in his golden mask.

"Everly," I said, sliding his hands higher up toward my waist.

"What do you like to do, Miss Everly?" he asked with a shaky chuckle.

I had to force myself not to visibly grimace. "I enjoy learning about current events," I said, seeing an opportunity. "Did you hear about the young boy in Fallmont? The one found protesting?"

"Oh yes! Everybody has heard about that. It's a pity about that young boy." He sucked his lips in with a wet slurp. "He was a lovely boy."

I'm not sure this is worth it.

"It's just not fair that they exiled a minor. Do you think maybe they're taking the exile town system a little too far now?"

"Best be careful talking about that," Fruit-Head's face grew somber. "This isn't the place for talk like that."

"What do you mean?" I asked, looking around to see if anyone was listening in.

"You're probably too young to remember Alexandra Delinquez." He traced a hand over my arm and I suppressed an annoyed whimper. "Oh yes, you're definitely too young to remember her."

"Who's that?"

"She used to be the leader of Eastmeade years ago. She was actively against the exile town system—the only leader since the war to disagree with it. After a while, there was a huge trial against her by the other city leaders. The details of the case were never made public, but she was eventually sent to Ironwood. I guess whatever it was must have been pretty dark."

Apparently, having an unpopular opinion is the worst crime of all.

"Is she still in Ironwood?" I asked. *If we could free her and get her to join our efforts—we could be unstoppable! If the people could hear from another true victim of this system…*

"Dead," Fruit-Head said bluntly. "No one makes it long in Ironwood. I think she lasted about three years before she was reported dead."

That idea died about as quick as it came on.

"Oh," I said flatly. "Do you think her arrest had anything to do with speaking her mind about the exile town system."

"Pretty girls shouldn't cause such a fuss," he said, reaching a finger up to my lips to hush me.

"Back off!" I finally snapped, pulling myself from him and storming off to find a bathroom.

Before I reached the restroom door, I felt a strong grip on my forearm.

"Everything okay?" Zaire asked, looking at my arm apologetically as he released his grip.

"That man is a perverted creep," I said. "I just need a moment. Wait here—please."

He nodded as I disappeared into the bathroom. The bathroom had red ornate wallpaper that matched the rest of the building. I managed to squeeze myself into the furthest of the four stalls. I took a deep breath and fanned myself with my hands, trying to calm my nerves and ease my jitters. Right before I unlocked my stall to step back out, I heard the main bathroom door open as two women entered together, arguing with each other.

"You can't honestly tell me you believe that horsesh—"

"Language!" the second woman hushed her friend.

The first woman grumbled impatiently. "All I'm saying is that you're gullible. Those letters were probably just some stupid prank pulled by some kid who's bitter that they got in trouble for something and they just don't realize how lucky they are not to have been exiled for it. But they probably realized they won't get away with it forever!"

"But I showed you the second one! About the young boy that was exiled! He was a minor and was exiled anyways!"

"Bullsh—"

"*Karen*!"

"Bull*crap*. That's against the law. And even if it did happen, I'm sure there was a good reason for it. The punk was probably just friends with the other little punk leaving the letters in the first place."

"Geez. Have a heart. You can't tell me you never did anything reckless as a kid."

"Sure I did. I dated Bobby Springs. And his brother. And kissed their dad. But they don't exile people for that kind of stuff because it's harmless," Karen said. I could hear the pop of a lipstick cap.

"Mrs. Springs might say otherwise."

"All I'm saying is that the exile system has worked for years. You paid attention in history—I know you did because you got an A in Mr. Sturgest's class—"

"Don't even try to make a point using history to back you up. I know you didn't pay attention in that class!"

"I got a B+!"

"Only because you were screwing the teacher."

The lipstick tube clattered back into a makeup bag. "Just listen for once! Crime rates were *never* this low in all recorded history, like, ever. The exile towns work wonders."

"But think about how many people never get to see their families again because of one action! Like that man in the first letter who defended a girl in a bar and was exiled for it!"

"I will admit, I'd love a man like that," Karen gushed. "Even if he's completely fictional, like your letters."

You couldn't get Paren even if you knew he was real.

One of the sinks turned on, making it difficult to hear the next thing Karen's friend had to say.

I've been in here a long time.

I shuffled around in the stall, bending over to flush the toilet. I ruffled my dress around to sound like I had actually been using the toilet rather than eavesdropping. After an appropriate amount of rustling, I pulled off my gloves, tucking them under my arm. I unlocked the stall and stepped out, keeping my face down.

The two girls grew silent and I saw their eyes behind their masks follow me to the sink. I began to wash my hands as the two stared out of the corners of their masks a moment longer.

Do they know who I am?

They both began to pretend picking through their makeup bag as I dried my hands.

"Do one of you ladies happen to have a mint?" I asked sweetly, trying to ease any suspicions. "I had one of those oniony pastries they were passing around and I can't get rid of the taste."

The girl nearest me, her gown and mask a shimmery rose gold, dug in her bag and pulled out a peppermint, holding it out to me.

"Here."

You must be Karen.

"Thank you," I said reaching for the mint.

"Ew," she said, holding tight to the mint and staring at my stained hands.

I felt my jaw drop as I realized how stupid I had been.

"Birthmark," I said quickly. "It sucks." I put the gloves back on.

The friend whapped Karen's shoulder and looked at her in disbelieve. Karen responded with a defensive shrug as I scurried out the door.

Back in the main room, I spotted Zaire chit-chatting with a lanky woman with asymmetrical strawberry blonde hair.

"Everly!" he called to me, waving me over. "I'd like you to meet a close friend. This is T."

"Big fan," T smiled, revealing abnormally white, square teeth. "I was just telling Zaire that Raine Velora has a speech scheduled shortly. For your sake, we are going to make sure you're positioned near the back of the crowd. You shouldn't even see her face during the speech, and it should be relatively brief."

Zaire put a hand on my shoulder as if trying to reassure me, but frankly, it just seemed awkward and stiff. Normally, Zaire uses a lot of eye contact—almost too much at times. This time, he was hardly looking at me.

"I'll be fine," I said. "I might need more champagne though."

Zaire chuckled nervously before flagging down a boy carrying a tray of flutes.

Just as I started to tip back the glass, there was a loudening, rhythmic clinking of glasses. I slowly lowered my glass, feeling the champagne hit my stomach like a rock.

T slipped her fingers between mine, pulling me along beside her and stopping when we had reached the outside of the growing circle of guests. She and Zaire stood on either side of me, their arms linked in mine as if holding me in place.

Then, I heard it.

Her voice felt like it cleared the room of everyone except her and I. My fingers and toes grew cold and began to tingle; my vision began to blur around the edges and I had to deliberately remember to breathe.

T reached her other arm over and pinched my side aggressively.

"Ow!" I grunted, but my vision cleared and the feeling slowly began to return to my extremities.

Focus.

I redirected my attention back toward the source of the horrid voice. There was a solid wall of people in front of me, so I couldn't see her. Another deep, shaky breath, and I tried to focus on the words coming from her hateful mouth.

"Thank you all for coming out tonight!" she exclaimed, her enthusiasm dripping with insincerity. "This event is my favorite part of the year, and I'm so glad each and every one of you was able to make it here. A special thank you to our host, Mr. Patrick Redelle!"

What a dick.

I used to work as an in-city messenger through Redelle when I lived in Rockhallow, until he played an integral role in my exile. Maybe I was a bit unjustly bitter toward him—it was pretty obvious I was guilty—but that doesn't change the fact that he took me from my family and my home forever.

"As I'm sure all of you are aware, there have been a lot of concerns regarding security in the New Territory recently due to dissenting exiles," Raine continued. "I would like to assure all of you that every measure is being taken to protect our citizens and our homes from this new threat."

I tried to resist rolling my eyes as I listened.

"In order to combat the rising conflicts in and out of the cities, all New Territory officials have been trained and ordered to arrest dissenters on site. Typically, we would not take such extreme measures, but this is for the safety of everybody. If someone begins to express a distaste for the exile town system and the leadership of the cities, time has proven that these people all eventually grow aggressive about their views. These criminals are influencing our neighbors, our friends, and our families to act out in hate for their government that works tirelessly to protect them."

Raine is going to start exiling people for having opinions? There's no way people are going to go for that.

"By any means necessary, we need to stop this kind of behavior before it escalates." Raine concluded her proposal and the gala guests erupted in applause. Some people went so far as to shout out their support for Raine, praising her for her wise and bold leadership. I turned to quietly protest to Zaire, but he stopped me before I said a word, challenging me with widened eyes.

"In response to this increasing concern of security, we have worked diligently to improve our video communication methods!" Raine continued.

Crap. I wasn't paying attention.

"As much as we would love security cameras throughout the city streets, we unfortunately lack the necessary resources for that kind of supply at the moment. However, our talented young men and women on the technology development team have recently configured the CLVCS to work more efficiently!"

The crowd clapped politely, and a few people elicited excited cheers.

"CLVCS?" I asked Zaire under my breath.

"City Leader Video Communication System," he answered quietly. "The city leaders have cameras and TV screens that allow them to discuss issues and news without having to do a lot of travelling."

"They have also finished putting together a couple functioning skyscraper screens to bring Rockhallow and Nortown up to speed! Hopefully, this will help boost the success of newer businesses in our two smaller cities. We have seen much success with this in Fallmont, as I understand Eastmeade has as well. These screens will be installed—"

As I continued staring ahead into the backs of the guests in front of me, trying to listen, a few of the people ahead of me shifted on their feet, creating a small gap between them. In this gap, I spotted Raine's thick, raven-feather curls and pasty skin. Almost as soon as I could see her, I felt the acid race up my throat just before I spewed all over the people in front of me.

Before I could process what exactly had happened, T and Zaire jerked me from the crowd. With them on either side of me, they nearly carried me out of the building, leaving some of the splattered guests screaming in disgust. Two officials stood at the door, eyeing me up and down as T and Zaire supported me.

"Too much bubbly," Zaire said to them, his eyes begging them to let us leave.

They immediately threw open the doors for us.

"Feel better, ma'am," one of them said politely.

The heavy doors slammed shut behind us, leaving us alone in the darkness of the modest city square.

"Help me get her to the truck, please," Zaire asked T.

"I'm fine!" I insisted.

"You just puked all over half of the most important people in the New Territory," Zaire said. "We're going to help you to the truck and I'm going to get you back to your friends."

I grumbled in defeat as they walked me slowly down the street, back toward where we parked. At the truck, T opened the passenger door as Zaire eased me into the seat and shut the door behind me. He hugged T and she gave me a sympathetic wave goodbye as she turned and made her way back to the gala.

"I'm not drunk," I insisted as Zaire climbed into his seat. Cranky, I took my heels off and chucked them into the backseat.

"Whatever you say." He refused to look me in the eye as he turned the key in the ignition.

"I'm not!"

"Tell that to the unfortunate people who were caught in the splashzone."

"I saw Raine through a gap in the crowd. Next thing I knew, I was sick."

Zaire sighed, pausing before he put the truck in gear.

"Whatever," I huffed, crossing my arms in defiance as I turned to look out my window, watching the buildings pass slowly as Zaire eased the truck down the street.

As we turned a corner, I spotted a stocky figure in the distance, their back to us and their arm held out in front of them. The closer we got, the more I could make out their actions. In front of the figure was an unfinished graffitied sun. I gaped unblinkingly at this person as we got closer.

I turned to Zaire to see if he had noticed, but he seemed unphased by the occurrence. As we got closer, the artist completed their painting and turned in our direction, spotting us and turning again to disappear into a narrow alleyway. His exit was quick, but not quick enough where I wouldn't be able to recognize the familiar face.

"Stop the truck!" I screamed, flailing at Zaire.

"Don't you dare puke in my truck!"

"Let me out!"

Zaire began to stop the truck, but before it had fully braked, I threw my door open and leapt from the seat, taking off down the alley in my gown, my bare feet smacking against the rough pavement.

"Wait!" I called down the alley.

I could hear his pace quicken as he kept ahead of me, dropping the paint can with a rattle on the ground. I called after him again, trying to keep up.

"Dad!"

SEVENTEEN

The sound of his running stopped suddenly as he stood in place, his back to me.

"Dad?" I said, this time more delicately as I stopped running and carefully walked toward him. I loosened the knot at the back of my mask, taking it off and letting it fall to the ground.

"Eos?" he asked, turning to look at me. When his caring eyes met mine, the worry in his brow melted and his lip quivered. He stood there, speechlessly gaping at me for a moment. He opened his mouth a few times, trying to form words.

Unable to speak, he threw his arms around me.

"I missed you so much," I sniffled, my throat and eyes burning as he held me close, his strong hands flat against my back. I could feel him bury his face in my hair as his body shook.

"I'm so sorry," he said weakly, his voice breaking.

"For what?" I asked softly, hugging him tighter.

"For abandoning you the day you were exiled. For not even saying goodbye. For everything. You have every right to hate me for what I did."

"I could never hate you," I said, sinking my teeth into my lower lip to keep from crying, but the surging water in my eyes allowed a single thick tear to escape down my cheek.

"I never thought I'd see you again," he said, pulling away from the hug and holding my hands in his as he looked at me. "You look so different! Your hair is beautiful, baby girl!" He smiled proudly at me, his eyes red. "What are you doing back here though? What if someone recognizes you?"

"That's why I did this," I fanned out my short black hair. "And what about you? Graffiti? That isn't like you!"

"The letters," he started. "Those were you, weren't they?"

"How do you know about those?"

"Someone from work. Their brother is a driver. Says he got ahold of one while he was in Fallmont after he heard the rumors over there, so he brought it back to his brother, who shared it with the rest of us. A lot of the guys at work support you in this."

"How did you know they were mine?"

"How could I not?" He beamed at me. "I know you better than anyone—I knew the moment I read it. Plus, it helps that you used our last name on them." He chuckled shakily.

"Is everything okay?" I heard Zaire call from behind.

"Better than okay," I replied with a loud sniffle, still facing my dad.

"Who's that?" Dad asked.

"A good friend." I smiled.

A moment later, Zaire approached us.

"Who's this?" Zaire asked, his stance defensive.

"Zaire," I said. "This is my dad."

Zaire's eyes widened as he looked back and forth between my dad and me.

My dad filled me in on how horrible my mom felt about not letting me in the house after my trial. He said she hasn't been the same since—she mostly sits in silence in my old room. According to him, she was in extreme denial after my sentence. She couldn't face the fact that she could no longer protect me. Since hearing about my letters, she had grown irritable and distant. Dad claims she's proud of me for standing up for what's right, but she's terrified of how involved I've become. After word got to Rockhallow about the letters and the Dawn and Raine graffiti, my dad started tagging buildings with sun paintings to encourage people to stand against Raine's corruption.

"I'm so proud of you," he said, pulling me in for another hug. "But you need to get out of here, and I need to get back to your mother."

"Will you tell her I forgive her?"

He smiled softly and nodded.

I picked my mask up and retied the ribbon before Zaire and I returned to the truck and my dad disappeared down the alley. The entire ride back to the ruins, I kept my face turned to the window, unable to shake my smile. The desert around us was dark, but every so often, I'd catch a reflection of myself in the glass. When we finally reached the ruins, Zaire opened my door for me and helped me out.

At the sounds of the truck doors and engine, Paren peered through a crack in the front door before excitedly bumbling outside to greet me.

"How'd it go?" he asked, handing me my bag, in which he had folded and placed my street clothes.

"Could have gone better," Zaire said. "You going to be able to give me directions to the new place?"

The drive was short and Paren was able to direct us to our new home without difficulty. Zaire's eyelids were drooping and his words were short as he said his goodbyes, leaving me with a hug before disappearing into the dark of the desert in his truck.

Paren guided me into the house, which looked similar to many of the other ruined houses I've seen before, but moderately larger than the previous one. This one had a second story, but just like the other, this one had blackened walls, a questionably unstable ceiling, and dust everywhere. *No surprise there. Shelter is shelter though, I suppose.*

Inside, all of our friends were split into the various bedrooms, with a few people spread out and sleeping in the living room. I said goodnight to Paren before heading to the bathroom to change out of my gown. I navigated the new house in the dark, using the moonlight cast through the windows and closing the bathroom door behind me once I found it.

"Woah!" I exclaimed, my heart jumping as I noticed someone passed out fully clothed in the empty bathtub.

"Hey, Skunk," Skylar grumbled. "Have a good time at your party?"

The moonlight colored her blue-white as she leaned clumsily over the side of the tub, squinting at me. Her arm appeared over the tub ledge. In her hand was a bottle of liquor that she clinked noisily against the wall of the bathtub.

"Guess I can't call you Skunk anymore, huh?"

"How much have you had to drink?" I asked, taking the bottle

from her.

She belched and slouched back in the tub.

"Skylar," I said, leaning over to get a better look at her. "Are you okay? This isn't like you."

"What *is* like me?" she whined like a cranky child, crossing her arms as she slouched deeper into the tub.

"What are you talking about?" I said. "You're the level-headed one. The one who says what needs to be said even if no one wants to hear it. You're not the one to get drunk and mopey in a bathtub."

"I'm tired." She tilted her head with a flop, looking at me with sunken eyes.

"Let's get you out of the bathtub and somewhere a little cozier then." I offered her my hand.

"No." She sighed. "I mean I'm *tired.* This whole thing. I'm not sure it's going to work, and I think the more people that join us, the more likely we all are to get hurt. I can't do this anymore."

I felt my throat tighten as a weight grew in my chest. "You're giving up on me?"

"Not on you," she said. "On this. The letters, the hiding, the worrying, the sneaking into Fallmont. I'm done."

"I understand—there have been plenty of times I've wanted to give up—times I've wanted to run off in the middle of the night while everyone is sleeping and never look back. But I can't do that. People are counting on me, and on you."

"Whether or not you guys succeed is not dependent on me."

For a moment, I imagined what it would be like to leave all of this behind and get as far away as possible. Even knowing that I likely wouldn't make it far from the New Territory, I couldn't deny the rush of excitement and relief at even the thought of leaving.

I gnawed on the inside of my cheek, my eyes stinging. "Where are you going to go?"

"Fortitude," she said, handing me the bottle. "That's the best place for us, and you know that."

"It was for nothing, then," I said.

"It was encouraging to see how many people support us and are against the exile town system, but there aren't nearly enough to overthrow it. It wasn't for nothing though—we still changed the minds of some citizens."

"I don't mean the letters."

She turned to me, confused.

"Zane," I said, my voice cracking.

"Don't pull that on me," she growled, trying to sit up, using the ledges of the tub to balance. "That's not fair! That wasn't up to any of us. Don't act like that didn't hurt me too. And do you honestly think that getting caught and killed would make his death any more worth it?"

"If I hadn't had the idea that I could even make a difference, Zane and I would still be in Fortitude right now," I said softly, leaning against the wall and sliding down until I was sitting on the cool tile floor beside the bathtub. "Maybe if I had been the one at Raine's desk… if Zane had been the one at the door instead. Things would be different. He would know what to do."

"You can't do that to yourself," Skylar said, pawing at the bottle in my hand. I glared at her, blinking through tears before taking a generous swig. I handed her the bottle and she held it up. "For Zane." She took a drink.

"For Zane."

"They need to know," he said sweetly, his soft lips brushing my ear. "I know you can make it right."

My eyes were slow to focus, making out my surroundings. I was on my back in the middle of Fallmont's city center, staring up at the skyscraper screens around me. Zane wasn't by my side at all, but instead, was illuminated on each of the screens in an identical image to each other. When he moved in one screen, he moved in all of the screens simultaneously.

"I can't do it without you," I admitted, stuck on the ground.

"You have everything you need to win," Zane smiled confidently, a familiar and reassuring twinkle in his eyes.

"Skylar is leaving," I said. "I don't have you anymore. It's only a matter of time before everyone leaves. If you were alive instead of me, they'd have a real leader."

Zane shook his head—a dizzying effect as each screen mimed the imagery.

"What do you know?"

"I—" I stuttered, unable to answer him.

He backed up in the screen, motioning outward with his arms and looking to his right, creating a ring of Zane on the skyscraper screens.

Just then, the image on the screens fizzled out into static, and I jolted awake.

I know how to overthrow Raine.

EIGHTEEN

"Finally awake?" Bexa stared down at me, a goofy grin creeping across her face. "You're going to want to get dressed."

"Why?" I asked, looking across my body, still in the red and black gown. "What's going on?"

"You'll see," she smiled. "Just get dressed."

After trading the gown for jeans and a tank top, I made my way into the living room, which was full of at least two dozen people, many of whom I recognized: the usual group, plus some old friends—Cameron, Astraea, and Tophian. There were a handful of unfamiliar faces as well.

"Who are all of these people?" I pulled Bexa aside as she tried to join the crowd that was excitedly babbling around the front door. "How are we supposed to feed everyone?"

"Zaire brought a ton more supplies!" Bexa motioned to a stack of boxes against the wall. "Zaire and Legend have been bringing people in all morning! Word has been getting out about our mission, and a lot of people wanted to join."

"This is great and all, but don't you think it's going to be a bit harder to hide th—"

"Cindee?" I heard Braylin gasp.

I turned just in time to see the familiar bubbly, braided blonde step through the door, only to lock eyes with her brother across the room. Cindee's mouth hung open as she dropped to her knees, burying her face in the ground with a burst of sobs. Braylin bolted over to her, shoving a few others on his way to his sister. He sunk to the ground with her, throwing his arms around her, his face contorted in a mixture of an ugly wet cry and an elated grin. The people around them clapped excitedly for them, many with sympathetic tears in their eyes. Next through the door were Gwenn, Eve, Legend, and Zaire.

As Legend and Zaire walked through the doorway, the house erupted in excited cheers. Legend grinned wildly, bowing every few steps he took on his way toward me, with Zaire behind him laughing and rolling his eyes.

"I heard you were quite the party animal last night," Legend teased.

"I think I know how we can win this," I said, getting straight to the point.

"Wait," Bexa said. "Braylin is excused from this meeting due to his nice little family reunion, but shouldn't Skylar be here to hear this?"

I felt that same weight in my chest from the previous night. "Skylar told me last night that she was done—"

"—done goofing around. I'm definitely ready to take down Raine," Skylar cut in, appearing from one of the bedrooms. She threw me an apologetic glance from the corner of her eyes. "What's the plan?"

"It isn't so much of a plan yet as it is an idea," I said.

I filled Bexa, Legend, and Skylar in on what Zaire and I had heard the previous night about the updated CLVCS and the new skyscraper screens, describing it in as much detail as I could recall.

"I don't exactly see where you're going with this, but I'm listening," Zaire said.

"What if we can get into Raine's office and broadcast from her camera to the skyscraper screens in all of the cities?" I said. "We haven't been able to get letters to the other cities. Even though a few letters have trickled in, this would be huge. This would broadcast the message to everyone in the New Territory, and it would show them all that this isn't just some kid goofing around—it's an entire population that has had their lives destroyed by Raine Velora."

"The skyscraper screens don't broadcast from Raine's camera," said Skylar. "They're usually just advertisements."

"Could we somehow link the camera to their network?" I asked, turning to Legend and Zaire, who then looked to each other.

"If there's a way, we'll find it," Legend said confidently. "We just need some time—it's a delicate task, as you can imagine. Leave it to us."

"So, what's next?" asked Bexa.

"Waiting to make sure this plan is even feasible," I sighed. "But so far, it's the best thing we have. I believe the best use of our time until then is to work on another letter. At the gala, Raine mentioned ordering officials to arrest anyone who outwardly disagrees with the exile town system, so I'd say we can start with that."

"What?" Skylar gaped. "How can she get away with something like that?"

"That's not even the worst of it," I grumbled. "The people there actually supported her idea."

"That's ridiculous! Is she just going to fill Clamorite with citizens just because they disagreed or something?"

"I'm not sure what exactly she has planned, but whatever her idea is, it's garbage. I feel like it's our responsibility to let the people know what their leader just proposed."

"How can I help?" Bexa asked.

I instructed my friends to find a newer group member with a good story about Raine mistreating exiles, asking them to work together to write the third Dawn Letter with a personal story and the news of Raine's decision. Everyone agreed to help transcribe copies, and we were confident that plenty of others in the group would be willing to help as well.

When some of the chatter had died down, I noticed a subtle but constant scraping sound by the front door. I looked up but didn't notice anything that could explain the noise. One by one, others began to notice the noise, looking from the front door to the group, as if expecting an explanation. Paren took a few steps to the door, looking back hesitantly at everyone before slowly turning the knob and opening the door.

Paren had hardly cracked open the door when it swung inward. He pulled back just in time to dodge getting smacked by it as the wind blew it in with a gush of sand.

Iris and Arke were nearby, jumping to Paren's aid and forcing the door shut. Startled, everyone's focus was on the small mound of sand that had rushed into the house in the short time the door was open.

"I'm not driving in that," Zaire said, turning to Legend.

"It's fine," Paren said, smoothing out his hair. "We'll just wait for the storm to pass before anyone goes anywhere."

I exchanged a look of inconvenience with Skylar.

"It'll pass," Skylar said. "Want a drink?"

Skylar and I took a bottle of whiskey into what appeared to be an old game room toward the back of the house, where the chatter of everyone else was muted.

She shut the door behind us with an exasperated huff. I flopped back on a cushy leather couch and dust puffed up in a cloud around me. I let out a few sputtering coughs, reaching for the whiskey in Skylar's hand.

Skylar rolled her eyes and laughed at me as I choked down a swig, still coughing.

"How aren't you hung over from last night?" I asked her.

"Practice." She shrugged. "Also, who said I'm not hung over?"

I scoffed. "What made you decide to stay?"

"I couldn't really leave," she said. "We're doing something huge here, and I need to be a part of it."

"I'm glad you didn't leave," I said, cringing at my open vulnerability and the aftertaste of the whiskey.

"I guess I'm glad too," she said, snatching the bottle. "If you're going to start talking this sappy crap with me, I'm going to need this."

An hour passed before Skylar rejoined everyone in the main room. I saw Bexa and Paren chatting in the corner and decided to join them. On the other side of the room, I could see Legend and Zaire hanging out on one of the couches.

"Why are they still here?" I asked.

"They can't leave," Bexa said. "The storm has only gotten worse."

I paused, trying to listen to the weather outside.

"You won't hear it over everyone talking, but it's really bad out there and it shows no signs of slowing down."

I turned to Paren who nodded in agreement.

"I'm sure it'll pass in a few hours," I said calmly. "We should make use of this time and get everyone working on the next Dawn Letter."

Bexa and Paren agreed and separated, each approaching different newcomers to find the best story to include in the new letter. It turned out that some of the new people were chattier than expected, but eventually, Paren came to me with a story.

"Him," Paren pointed to an older gentleman in the kitchen. "He's from Delaisse. He has a rare genetic condition and grew up on a lot of medication to help manage his symptoms. His aunt was concerned—she was convinced that a good diet would magically cure him, and when he insisted on continuing his medication, she reported him for drug abuse. I guess he was on some pretty heavy pain killers, but nothing that wasn't necessary for his condition."

I felt the weight of his words in my chest, and my anger for Raine burned on my face. I paused for a moment, processing the man's story before nodding.

"How much paper do we have?" I asked Bexa. "Pens?"

"Plenty," she answered, pulling a box out of the supply pile.

Bexa and I began to assemble a team of people to help us write while Paren drafted the first copy. Hours later, after the immense help from our team, we had a sizeable stack of completed letters.

"Do you think the storm has calmed down at all yet?" Arke asked, massaging a blister on her hand from the pen.

The room quieted as everyone tried to focus on the sound outside. As the chatter died down, the sound of the roaring wind seemed to intensify as it ripped past the house.

"Guys!" I heard a voice break the eerie silence of the room. I turned to face the source, spotting Braylin poking around the side of the hallway. "You're going to want to see this."

I followed him down the hall with everyone trailing behind me. He led us to the stairs, which were tucked away behind a door in a hallway of their own. At the top of the stairs, sand was piled high. Every few seconds, some of it would shift and tumble like waves down another stair.

"Broken windows," Paren said pensively.

"Let's just keep the stair door closed," I said. "The upstairs is probably completely full of sand, so it might be unusable after this anyways."

Braylin obeyed, closing the door just as another ripple of sand rolled down a stair.

The sandstorm continued well into the night. At one point, it seemed to be dying down. The sounds of sand and fierce wind against the side of the house turned to gentle rustles, and we were finally able to safely open the door. When Legend and Zaire tried to get to their truck though, they found that it had practically been covered. We all aided them in digging away sand, but before we could finish, the wind began to pick back up, throwing sand in our eyes and mouths. Blindly, we stumbled back to the house and swarmed the door—everyone piling inside and slamming it shut behind us.

"Did you know there's a basement?" Braylin asked me as I shook sand from my hair.

"What?"

He motioned for me to follow him. He led me into the room Skylar and I had been drinking in.

"There," he pointed to two doors at the far side of the room.

"I thought those were closets."

"That one is," he pointed to the left. "Not the other one."

I approached the door and opened it, revealing a dark stairwell.

"You coming?" I asked, looking back at him, his arms crossed tight and eyes wide.

"I'll be fine here."

"What's up? There something down there?"

"Oh," he chuckled nervously. "I just haven't worked up the nerve to go down there. My grandparents had a basement and I managed to go my entire life without going down into it. I'd like to keep my record of avoiding basements."

I sucked my teeth and nodded, studying his face. "Whatever." I scoffed, turning back to the dark stairs and carefully descending them.

With each step, I plunged further into darkness, eventually unable to see anything but the light at the top of the stairs. Braylin's cautious face appeared tentatively in the doorway, looking down at me.

"What do you see?"

"Nothing, really," I answered. "It's too dark."

I reached my hands out in front of me, blindly pawing at air as I walked deeper into the basement. As I walked farther, I suddenly felt my ankle catch on something, sending me face-forward onto the cold concrete floor with a violent thud.

"Eos!" I heard Braylin call. "Is everything okay?"

"Yeah," I managed to grumble, pushing myself to my feet and flexing my sore wrists, which had managed to break the fall.

A few slow steps deeper into the basement, I felt a wall in front of me. I placed my palms flat against it, feeling around to follow the wall. Then, I felt something different. I paused, giving myself time to run my hands over the strange protrusion on the wall. It felt like a metal wheel. I wrapped both my hands around the cool metal and turned until I heard a deep clunk from within the wall.

I blinked my eyes and squinted, trying to at least make out outlines in the dark basement, but still couldn't see anything. Pulling carefully on the wheel, the wall in front of me began to move forward with a pained squeal. When I opened the strange hidden door, a light began to flicker on in the room before me. My eyes burned from the sudden light—I squeezed them shut. *There must be some kind of generator.*

I shuffled forward slowly into the room as I let my eyes flutter, allowing brief bursts of painful light in at a time. By the time I was able to hold them open and see, I had stepped completely into this new room. Upon seeing my new surroundings, I instinctually covered my mouth with both hands, staring in horror at the family of skeletons lying in the corner.

I shook my head, as if denying what I saw would suddenly make it disappear. There were two larger skeletons seeming to huddle around a slightly smaller skeleton and two others that were undeniably from children. I looked around the room, seeing shelves full of empty cans and empty bottles. There were a couple bunk beds against the far wall and a couple children's toys scattered around.

As I backed out of the room, the light eventually went off on its own. When I had reached the stairs and rejoined Braylin back in the room, he immediately bombarded me with questions.

“Is there anything down there? Any supplies?”

“There’s a bunker,” I answered, feeling strange grief for the mystery family weighing in my chest.

“That’s awesome!” Braylin babbled excitedly. “That’d be a great spot to hide if we ever have officials find their way here. Were there supplies in the bunker?”

I shook my head, keeping my eyes low.

“That’s okay. We should have enough, especially with Legend and Zaire helping us. Why are you so upset about it?”

I looked up at him, his eyes surveying me as he waited for an answer.

“There was a family in the bunker.”

“Wait, you mean people are already living here?”

“I don’t mean it like that, Bray,” I said with a deep, shaky breath. “A family from the explosions. They must have hidden in their bunker, but I don’t think they felt safe enough to leave because of potential radiation or whatever else might have been out there. It looks like they ran out of supplies a long time ago.”

“Oh,” he said softly. He bit his bottom lip, kept his eyes low, nodded, and exited the room.

NINETEEN

One day passed with the storm hardly letting up, then another, and another. Four days into the storm, we finally had a moment of respite to clear Zaire and Legend's truck, which now looked like an immense sand dune in the middle of what once was a road. Once the truck was uncovered, Zaire and Legend climbed inside and promised to return with more supplies.

"Are you sure you're going to be able to get out?" I asked, eying the sandy road ahead.

"We'll manage," Zaire said confidently, turning the key in the ignition. The engine made a pathetic sputtering sound and Zaire stopped turning the key. He shot his brother a concerned look before trying again with the same result.

"What's wrong with it?" I asked.

"Probably all the sand. We'll get it working— I do this kind of stuff for a living," Zaire said, walking around to the back of the truck and opening the trunk.

Legend and Zaire worked together quickly as the rest of us watched cluelessly.

"Give it another go," Zaire said a few moments later, handing Legend the keys.

Legend sat down and gave the keys a turn. After a brief whine, the engine roared to life and the two brothers smiled, applauding themselves and the truck.

"I'll give it a better inspection and cleaning when I get back to the shop," Zaire said, returning the tool to the trunk. "This will do for now."

"We better get going," Legend said. "No telling if the storm is going to pick back up."

"Stay safe!" Zaire called to us, hopping in the truck and shutting the door behind him. Legend waved to us all from behind the passenger side window as we watched them carefully maneuver the truck down the street and into the desert.

As we watched the truck grow smaller on the horizon, the wind occasionally whipped around us, reminding us of its presence.

"How are we on supplies?" Skylar asked me, leaning against the wall of the house.

"Well enough to last another day or two. Longer if we ration carefully."

"Might want to start rationing," she advised.

"Zaire and Legend will be back with food. I'm guessing two or three days at most."

"I'm not sure if they'll be able to get back over here anytime soon," Skylar said, pointing toward the desert opposite where Zaire and Legend disappeared. In the distance, I could make out what appeared to be a tornado.

"That looks pretty far—maybe it won't come this way?"

"Best to prepare for the worst."

"If it hits the ruins, we're screwed anyways."

"Way to be the optimistic one," Skylar said, rolling her eyes and reentering the house. I stayed a moment longer outside, trying to gauge the direction of the tornado, but the wind around me began to grow too violent again, forcing me back into the house.

"What's this I hear about a tornado?" Paren asked me immediately, before I even closed the door.

"I don't think it's headed this way," I said, brushing past him.

Once inside the house, I noticed a bunch of people huddled over the boxes of supplies, pushing and clawing at each other as they dug through the boxes.

"Hey!" I shouted at them in vain. "What're you doing?"

I ran over, pushing apart two women I hadn't officially met yet who were fighting over a can of soup.

"What the hell is this about?" I demanded. The exiles stopped to stare at me, their arms loaded up with food and water. A loose can tumbled from someone's arms and rolled across the floor. The room was silent and still as everyone stared at me.

"The storm," muttered one of the women from the fight.

"We don't know when they'll be able to bring back supplies," the other clarified.

"Let me get this straight… You figured it would be a good idea to horde as much as you could so everyone else could go without?" My accusation was met by blank stares and silence. "You figured, as long as you get to eat well and stay comfortable, it doesn't matter if everyone else has to suffer through the hunger pains?"

One of the women pulled her armload of food in toward her chest defensively.

"Like hell." I swatted her arms, sending a cascade of food onto the ground around us. "If any one of you thinks you're better than the rest of us, if any one of you thinks you can eat while the rest of us starve, I'll throw you out into the storm myself, got it?"

More silence.

"We don't know how long this storm will last, but this might not even be a true issue—let's not resort to fighting like savages at the mere threat of a tornado," I said.

The silence broke as the room erupted in nervous chatter.

"What tornado?" called Cindee.

I groaned.

"What Eos means to say," Paren started, joining me at my side. "Is that this storm is getting worse, but there have been some moments of peace. Zaire and Legend have been able to leave during one of these moments of peace, and I'm sure that, if the storm continues, they will be able to return during one of those moments as well. There is plenty of food and water to last everyone for a few days—we have to be responsible with it. No hording food. We will ration it carefully, just to be proactive. Hopefully, the storm passes, and we can move on with our lives and keep moving with our plans."

Our small crowd quieted and some of the tension of the room seemed to melt away. The looters placed their findings back in the supply boxes and dispersed into the casually chatting crowd.

"How did you do that?" I asked, gaping back at the exiles, who seemed tranquil in the moment.

"I just told them the truth," Paren said with a shrug.

"So did I."

"I was a bit gentler about it, I suppose." He chuckled.

I thanked him for his help and, just as I was about to look for Bexa, there was a horrible scream at the door. With the door hardly askew, Iris stood, peering out the crack in the door.

"It's here!" She opened the door enough for me to see the tornado ripping up rubble along the edge of the ruins.

We're going to need that bunker.

I shouted for everybody's attention. When the exiles were quiet enough to hear me, I told them Braylin found a basement, and that there was a bunker with a generator hidden in it that could fit us all if we squished in tight. "The only stipulation," I said, "is that we need to move quick—the bunker has some skeletons in it, and I need help moving them so we can all fit."

A few people reluctantly volunteered, feeling pressured by the time crunch. I had them follow me into the basement before everyone else. We migrated the family of bones, placing them on the other side of the basement against a wall. Just as we were moving the last skeleton—one of the smallest ones—Skylar began to guide people downstairs and toward the bunker.

"Get in!" Paren commanded, just as we heard the twister near the side of the house.

The sounds of wood and brick being pulled from the walls echoed in the basement. Some of the exiles eased themselves down the stairs backwards, helping others carry the large boxes of supplies.

One by one, the exiles filed themselves into the small bunker. Some of the exiles climbed onto the bunkbeds to make room, and all of the supplies were stacked precariously in the corner to preserve space.

"I can't."

Cromwell looked at me from right outside the crowded bunker, his eyes scanning the room.

"We can make room. Everyone, squish in a bit more!" I yelled, the tornado growing louder and closer.

Everyone stood still.

"There's plenty of room for him," Skylar said from one of the bunkbeds.

"I'll be okay," Cromwell said with a somber nod.

"What's the problem? You can fit! Just hurry up!" I urged.

Cromwell's face looked flushed, and I could see sweat beading on his head. "I'm not good with tight spaces and crowds. I'll find somewhere safe and find you all after."

"Hey!" Paren called, wriggling his way out of the bunker. "I'm not leaving you alone."

"Guys—" Bexa warned over the roaring wind.

Without another word, Paren pushed the bunker door shut behind him with a deep thud, leaving him and Cromwell on the outside. The light above us flickered for a moment, but upon the first movement in the room, it buzzed and turned back on. Everyone was silent for a while, and the thick bunker walls blocked out any sounds of the tornado and chaos outside.

"How long do we stay here?" I heard Arke ask from one of the top bunks.

"I'm not sure," I answered honestly. "Probably a while, just to play it safe and make sure it has completely passed."

What would Zane do if he were stuck in a crowded bunker waiting for a storm to pass?

"Let's play a game," I suggested after another few minutes of painful silence that was only ever broken by occasional coughs and cleared throats.

"Tag, you're it," Skylar mocked.

I stared back at her, unamused, before detailing the rules of a word game I remembered playing as a child, where you go around listing things you're buying from the store. You start with the letter A, then B, then C, and so on. Each person gets their own letter, but the catch is—they have to repeat all of the items on the list before their letter.

"—lettuce, macaroni…N…noodles," Iris said as it got to her turn.

"Macaroni and noodles are the same thing," Arke said flatly. She turned to me. "This game is lame. It's been a while—can we at least check if it's safe?"

Everyone looked to me for a decision.

What would Zane do right now?

I looked to Skylar for a hint on what to do, but her expression was unwavering.

Zane would probably want everyone to be patient and wait a bit longer to be sure it's safe.

I began to open my mouth to speak, but slowly closed it as I reconsidered.

I'm not Zane. I make my own decisions.

I nodded once, turning to the heavy door and slowly pushing it with my weight. It wouldn't budge. I sniffed, rolled my shoulders, and pushed again, this time with a bit more force. Still, the door wouldn't move.

"Can you help me out a bit?" I asked one of the nearest exiles, some guy I had yet to get to know. He pushed against the door with his shoulder, bracing his feet firmly against the ground. We both continued to push, a vein beginning to bulge on his forehead. He stopped and looked at me, shaking his head.

"What's going on?" I heard a voice from the far end of the room.

I looked around at the concerned faces around me as I grimaced.

"We're stuck."

"Someone else help her!" one of the exiles pleaded pathetically.

"It's not going to move," I said. "It won't even budge."

"Is it locked? Maybe you need to unlock it?" someone else suggested.

"We're going to die in here?" another whined.

The room erupted in panicked chatter as a bunch of people began to force themselves forward to try their hand at the door in vain, shoving me in the process and trampling others as they swarmed.

"Hey!" I yelled, trying to get everyone's attention as they continued to push and shove each other out of the way to try to open the door, which would only shift a hair—just enough to mock each person's attempt with a grinding click.

I looked over my shoulder to see Skylar, still sitting on one of the bunkbeds, watching the small mob with disinterest and disappointment. When she noticed I was looking at her, she rolled her eyes, shrugged, and wiggled a flask at me before taking a drink. Feeling my lips flatten together, I scanned the bunker, spotting an incredibly thin clearing by the supply boxes. Using my elbows as a shield, I barreled my way toward the supply boxes just to get some space.

After time, the exiles began to give up the battle with the door, retiring in reluctant submission to their situation. For a while, I enjoyed the silence and stillness while everybody sat or stood in their own thoughts, likely going through their own list of what-ifs. An hour passed like this, with not a single word spoken.

"What are we supposed to do?" someone asked the obvious.

"Maybe the wind is right against the door," I suggested. "Let's give it a bit longer and then try again."

A bit longer turned into a while, which turned into a long while. No one wanted to be disappointed by the door again. Eventually, a couple of the exiles nearest to the supply crates with me began to rummage into the boxes, pulling out food and supplies, shoving them greedily into their pockets.

"What do you think you're doing?" I challenged them.

"You know what?" one of them started. "You're not in charge here. You might think you are, some of these people might think you are. But you aren't."

"No one is 'in charge,'" I corrected him. "But those supplies belong to everyone, and I'm going to need you to put those back."

"You're just like her, aren't you?" he said with a snarled lip.

"Just like who?"

"Raine," he hissed, shoving his hands back in the supplies.

I pulled his hands back. "What are you talking about?"

"She cut back our rations too," he said with a scoff. "That's why a lot of us left the exile towns just recently."

I couldn't form words, I just felt disgust.

"I'm so sorry," I said. "I had no idea she did that."

"It was to our benefit," Fabian called over. Everyone's heads nearly snapped as they all glared at him simultaneously.

"Excuse me?" the ration-thief said.

"Let me clarify," Fabian said, his pasty skin rapidly turning bright red. "The ration amendment is incredibly inhumane, but think about how that makes Raine look. Word has gotten out to some of the citizens and even more people are realizing how terrible she is. It's helping our cause, if nothing else. And hopefully, we can get the exiles out of the towns soon enough so they don't have to worry about it long, right?" He swallowed nervously.

"That's true," I said softly. "No matter how Raine is handling things though, our primary concern right now needs to be surviving in the present moment, and we can't do that if just a couple people steal all of the rations for themselves. Put the stuff back."

I stared at the thief, forcing myself not to blink or look away. For a moment, he stared back as if testing me, but the corners of his eyes began to squint as a wicked smile grew across his face. He slowly raised his middle finger between our two faces before proceeding to fill his pockets, the other surrounding exiles joining in the chaos.

Scanning the room for someone to help me, I spotted Skylar crawling out of the bunk bed and worming her way to the door.

"Enough is enough," she grumbled, rolling her hand to crack her wrist as she approached the door.

At the door, she wiggled the handle wheel, turning it in either direction as she pushed with all her strength, her feet sliding against the concrete until eventually, the door—and Skylar's balance—gave way. Skylar toppled over through the door, nearly colliding with Cromwell and Paren.

"You're alive!" Braylin exclaimed upon seeing our two friends, who were in obvious shock.

"What's going on?" Paren asked, his eyes scanning over the panicked looks on everyone's faces.

I looked over at the looters, my lip snarled as I debated ratting them out.

"Nothing," I resigned.

"How long ago did the storm end?" Skylar asked Paren and Cromwell, who helped her to her feet.

"Quite a while ago. We found somewhere to hide for a while, and when we were sure it was cleared up, we came back to check on you all," Paren said.

I looked around behind him and found that I was able to see the basement. The ceiling above had a few cave-ins, allowing light to stream in through the broken floorboards above. The basement was fairly empty, except for a few old pieces of furniture and knick-knacks. There was a layer of sand across the floor, and there was a broken armoire beside the bunker.

"The storm must have knocked that thing in front of the door," Cromwell said, pointing to the armoire. "There was a bunch of stuff blocking the door. We figured, once we saw the mess, that maybe you guys got stuck in here."

"You figured right," Skylar said, kicking some of the shards of wood aside and pulling the door open wide, allowing out a rush of claustrophobic exiles.

"How's the rest of the house?" I asked, standing aside as everyone shoved their way out of the bunker.

"Not great," Paren answered. "There's another house on the other side of these ruins that we might be able to make do with, but it's not ideal."

"Lead the way."

Everyone managed to settle into two neighboring houses on the other side of the ruins. The next few days were spent writing letters and carefully rationing supplies while we waited. After much debate, we were able to retrieve the stolen supplies from those who had pocketed things while in the bunker. It seemed as if arguments were constantly breaking out over supplies, but with help, I was able to keep the exiles under control so we could stretch our rations as long as possible. We kept three exiles on watch at all times at the previous house, just to make sure we wouldn't miss Zaire and Legend. Three days passed before we finally heard the rumble of a truck engine.

Please be Zaire and Legend. Please, please don't be officials.

The door opened, and our three exiles who were on watch last cheerily strutted into the room, arms full of supplies. I felt my racing heart beat a little slower as I sighed in relief. Zaire and Legend followed behind the others, boxes stacked high in their arms, stumbling blindly into the ashy living room.

"Bless you!" Cindee praised, running to help Zaire with a box that was teetering at the top of his stack.

When they had finally set all the supplies down, Zaire made a beeline for me.

"Fallmont is a mess right now," he told me.

I stared back at him, waiting for more details.

"The storm, for starters, caught everybody by surprise. There wasn't a ton of damage inside the city itself, but there's sand *everywhere*, and some of the houses in one part of town got the brunt of the storm. But even beyond that—Raine has absolutely gone off the rails."

"What's new?" I snickered at my own joke, but I was met by Zaire's unamused eyes, blinking back at me impatiently. "Sorry, continue."

"You remember what she said at the gala? About arresting people for speaking against the system?"

I nodded.

"Fully implemented. Some officials have even gone out of their way to go hunting for sympathizers outside of their usual working hours. It's become some kind of twisted game for them to see how many they can find."

I didn't know how to respond, so I just gaped at him. *We have no chance—even if people agree with our cause, now they definitely won't act on it.*

"There's a bright side," he said.

"How?"

"More sympathizers."

"Again I ask—*how?*" *Are people really that dumb?*

"More and more people are realizing how psychotic Raine is and how this system is outdated. People who were on the fence before now understand and are on our side!"

"But they can't do anything about it or they'll be exiled, so it doesn't really matter anymore, does it?"

"Did it ever matter before that there were consequences? That part hasn't really changed as much as you think it has. They might not do anything about it now, but I think it's important that you continue rallying people and prepping them for a rebellion."

My skin grew cold at the word.

Rebellion.

It sounded so made-up—like nothing we would ever even joke about doing. It seemed so far-fetched. *But here we are, and rebellion isn't so much of an "if" as a "when."*

"What about the camera?" I asked.

"Woah," Zaire laughed. "It hasn't been that long. That'll take some time. We've got some friends who are looking into it for us, but it'll take time. If they go about it too fast or without enough care, Raine or her cronies are going to notice. If they notice, we're done. All of us."

I nodded solemnly.

Legend and Zaire said their goodbyes and they began to make their way to the truck after the supplies had been loaded into the two houses. I followed them outside, thanking them endlessly for their help. Both boys gave me hugs before taking off in their truck once again.

Upon reentering the house, I was immediately bombarded with questions from Gwenn, Eve, and Cindee, who approached me with arms linked.

"We want to be a part of the delivery team," Gwenn smiled, her eyes full of fire. "We've heard the risks, but we want to help deliver the letters."

"I—" I started.

"*Please?*" she whined, batting her eyelashes.

"Sure," I shrugged. "I don't particularly care who delivers them, as long as someone with experience goes with and as long as everyone is careful. No matter what happens, you can't give up our location or any of our plans—got it?"

The three girls nodded energetically.

"Who's taking you who has gone before?" I asked.

Eve pointed into the cluster of people in the living room. I couldn't tell who she was pointing to.

"That short kid with the black hair? I don't think he's ever come with."

"No," she clarified. "The blond boy with the glasses."

"Fabian's taking you?" I could hear the surprise in my voice. I thought for a moment. "You know what? Okay. Go for it." *He's proven himself multiple times—I can trust him to lead a group by now, right?*

Eve and Gwenn trotted away to join a group of letter-writers in their efforts, while Cindee patiently waited for them to leave, her eyes locked onto mine as if begging me not to move.

"Is everything okay?" I asked.

She nodded, her eyelashes fluttering.

I looked away from her and back to her, still waiting.

"Did you need something?"

"I'm waiting," she said with a soft smile, her eyes flicking toward Skylar, who was approaching us with a lazy swagger.

"Hey, did you hear that the team is thinking they'll have a load of letters ready by tonight?" Skylar asked, motioning to the group of people writing frantically.

"I'm aware," I said. "Can you give us a moment, Sky?"

She cocked an eyebrow at us before giving a dramatic huff and walking away. I looked at Cindee expectantly.

"Have you given any thought to what you want to happen after the rebellion?"

"Excuse me?"

"After we overthrow Raine," Cindee said confidently. "What do you plan on doing?"

"I'm not sure I get what you mean," I hesitated.

"You're essentially planning to overthrow the government as we've known it—you'll need something in its place."

"You mean a leader?"

"Mmmm," she thought. "More than just that. That's just the beginning."

"I guess it's up to whoever the new leader will be," I said.

"Don't you think they'd want you to lead?" she asked.

"Would you?" I smirked.

She paused uncomfortably.

"It's okay," I said.

"Sorry."

"I guess reinstating the prison system would be the next step. There will still be crime, but I think that's the fairest way to deal with it. Give all the exiles retrials—I'm sure some still deserve to serve time, but others' freedom is incredibly overdue."

Cindee nodded, seemingly satisfied but still pensive, as if I was missing something she was looking for. When she had determined that she wasn't sure what that was—or that she wasn't ready to share it with me—she retreated to her friends and took up a pen and paper.

When the sun slithered below the horizon, the writers concluded their letters, folding them and distributing them to those who would be delivering them that night—Gwenn, Cindee, Eve, Fabian, Arke, Iris, and a few others that I didn't know.

"You sure you don't want to join us?" Gwenn offered as she stepped through the front door after the others.

"Be safe," I said with a light smile as the door closed softly behind them.

TWENTY

The night was quiet. Many of the exiles left for the second house, leaving me and a few others in the first one. I spread out my blanket on the floor and curled up, trying to get some rest.

Unable to sleep, I lay there, profoundly aware of the stiff, cold ground beneath my blanket. I stared up at the ceiling, a few holes in the roof exposing a view of the stars beyond it. My mind, in the emptiness of the moment, flickered back to the time Zane and I shared a blanket under a damaged roof like this. A chill rippled through my spine and I shuttered.

I miss you.

I continued to stare off at the stars, adjusting my already uncomfortable angle on the floor to better see through the cracks and holes.

I'm so sorry.

My eyes began to sting, but I refused to blink. The more I stared at the stars, the more alone I felt and the more his absence felt like physical aching.

I deserve to feel this.

I felt my body give another shudder and then a deep lurch. A singular sob. I fought it, holding my breath but feeling my chest and legs shake. One of the stars seemed to twinkle through the crack in the ceiling and I blinked. A warm, thick tear rolled down my cheek and I gave into it, trying to keep the sobbing as silent as I could so as not to wake the others.

Through the thick tears, it became difficult to see the stars.

It's all my fault.

I lay there, feeling sorry for Zane and feeling sorry for myself. I let out a couple more gasping sobs before biting down on my lip, drying my tears, and forcing it all back deep down. If I wasn't tired before, I certainly was now. In defeat, I rolled over, trying to ignore the stars above.

For the first time in a while, the air outside was completely still, leaving the house in eerie silence. Whenever someone stirred in their sleep, I shot up, my head spinning as I tried to make out my surroundings. Each time I awoke from restless half-sleep, I grew more and more exhausted until I finally drifted off.

"Hey," he said gently, his soft lips brushing my ear. He twirled a loose strand of my hair as he waited, my eyes slowly opening groggily.

"Hey," I groaned, rubbing my eyes and rolling over to face him.

"Why do you keep doing this to yourself?" he asked, his brown eyes comforting me in the moment. *Where are we?* We were in a white bed in the middle of a spacious, empty room with large windows on all sides. Wispy white curtains fluttered around their open windows, obscuring the view outside.

"Why do you keep doing this to yourself?" Zane asked again, tucking the strand of hair behind my ear as he watched me.

"Doing what?" I asked, focusing my attention back on him.

He smiled innocently. "It wasn't your fault, and you know that."

The reality hit me, weighing like bricks in my throat and my stomach.

"You're wrong," I said.

"Think about it."

I lay there, thinking back on the moment in Raine's office. The feeling of the doorknob in my hands, the sound of the gunshot, the sight of Zane across Raine's desk.

"You're not really dead," I said, the words feeling thick in my throat.

A small smile twitched at the corner of his lips. "Keep thinking."

"I'm a monster," I said, my face growing hot, a muscle in my arm beginning to twitch. "I'll never forgive myself for coming up with that stupid idea. But Raine is an even bigger monster and I can't wait to throw her decapitated head from the top of a skyscraper."

He made a soft hushing sound, tracing a finger down my cheek. "Keep thinking."

"Maybe if I had been the one at her desk. If you were at the door—you'd be alive right now. I'd give anything to redo that moment."

"But you can't," he said, his voice reassuring, rather than accusatory.

"I'm so sorry." My eyes began to sting again just before thick, warm tears raced each other down my face. I felt my body tense as I gave into the involuntary sobbing.

"For what?" He let out an airy laugh as he caught a particularly large tear with his finger.

"I'm sorry that I made you come with me."

"You never made me do that."

"I'm sorry I wasn't the one by her desk instead."

"That wasn't your choice."

"I'm sorry I ever followed you out of Avid in the first place."

"I'm not."

Blinking back the tears, I fixed my eyes on his again.

"None of this was your fault. Meeting you was the best thing that could have ever happened to me, no matter how things went," he said. "I'm so proud of how far you've come."

I scoffed. "I can't do this without you."

"You have to."

Just then, searing white light filled my vision before dissipating into blackness. I sat up, my cheeks feeling warm and wet, the familiar weight residing in my throat. Frozen, I continued to process for a moment before an idea struck. Scrambling from my bed, I scurried over to the supply bins, fishing out a pen and paper. I placed the paper on the kitchen counter and squinted, trying to focus on my handwriting despite the dim moonlight through the windows and the holes in the structure of the house.

This will be my last letter.

By now, you've read the stories about exiles... no... people who were mistreated by Raine. Some of them are your family, your friends, your neighbors. There's no way you could be oblivious to the corruption anymore, but I have one final story for you.

Zane Hess was one of the best people I have ever met. I hope after this, you see the corruption we live under. Zane grew up with a sick older brother. His family couldn't afford basic necessities after the medication costs, so Zane had to resort to stealing to help provide for his family, even at a young age. He got away with it for a while, but as a young adult, he was caught and exiled to Avid, leaving his family without vital provisions.

If the story of his arrest isn't enough for you, there's more.

When I made the dangerous trip into Fallmont as an exile to plead for the reinstatement of the prison system, I was not alone. By his own goodness, Zane decided to come with me. We did not draw weapons, we did not threaten, but when we came to speak to Raine in peace, she pulled her gun and shot Zane, leaving his body strewn across her desk as her officials dragged me off to Ironwood.

Is this the kind of life we want? Is this the kind of life you want for your children? Do you want them to grow up under a leader that sends them off to exile towns for life or even shoots them, just for sharing their differing ideas?

If you're with us—if you believe it is time for Raine to fall—wait for our instructions.

Just as I put the letter in my pocket and pulled out one of the kitchen chairs to sit, a group of people crashed through the door. The hair on my arms stood straight as I gaped in shock at the two larger guys helping carry someone through the doorway.

"Get up!" one of them barked at Skylar, who was sleeping on the couch. She sat, dazed for a moment before scurrying off the couch at the sight of the limp body.

The two carriers placed the body gently on the couch as Paren pushed his way over.

"What happened?" he asked, crouching and taking a closer look.

I wanted to know who it was, but fear glued me to my seat in the kitchen.

"We were delivering letters and they came out of nowhere," Cindee said through blubbering whimpers, followed by a wet sniffle. Eve pulled her in close, rubbing her back and whispering something in her ear.

"Who did? What happened?" Paren pried.

"A t-truck," Cindee sniveled.

"A truck?" Paren asked, pausing. "I don't understand. No one except officials drive trucks for the most part, right? How did this happen?"

Cindee just nodded, her curls quivering with every movement.

"It was an official?"

She nodded again, her chest heaving over and over as she tried to catch her breath. "They k-killed her." Another sniffle. "They killed Gwenn."

"She's not dead," Paren said, his tone contradicting the optimism of his words. "But I don't know how to help her."

"I know someone who might be able to," my mouth said before my brain could catch up. “Someone pick her up. Follow me. Just a few of you—I don’t want to draw attention to us.”

Two other muscular exiles offered to take a turn carrying Gwenn. Eve, Cindee, and the two new carriers followed me as I rushed out the door, leaving the rest of the room in speechless shock.

When we reached the gates of Fallmont, I pulled out the Skeleton Key and opened the gate, letting everyone slip inside before sealing it up behind me. I pointed in the distance as I continued to lead the group, hugging the walls and using everything we could as camouflage. As we navigated down the street, I noticed more Dawn graffiti than the last time I was in Fallmont. In a few places, some of the Dawn Letters were posted sloppily across brick and concrete walls as if someone had pasted them there in a hurry along the entire stretch of the street.

“Woah,” one of the carriers said softly, taking in the sight as we hurried past the graffiti.

“What’s with the graffiti? It never looked like this when I lived here.”

“Dawn graffiti,” I replied in a whisper.

“Looks like you’ve got some supporters,” he replied.

“I’d say more than *some*,” Eve said.

We continued down the street until I recognized where we were.

“That one,” I said in a hushed tone, pointing to a small house. My eyes fixated on the shards of colorful broken glass set against the windowsill—the rest of the glass on the lawn had been cleared. “Inside!” I hissed, clarifying my directions after my initial instructions were met with confused glares.

“Wait—” I said as Eve began to raise a fist to knock on the door. “Get down and wait.”

I directed them to crouch behind some nearby bushes, practically holding their breath as they waited. I hurried around to the side of the house, toward the side window. Carefully, I slid it open just enough for me to wiggle through, my foot getting slightly caught in the curtain in the process. After closing the window behind me, I made my way through the house and to the front door, unlocking it and holding it open, waving for the others to enter. I allowed everyone to file in quickly before locking it behind us.

Gavin and Mallory stood in their living room, stunned as the two carriers set Gwenn, who was still unconscious, on their couch.

"You're a nurse, right?" I asked Mallory, who replied with wide eyes and a tentative nod.

"She was hit by a truck. She's a friend." I allowed my eyes to do the pleading.

"I—"

"We have nowhere else to go," I reminded her.

Mallory nodded solemnly, approaching Gwenn. She delicately held open Gwenn's eyelid for a moment as she began asking us questions about the accident.

"We need to get her to the hospital," Mallory insisted, still inspecting Gwenn's body.

"They can't know we're here. Not an option. She's an exile."

"She could be bleeding internally—she needs someone who can properly examine her! She needs medical equipment!"

"No." I stared at her unblinking.

"I can bring just her—I'll say she knocked on our door and that I don't know who she is or where she came from. When… if… she comes to—I'll tell her to pretend she forgot who she is. They'll take care of her," Gavin offered.

"I don't know if she'll need to pretend," Mallory said solemnly.

For the first time since they brought Gwenn back from the delivery, I took a true look at her. Her face, swollen, battered, and scratched, was frozen in place. There was a deep gash across her cheek up to her forehead with gravel and sand stuck in the wet blood.

"Brain damage?" I asked, unable to take my eyes off Gwenn.

"I can't say for sure, but I would assume so. Her abdomen is really swollen too. If you want to even give her a fighting chance, you'll let us take her to the hospital."

I nodded, stepping away from Gwenn.

"Do you need help?" one of the carriers asked.

"Bad idea," I warned him.

"No, thank you," Gavin confirmed, laying out a blanket on the floor. "We don't want you guys to get in any kind of trouble for being here. Not worth the risk. We can handle it."

He lifted Gwenn and laid her gently on the blanket. He grabbed the corners of the blanket toward Gwenn's head as his wife lifted the corners at her feet.

"Door," Gavin said as the two waddled through the living room, carrying Gwenn on the blanket between them.

I opened the door, let them out, and locked it.

We decided to all stay together in the house to wait until they returned, however long it would take. Though I felt guilty about finding any gratitude in such a situation, I couldn't deny being somewhat relieved to spend time in a structurally sound house with running water.

While the others were socializing in the living room, trying to distract themselves from the situation at hand by nervously chit-chatting about some parties they had been to before each of them was exiled, I snuck off into Mallory and Gavin's bedroom. Checking over my shoulder, I slid the safe away from the wall, revealing the hiding hole. I crawled into it, searching for the bucket of syringes. When I found it, I pulled it out of its hiding place and into the light. In the bucket with the syringes were some tiny empty bottles of medication. I carefully plucked one from the bin, avoiding the needles. With the little bottle between my fingers, I turned it over to read the label. There was a long name on the bottle with some random numbers. When I heard footsteps in the hallway, I quickly threw the bottle back in the bucket, the bucket back in the hole, and the safe back in its place.

"Everything okay?" Cindee asked, poking her head out from behind the door just as I had stood up.

"Yeah," I said a little too quickly.

"You sure?"

I nodded. "Just wanted some space."

She threw her arms out wide, her bottom lip beginning to quiver.

Crap.

"I'm scared too," she said pathetically, wrapping her arms tight around me.

I awkwardly patted her hair, which was frizzing out of her braids. "It'll be okay," I said unconvincingly.

"You think so?"

"I do," I said, feeling immediate guilt. *It seems like the right thing to say, right?*

When she had calmed down a bit, we rejoined the others in the living room. Eve had fallen asleep with her head in the lap of one of the carriers, who was bouncing in and out of consciousness. The other carrier, a shorter, heavier-set guy, fiddled with an unfinished puzzle on the coffee table.

Time trickled by slowly, and nobody felt up to starting another conversation. A few of us took turns showering, silently grateful for the opportunity, despite the circumstances. When I had finished showering, I returned to the living room to see that the other carrier and Cindee both dozed off as well, leaving me as the only one awake. I paced around the room, trying to stay awake. Eventually, I heard the doorknob jiggle as someone tried to unlock it. Seconds later, Mallory and Gavin slipped in the door, closing it behind them.

Eve, Cindee, and the carriers awoke to the noise, and everyone stood, eagerly awaiting an update. Speechless, we stared at the couple. Mallory's eyes were bloodshot, her nose red, and a dirty tissue in her right hand. Before anyone would speak, she looked between me and the others and slowly shook her head, giving a single whimpering cry.

Instantly, Cindee and Eve burst into tears and hugged each other. My throat burned as I swallowed my sadness.

"I'm so sorry," Mallory apologized. "I thought if we could get her help that maybe she'd have a chance. I feel absolutely horrible."

"It's not your fault," I said. "You were just trying to help—we appreciate it." I felt like my voice sounded unnaturally void of emotion as I tried to keep it together for Cindee and Eve.

"They said she suffered extreme brain damage because of the impact," Gavin said. "The doctors don't think she felt any pain after she was hit."

I could tell he was trying to be comforting, but his words sent Cindee and Eve into another fit of pained wails at the loss of their best friend. I looked at him and grimaced, putting a finger to my lips to politely hint that he should keep the gory details to himself.

"*Sorry*," he mouthed. I nodded.

"You guys can stay here as long as you need," Mallory offered. "Let me make you some tea." She scurried off to the kitchen, which was soon filled with the sound of clinking teacups.

When she returned, she held a tray full of steaming little cups. The spoons in each cup clattered as her hands shook.

"Sugar?" she asked as everyone took their cups. *For a nurse, the poor thing doesn't handle death well.*

I motioned for Gavin to follow me into the bedroom while Mallory was tending to the others. He followed, one of his eyebrows raised skeptically. Once in the bedroom, I shut the door behind us.

"You never told Skylar and me about the syringes," I reminded him, my voice hushed.

"You're asking about that *now*?" he asked, his voice hinting at a bit of disgust. "Eos, you just lost a friend, do you really think now is the time?"

"I'm sorry. I'm trying to keep it together for their sake—someone has to. I really can't afford to think about how much we have all lost right now—I can't handle it. So please, just humor me."

He stared at me, processing.

"Sometimes, when things get quiet in the ruins, my mind starts to drift off and wonder what you could possibly have a bucket of syringes for. Are you a drug addict?"

"What?" he sputtered in shock. "No!"

"I mean, you have to at least understand how bad this looked from our perspective."

He grumbled. "They're for my medication."

"Medication? Why is that the kind of thing you're hiding from your wife?"

"I've been sick since I was young, and I was on medication for years. It helped and the doctors thought I was getting better—and I was—for a while, so I stopped the medication. I started to get sick again a few months ago, so the doctor put me back on my meds."

"That seems like the kind of thing you should tell Mallory," I said sternly. "What if she were sick and didn't tell you?"

"With the baby and with everything happening out there right now, Mallory is stressed enough already. I don't need her stressing about this too. I'll be fine. It's just a condition I have to live with, and they said I'll probably need to stay on the medication the rest of my life, but it's not the worst thing in the world. I plan to tell her after the baby and after things calm down one way or another. Please," his eyes were desperate, "don't tell my wife. She doesn't need to know right now. I'm fine."

I looked over him as I processed. His posture was hunched in submission, his eyes locked on my face as if he couldn't breathe until my next words, and his hands wrung each other in front of his chest.

"Fine."

"Thank you!" He hugged me, and I felt an unwarranted wave of comfort wash over me. I threw my arms around him in return.

"You're welcome," I muttered into his shoulder.

"I should get back to Mallory," he said, pulling away.

I dropped my arms and backed up awkwardly. "Good idea. She seemed like kind of a mess. Is she like this when patients die too?"

He smiled softly. "Pretty much—to some degree or another. She has a really big heart."

Gavin and Mallory allowed us to spend the day at their house, and we used the day to catch up on sleep. Everyone took turns with the shower until the hot water was depleted, and even then, Eve decided to shower. I could hear her excited "woohoo!" as she stepped into the cold water, stunned by the cold but grateful to be clean. When the sun finally crept back past the horizon, we thanked our friends for their help and hospitality and went on our way.

When we reached the ruins, it hit me that one of us would have to share the news about Gwenn with everyone. Seeming to read my mind, Eve put her hand on my shoulder, looking at me sympathetically as I stood frozen at the front door.

"I can tell them," she offered.

I nodded, opening the door and allowing her to step before me.

Inside, everyone eagerly crowded around us, bombarding us with questions about Gwenn, about where we went, about why we were gone so long.

"Gwenn didn't make it," Eve said, her voice steady. "Eos brought us to some friends, and they saw to it that Gwenn received medical attention, but it was too late. We decided to stay there for the day where we were safe while it was light out. I'm sorry."

Cindee wrapped her fingers around one of Eve's hands. Eve's empty hand twitched, as if longing for the closeness of her other best friend. She brought her empty hand over and covered their joined hands with a pat.

"Thank you," Eve said to me.

"I'm sorry—"

"Nope," she interrupted. "You don't get to be."

Before she could walk away, there was a loud bang followed by the sounds of shattering glass. Across the room, one of the oldest exiles fell instantly to the floor, a crimson stain growing on his pastel green shirt.

"Get down!" Paren commanded, and just as another shot rang out, everyone ducked to the floor. Glass flew from the window as the weak, old panes gave in.

"Is the back clear?" I hissed across the room to Skylar. She scampered off for a moment and returned, shaking her head.

"Step out of the building—all of you!—with your hands up!" a voice boomed from outside. "If you try anything, we will put bullets in every single one of your skulls."

A cold chill raced down my spine as I weighed our options. *Do we even have any options?*

"Does anyone have a lighter?" I asked, my mind racing.

"Here!" I heard a hushed voice call, followed by a basic black lighter sliding across the ground.

"*Alcohol!*" I called next, still keeping my voice down. "Two bottles of it."

Almost immediately, two bottles of booze were passed up to me from the supply crates.

"You have one minute to make your choice!" the outside voice warned.

I peeled my t-shirt off and used my dagger to rip it. With a scrappy rope of cloth in either hand, I shoved the fabric down into each bottle.

"Be ready. I'm going to light them both. Get this one to Skylar quick. When I give the word, Sky, I need you to throw it as hard as you can at the nearest official out back. Everyone else—be ready to run!"

Without waiting for confirmation or questions, I lit both of the Molotov cocktails, immediately passing the first down to Skylar, who was poised to open the back window. I pulled out my gun, aiming ahead of me as I hurried to the front door. An exile nearest the door slowly cracked it open for me.

"*Now!*"

TWENTY-ONE

I lobbed the explosive at a cluster of officials and the bottle made a *clunk* as it hit a helmet and fell to the ground. Panicked, I stared down at it, the fire still burning at my shirt scraps. Without letting another moment pass, I fired my gun at the bottle, sending a wave of flames outward. The weak and cracked windows nearest the front and the back of the house shattered inwards and a few of the exiles screamed. Flames licked the doorframe as I stood just inside, barely shielded by the door itself.

"Are they dead?" someone called out to me.

"I don't know," I answered, unable to move the fiery door to peer outside.

I heard a wail come from the back, but it sounded like it was outside. I turned on my heels and raced toward Skylar's window, but she wasn't there. I peered outside the obliterated window, spotting Skylar wrestling with an official. She snarled and screamed like a rabid animal as she clawed at the official pinning her down.

My heart shaking my chest with every adrenaline-fueled beat, I launched myself out of the window, tearing off into the sand behind the house and charging toward the official. The impact knocked him off Skylar, but he reacted swiftly, throwing me to the side almost instantly. Reflexively, I rolled over and threw myself at him again, my fist sailing toward his jaw. Again, he reacted quickly and threw me to the ground. He pulled out a knife from a pocket on his thick black vest as he straddled me, pinning my arms with his knees.

I cried out in pain as he let his weight sink into his knees. In response, a hint of a grin twitched at the corner of his lips, just before a thick spurt of blood shot from the side of his head. Seemingly in slow motion, his expression frozen, he slumped forward, falling onto me. Blood leaked from his temple, dripping across my cheek and into my hair as I struggled to get out from under him. Skylar approached, a pistol in her hand as she shoved the official's corpse off me.

"Get up," Skylar said, reaching her hand out to me, pulling me to my feet. "We still have to check on the front."

We ran around the side of the house, peering around the corner just as several officials, their uniforms singed by the flames, charged down the street and into a truck. The truck then tore down the road.

"We need to relocate," I stated the obvious.

Skylar turned to respond but paused and stared at my bare abdomen.

"What?" I asked, looking down. "Oh, God."

A sizeable gash contrasted against my pale stomach, undoubtedly from jumping through the broken window. A loose chunk of skin flapped at its bottom edge as I breathed.

"We need to get you inside," Skylar said, her voice edging on panic. "Now."

Now that the adrenaline was beginning to fade from the attack, the pain was starting to seep in, spreading slowly over my body until it felt like my innards were on fire.

I let out a pained whimper as I tried to take a step forward, feeling the cut stretch as I moved.

"Sit down—I'll go get supplies," she said, shielding her eyes from the gore with her hand.

"I can walk," I groaned, shuffling slowly across the pavement. "It's not far."

"Hey!" Skylar called, spotting Paren as he stepped through the front door, the flames replaced by soot. "Get her inside!"

Without a second thought, Paren raced over, scooped me up—to which I protested with a blubbering "no!", and carried me inside. He set me down on the couch and hurried off to the supply crates, returning with alcohol, bandages, a needle, and thread.

"Nope."

"You need stiches," he said confidently, his face twisting into obvious upset.

"Nope, nope, nope," I said, blocking my wound with a dusty pillow. "No needles."

"You don't really have a choice here," he said. "You can't leave that wound open."

"Do you even know how to give someone stitches?" I cried.

"Erhm…"

"Paren! No!" I squealed, clutching the dusty pillow tighter.

"I watched my mom sew all the time when I was a kid—I made a couple little crafts. How different can it be?"

"Very! This is skin! Unless you did crafts with human flesh, you need to find someone else to do this!"

"Fine," he forfeited. Raising his voice, he called out to the entire house, "Does anyone know how to give stitches?"

Silence. Horrible, horrible silence.

"I'm your best bet," Paren said. "Take a drink."

He handed me a small bottle of vodka and I groaned as I took a mouthful, feeling it sting my throat. Paren stuck out his hand to take the bottle back. He waved over a couple of the more muscular exiles, including Cromwell and Bexa, who held my shoulders, arms, and legs down.

"This seems a bit excessive," I complained.

Paren raised one eyebrow, his face unamused as he turned the bottle of vodka upside down over the gash. With a throat-scratching scream, I began to try to pull my arms out from under Cromwell's grip in vain. I continued to flail and scream for a few moments until the pain began to dull ever so slightly. At this point, all of the exiles were crowding around me, and Paren had to continually beg them to give us space.

"Bite this." He handed me a wadded-up shirt.

I took a deep, shaky breath before clamping down on the t-shirt with my teeth, which squeaked against the dry fabric. *This tastes like sweat. This is a used shirt.*

"Don't let her look," Paren advised our friends. Skylar took the dusty pillow I had discarded, holding it at my chest to block my view.

I waited in agonizing impatience, just wanting to get it over with. I tried to focus on the gross taste of the sweaty shirt, but I could feel my whole body twitching with nerves as I watched Paren's face. I could see his jaw slide from side-to-side as he ground his teeth. He unraveled some thread and poured alcohol over it and the needle. Apologetically, he looked at me before turning his attention back to my wound. Seconds later, I felt the horrible piercing and I let out a muffled scream.

"So, where'd you learn how to make a Molotov cocktail like that?" Paren asked. I stared at him, gag still in my mouth. "Oh yeah. Sorry."

Another pierce.

The sounds of my hyperventilating through my nose filled the room as everyone was silently observing. I glared at some of the exiles who were staring at me, whispering to each other. A bead of sweat rolled down my brow and along the corner of my eye, forcing me to blink as I continued to feel the occasional poke of the needle.

"Done," Paren said with a sigh, as if he had been holding his breath the entire time.

Bexa, Cromwell, and the others released me, and Skylar set down the pillow. Tentatively, I looked down at my abdomen.

"Green? You used *green* thread?" I squinted at him and his face turned bright red.

"I—"

I burst out in painful laughter, clutching my wound as I did. Paren looked relieved and the red washed from his face as he let out a nervous chuckle.

"I like it," I said. "Thank you. School, by the way."

"What?"

"I learned how to make a Molotov cocktail in school," I grinned proudly. "They didn't mean to teach that to us necessarily, but I saw a picture of one in a history book and I asked what it was. Mr. DeSante taught us a lot more about them than I expected. Turns out he was a weapons fanatic."

"When they tell you that you need to study for your future, I don't think they anticipated you using that tidbit," Paren laughed, motioning for me to sit up. He began to wrap a large medical bandage around my abdomen, covering my wound and my green stitches.

"How did they find us here?" Skylar asked, sitting beside me. "You shouldn't have even needed to use that knowledge. We just blew up a bunch of officials, and the survivors are probably getting reinforcements right now. We need to go before they come back."

Skylar and Paren rounded up the entire group of exiles, directing them out of the ruins and into the desert. Paren carried me, despite my persistent protests that I would be fine to walk. Concerned I would pop my stitches, he continued to carry me until his arms began to shake. Most of the other stronger exiles were tasked with carrying the supply crates, so he set me down and offered to help me walk for a little while before picking me up and carrying me again.

As we trudged through the desert, constantly scanning the horizon for ruins, I let my eyes wander to the people in our group. Skylar looked exhausted, but she was tough—she held her head high, nose turned up as if expressing that she was better than the desert and better than everyone around her. Braylin followed behind Cindee and Eve—he hardly let his sister step two feet away from him since the incident with Gwenn. Fabian was walking and chatting with Iris, who bit her lip all too often when he was talking. Playfully, she stole his glasses and put them on. Fabian giggled and pushed the glasses up further on her nose. This was the first time I saw Iris without her sister. Looking through all the faces, I realized I couldn't find Arke.

I began to grow nervous. *Did we leave her behind? Could there be more that we left behind?*

"Iris?" I called out, sitting up in Paren's arms to get a better look at the people around me.

Iris turned to look at me, handed Fabian his glasses back, and trotted over to me.

"Where's Arke?" I asked.

"She's right th—"

Her head spun around, making out the faces of those around her, unable to find her sister.

"I—" she began to panic, her smile quickly faded. "She was just here… I thought."

"I just now realized she was missing—I'm so sorry. If I would have noticed sooner I would've said something."

"I need to go find her," Iris said.

I wanted to convince her otherwise. I wanted to tell her that she was being foolish and would never find us again, that she would run out of supplies on her own, but I could understand. If it had been Zane, or Lamb, or Braylin, or even Skylar, I would have gone too.

“Take some supplies,” I said.

“My bag is already full—I should be fine.”

I nodded, offering her a consoling hand on her shoulder before she waved one more time to Fabian and departed. With her walking the opposite direction, it wasn’t long before she completely disappeared into the desert behind us.

After trekking through the desert for a day, we came across some smaller ruins.

“How are Legend and Zaire supposed to find us?” I asked Paren as he set me down near the door of a crumbling townhouse. I began to worry about the implications of us moving even further away.

“I’m sure they’ll understand that we moved when they see the pile of blackened bodies outside the house. They’ll come looking for us, and I’m sure they’ll find us eventually.”

Eventually, they did.

On the fourth day in our new home, a crooked townhouse with peeling putrid pink wallpaper throughout, a small group of us began to discuss rationing the remaining supplies. Just as I had jotted down some sloppy math on spare paper, trying to work out my thoughts on how to best manage with our remaining food, Zaire and Legend knocked weakly at the door.

“Eos? Skylar? Guys?” I could hear Zaire. His voice sounded dull, and it faded with each word.

I shoved my way past a few people to get to the door. When I opened it, the first thing I noticed was how hunched-over the boys looked. Their eyes sunken in, their once-vibrant ebony skin dulled with dust, they pulled their gaze up to face me.

“Thank God,” Legend groaned.

“We’ve been searching for two straight days now,” Zaire said. “We haven’t slept.”

“Why didn’t you go back to Fortitude or somewhere to get some rest?” I asked, pulling them inside.

“It would’ve taken too long to go to and from and we didn’t want to risk letting you guys starve or something,” Zaire said.

“If it would’ve come to it, we would’ve gone out for food!”

Braylin wet a couple rags with a water bottle and handed them to Zaire and Legend, who wiped the dust from their faces. They handed Braylin the stained rags with nods and weak smiles. He held the rags pinched in his fingers as he spun around looking for somewhere to put them, eventually settling on chucking them in a corner.

“It’s okay—we also have news for you,” Zaire said, his voice hushed. “Can we talk in private?”

“Supplies are in the truck!” Legend announced, sending an eager flock of exiles outside to fetch the boxes.

I motioned for Zaire, Legend, Braylin, Skylar, and Paren to follow me into one of the bedrooms. Turning the knob carefully, I shut the door quietly behind us to avoid attracting the attention of the exiles still in the house.

“We’ve got a friend who’s an official in Fallmont,” Zaire started. “We met with him right after we discussed the camera with you. He’s been looking for it since. We followed up with him before we ended up having to search for you guys. When we saw all of the dead officials outside the house, we knew something must’ve happened and we immediately started searching. We had no idea if any of you were hurt or if one of th—”

“The news,” I cut him off, waving my hand for him to hurry up.

Just rip off the bandage. Can we do this or not?

“He found the camera,” Zaire concluded. “It wasn’t easy, even as an official. Everything is on tight security—the most secure Fallmont has been in years.”

“So, we need weapons,” Skylar said, her lips flat and her eyes locked on Zaire.

"We need weapons," Zaire reiterated. "But Eos, there's m—"

"But where do we get that many weapons?" Braylin asked. "And should we arm everyone?"

"Yes," Paren said. "If possible. We shouldn't send anyone into the city who can't defend themselves."

"Woah, hold up," I said with a nervous chuckle. "You don't plan on running and gunning it, right? I know some of the people in there have done horrible things to us—" I paused for a split second as Skylar rubbed at her back. "—but there are also a lot of people there who agree with our cause, including some who have helped us, like Gavin and Mallory. We can't just go in and shoot up everyone."

"That's not what I'm saying." Skylar groaned. "We all need to be armed in case we're attacked. Only for self-defense. We try to keep the weapons concealed so there's a chance we aren't shot on sight."

"That's great in theory," Braylin said. "But won't we be shot on sight anyways just for being there?"

He looked eagerly at me for an answer.

"We wait until night," Paren suggested. "We sneak in and, as best we can, head for City Hall. We can have a team designated for holding back the officials—they'll go in first with weapons drawn. When they have things under control, another team can charge up to Raine's office and can hold off the officials upstairs, as well as Raine. Then, Zaire or Legend or their friend can connect the camera to the screens and Eos can broadcast her message."

Everyone was quiet for a moment, playing out the plan in their minds—imagining everything that could possibly go wrong, and there were a lot of possibilities.

Zaire attempted to break the silence, hardly getting a sound out. "Eo—"

"Can we have the camera set up beforehand? The less time we have to wait to get the message out, the better. The longer it takes, the more likely it is one of the officials will stop us and a lot of people could get hurt," Skylar pondered.

"I think we can arrange something," Legend said. "We'll talk to our friend."

"Eos!" Zaire boomed. "Listen to me! You're going to want to hear this—I think."

"What?" I retorted through gritted teeth. "Can it not wait until we figure this out?"

Zaire's eyes looked sullen and he gnawed on the inside of his cheek as he stared at me for a moment.

"Our friend shared some news with me. I don't know if it's true and I really don't want to give you any kind of false hope, but I'd be remiss if I didn't tell you—"

"Get to the point. Please."

"Zane might be alive."

Suddenly, the figures of my friends beside me grew blurry. There was a sharp ringing in my ears as I tried to muster enough saliva to force the lump in my throat down.

"What?" I managed raspily, the sound hardly coming out, but rather echoing in my head.

"That's impossible," Skylar said, her face growing red and a thick vein protruding on her temple. "That's a lie, and it's not fair to spread rumors like that."

"I'm not so sure it's a lie," he said softly, his eyes never leaving mine. "I can't promise anything, and my friend doesn't know Zane, so he can't say for sure if it's him… but he told me 'some guy' was shot by Raine, was given medical care, and was kept in a holding cell for 'emergencies.' Basically, a bargaining chip she kept up her sleeve. I think that 'some guy' might be Zane."

"It can't be," I said, my eyes on fire as the tears began to collect. I dug my fingernail into my palm, willing the tears not to fall. "I saw him. I saw the whole thing."

"You were in shock—you might not have remembered things exactly right—"

"I know what I saw!" A strand of spit flew from my mouth when I yelled, and suddenly the hot tears gushed over my cheeks. "Raine shot him in the head right in front of me!"

"Did you see an entry wound?" Zaire asked, his voice calm but his leg shaking as he watched me unravel.

"I—" The scene replayed in my head and I tried to force it to slow down, to zoom in on Zane as if I had some kind of memory magnifying glass, but I could only remember turning from the doorknob to see Zane splayed across Raine's desk, a growing puddle of blood forming around him. "No."

"Our friend told us that the guy in a long-term cell has a huge scar on top of his head from the gunshot, but there was no internal damage. I normally wouldn't have told you because I don't have a way to prove who it is right now, but Raine hasn't shot anyone else as far as I know and as far as our friend knows. It's risky for Raine to take drastic measures right now since so many people are turning against her and a lot more are on the fence about her leadership. Shooting someone could have some major downfalls for her. I don't think this guy could be anyone but Zane."

"Where is the long-term cell?" Skylar asked. "When we go to City Hall, we'll find him so we know for sure. Even if it isn't Zane, we'll release him. It sounds like Raine has done more than enough to him."

"There are a bunch of holding cells downstairs in City Hall. Just past those, there are a couple other secure doors belonging to long-term holding cells. They just have an extra door between the cell and the hallway. I'm not sure they've ever been used before now."

Downstairs in City Hall? Where I freed Paren? I was down the hall and Zane could have been just a few cells away? I was right there…

"Whether or not that guy is Zane, by telling her about this far before she can do anything about it, you've effectively incapacitated our leader," Braylin said defiantly, pointing to me just as I was lowering myself to the ground out of dizziness. "What good came of telling her this right now?"

"Now she has something more to fight for," Skylar said, and I remembered our conversation when she wanted to give up on the entire mission, and when I wished I could too. "Now let's talk about those weapons."

I remained detached through the rest of the planning, everything in my mind hoping that what Zaire said was true, all the while confident that it couldn't be. For a short while, I tried to snap myself out of it. *I have to focus. They need my help.* But no matter how hard I fought it, I kept sinking back into the millions of "what ifs".

"Your social skills suck, Zaire," Paren said. It seemed like a joke, but his stern expression was unfaltering.

"What did I do?" Zaire bemoaned, turning his palms outward. "You can't honestly tell me I should've kept that kind of news to myself!"

"You could have waited!" Paren argued.

"Until when? Tell me. Until right before you all go marching into Fallmont and need to have your wits about you? Until you're all already in Raine's office, 'Oh yeah! Eos! I forgot to tell you your boyfriend might be alive!' Or maybe I should've waited until the entire freaking revolution ends and everyone has calmed down? Just long enough that there is no one left checking up on him because he's Raine's prisoner, and if we overthrow Raine and no one goes to feed him, perhaps he'll starve by the time I tell her! There *is* no good time to tell somebody news like this."

"Stop—" I muttered quietly.

"You could have made sure it was true first! What if it isn't Zane?" Paren's hair seemed to be standing upright as he yelled.

"Stop fighting!" I squeaked. Everyone went quiet, and I sucked back a thick sniffle before speaking. "Thank you for telling me, Zaire. Even if it isn't true—I would've been mad to find out you kept that suspicion from me in the first place. Thank you."

Zaire turned to Paren with a smug grin and a raised eyebrow.

"Oh, stop that!" Skylar swatted Zaire with the back of her hand. "Not appropriate!"

"Focus!" Braylin asserted himself, banging a fist against the wall and catching everyone by surprise as some loose chunks of ceiling tumbled onto the ground. "We need to think about how we can even get that many weapons before we consider making another move."

"He's right," I nodded, still wiping tears from my cheeks. "Fabian might know where officials get their weapons from—they have to come from somewhere."

Paren left the room briefly, reentering moments later with Fabian, whose typically curly hair was looking matted and greasy from the extended time without a shower. I tried not to think about the constant stench that filled our house, which proved difficult with physical reminders of our filth. I considered myself fortunate that I have had a couple opportunities to shower at Gavin and Mallory's, and I often wished for more chances.

As soon as the door shut behind Fabian, Skylar got right to the point.

"Where can we find weapons?"

"What?" Fabian asked, taken aback.

"The officials get their weapons from somewhere, right?"

"I mean, there's a small manufacturing and storage facility in Nortown," he said to Skylar, adjusting his glasses as he waited for some kind of response. When he didn't get one, he continued. "When new officials are hired, or when an official is asked to switch duties—gate patrol, street patrol, supply runs, things like that—they are given new weapons. It depends on what they're asked to do, but I'm pretty sure most of that comes from the facility in Nortown."

Skylar was silent, staring Fabian down as she analyzed. "You came up with that answer awfully quick."

Fabian looked at her with disgust. "Really?" He scoffed. "I'm sorry! Did you not want weapons? Did I misunderstand the question?"

"How do we know you're telling the truth? How did you come up with that so quickly?"

"They sent me on a run to Nortown with one of the senior officers once to pick up a crate of ammo. I've been there, but he had me wait outside, so I don't quite know how much is produced there. You asked me a question, and I gave you the best answer I'm aware of. If you don't want my help, don't ask for it!" Fabian growled as he turned on his heel and stormed out of the room, leaving everyone except Skylar shocked and staring at the door as he slammed it shut.

"What the hell is your problem?" I hissed at Skylar. "What did he do to tick you off so much?"

"Nothing," she smirked. "But now we know he was telling the truth."

"Of course he was telling the truth! He's on our side!"

"Really?" she asked, turning her entire body to face me, straightening her posture and placing her hands on her hips. "Where was he when the officials attacked the house?"

TWENTY-TWO

"He was there," I said, my voice growing soft. "I'm sure of it."

Skylar's lips flattened as she locked eyes with me. I hadn't noticed how bloodshot her eyes had become. Thin wrinkles etched at the corners of them and deep purple circles shadowed beneath. Her cheeks looked thinner than I remembered, and there was a tiny sore on her jaw that looked like it had been picked open more than once.

"Where else could he have been?" I whispered defensively, as if no one else could hear me.

Skylar's only response was a subtle head tilt as if to tell me "you already know."

I shook my head, sucked in my lower lip, and left the room with an exhaustive sigh.

"Fabian!" I called to him from across the room.

He looked up from what he was pretending to work on, which appeared to be a sketch of something on a paper in his lap. When he realized who was calling him, the curiosity was replaced by annoyance and he reverted to his drawing. From a distance, it seemed like he was mindlessly making the same back-and-forth motion with his pencil just to appear too busy to be bothered by me.

I stormed over to him, trying to decide in the brief walk across the room whether I was mad at him for possibly being a traitor, mad at Skylar for being so skeptical of him, or mad at myself for allowing the paranoia to get to me.

"Where were you when the officials attacked the house?" I asked bluntly, keeping my voice down as I sat next to him against the wall.

"What?" he asked in dismay. "I was in the damn house! Where else would I have been?"

"I don't know. Skylar seems to think you weren't with the rest of us, and that's why she's a bit… hesitant."

"Answer one question for me—how would I have walked with you guys here if I wasn't there during the attack?"

Relief washed over me as I processed his comment.

"Okay," I nodded. "I told her she was being paranoid. Thanks," I put a hand on his shoulder. "I'm sorry about her."

Fabian let out a drawn-out breath and rolled his eyes before picking his pencil back up, continuing to trace one of the lines on his drawing over and over mindlessly.

As I stood, I noticed the dark sketch in his lap.

His drawing depicted a tiny doorway with a piece of cheese on a mousetrap in front of it. Behind the door was a little cartoon mouse reaching its pudgy fingers through the door with wide eyes. I looked over the drawing for a moment before returning to Skylar.

"He was here," I said as I shut the door. At this point, it was only Skylar and me in the room. "How else would he have gotten here with us?"

"He could've been with the officials just outside," Skylar said. I detected a slight twitch to her left eye.

I sighed and gnawed on my lip for a minute. "I really think you need some sleep."

"You're too trusting!" she warned. "Just because he was your childhood friend doesn't mean he's a saint!"

"I'm well aware, Sky, and he's betrayed me once, but I don't think he's who we have to worry about right now. Honestly, I know him better than I know a lot of the people here right now! I've known him for many, many years, but I don't even know the names of some of the people here. I trust him more than I trust some of these other people!"

"Someone told them where to find us! The attack was too planned—they knew exactly where we were! Someone told them!"

"We don't know that. They've been looking for us for a while—they might have had someone watching us. It doesn't mean anyone is a traitor."

"Where was that chick with the brown curls?"

"Who?"

"Freckly one," Skylar was flapping her hand as if to speed up her thoughts. "Has a sister—"

"Arke?" I asked.

"Yes!" Her reddened eyes bulged and she pointed a finger at me, her voice crazed. "Where was she? And pixie cut!"

"Iris," I said.

"They're both missing, and Arke wasn't there during the attack. It's her fault!"

"Calm down!" I said, taking a step closer to her and reaching out. I placed my hands on her shoulders, but she stopped me instantly with a sharp slap across the cheek.

I kept my face down as I felt my cheek with my fingers. The skin stung, and I felt my face begin to grow hot as I clenched my fist. I took a deep breath, trying to calm down before allowing my gaze to meet Skylar's again.

"Get over yourself!" she screamed at me. "You think you're always right, and you think you're such a great judge of people and of what to do, but do you realize how many people have died because of *you*?" Her words oozed with malice as she glowered over me.

Before I could speak up, Paren burst into the room and spotted me, my cheek red and Skylar practically baring her teeth at me like a feral cat.

"Are you guys okay?" he asked, freezing in the doorway, uncertain about coming closer.

I trotted over to his side, throwing a betrayed look over my shoulder at Skylar.

"We're fine," I said, continuing to stare at Skylar. "She just needs some sleep."

Paren looked back and forth between us for a moment before escorting me out of the room, leaving Skylar. I caught a glimpse of her as she melted face-first into the bed just before Paren closed the door behind us.

"We need to get those weapons from Nortown," I said. "We need to get as much detail as possible from Fabian so we can be prepared. I don't want Skylar coming with—we can't risk anything right now and she's a liability."

"What happened between you two?" he asked, tracing his finger over the welt on my cheek.

"She's just paranoid."

"About what?"

"She thinks Arke and Iris betrayed us to the officials and that's why we were attacked."

"That's ridiculous," Paren said.

I brushed the topic off, moving on to something else.

"I have another letter," I said. "It's the last one."

"We can't deliver another letter," Paren said with a grin as if I just told a joke.

"What are you talking about?" I stared back at him, my arms crossed.

"It's getting more and more dangerous, E," Paren said, his smile fading when he realized how serious I was. "Gwenn died. The next time we go to Fallmont has to be for the video on the skyscraper screens. We can't risk going in again before that."

I reached into my pocket, fishing out the wrinkled letter and handing it to him. He looked at me hesitantly for a moment before unfolding it and reading it. I watched his eyes trace along each line as he read, and they seemed to quicken the further into it he got.

"Make this the script," he said, giving the letter another look.

"What?"

"The script," he said, folding the letter and handing it back to me. "For the video. Tell his story on the video for everyone to see. I think it'll be more powerful if they see and hear an actual person telling this story."

He's right, but saying it all out loud seems so much harder than writing it.

I nodded, pocketing the letter.

"Get Fabian," I said. "We need to figure out a plan, and I don't want to waste time and risk getting found again."

This time, Paren, Fabian, and I were the only ones to talk, hoping to work out a rough plan before involving too many people at once.

Paren sighed. "We need more people."

Fabian and I muttered in agreement, and Paren called Zaire and Legend over.

"I heard there was a cat fight," Legend grinned, his eyes shimmering.

I scowled at him and Paren tried to redirect everyone's attention back to the issue at hand.

"How many exiles do you think you could get to join us for a revolution?" Paren asked.

"Big fan of brevity, this one," Zaire chuckled, pointing toward Paren with a thumb as he nudged his brother.

Paren cleared his throat and we stared at Zaire and Legend expectantly.

"I don't know." Zaire laughed as if he thought the request was ridiculous. "Probably a lot, honestly. Fortitude tends to make people a bit restless and reckless. How many do you need?"

"As many as you can get here," I said. "You can fit a few in the trunk, a couple squished in the front with you guys, and probably twice all that in the backseat. If we wait three days before we march Fallmont, about how many truckloads of exiles do you think you could get here?"

"I think I had a question like that in my math book once." Legend's laugh rang out, echoing throughout the tiny house, earning him a few confused looks from the others around the room who were casually invested in their own conversations.

"Seriously?" I asked, growing impatient and crossing my arms. My weight shifted to my right hip as I waited for a real answer.

Legend and Zaire's smiles melted.

"I can try to get thirty… maybe forty if they're willing to suffer an incredibly uncomfortable ride."

"That's not enough people."

"Are you kidding? How do you expect me to bring more people here with one truck in that short of a time?"

"We'll send a team to hijack another truck on a supply run. Avid's not far from here. What if we steal another truck?" I asked Zaire, my tone growing desperate.

He paused for a moment, sucking his teeth. "It could work."

"I'll work on it. We'll get one for you as soon as we can. Any clue when the next delivery is?"

"Today's Tuesday?" he asked.

I nodded.

"Guys?" Astraea called from the crowd. "Won't that draw attention to us and our location if a truck is reported stolen?"

There was a moment of silence as everyone thought about the idea logistically.

"She's right," I groaned. "We'll keep brainstorming, but no matter what we figure out, you have three days to get as many people here as you can."

"I need to get more gas if I'm going to make that many trips. Can I have four days?"

"Fine. That's it though. When can you leave?"

"Damn!" Legend laughed again. "Ready to get rid of us?"

"If you keep up the joking," Paren warned.

"Chill," Zaire advised. "We understand this is serious and we are taking it seriously—can't we have a laugh every now and then? Can't let ourselves get too dark. If you can't find some kind of happiness, what exactly are we doing all of this for?"

"One more thing," I started.

Zaire's eyes rolled dramatically and landed on mine.

"Do you have bags we could use for weapons?"

After we filled in the rest of the exiles on the general plan, the next four days were spent plotting our weapons heist. Several of the exiles grew up in Nortown and, considering it was the smallest of the cities, were able to recount an approximate map of the town by working together. None of them knew about the weapons facility except Fabian, who was able to narrow it down to a general area of the town.

"I wasn't allowed to follow the guy inside," Fabian said on day two. "I was still in training. He just needed someone to accompany him there and back, but not inside. I remember a lot of black glass, but the building was pretty tall and long. I'm not sure if the whole thing was the weapons manufacturer or not."

"Do you remember which door the official went in?" I asked.

Fabian shook his head, brows lifted apologetically. "The front one, I guess?"

"That's okay. We'll figure something out." I pointed down at a spread of several papers in the middle of the floor. We had sketched the map across the pages and used a darker ink to indicate our travel paths. "Even if we go at night, I think it's safe to assume there'll be some officials there. How do we distract them or get rid of them?"

"I really hate to bring this up as an example," Eve spoke up, lifting a hand through the crowd to get our attention. "But do you remember Mallory's plan to get Gwenn into the hospital?"

"Yeah," I said, narrowing my eyes at her as I tried to connect the dots. "She was going to have Gwenn pretend to have amnesia."

"What if one of us did the same?" she asked me.

"I'm not sure I follow."

"If one of us can look battered up, whoever it is can walk right inside and act like someone desperate looking for help. They can pretend they don't remember who they are or how they got there or whatever and see if the officials can take them to the hospital. At some point along the way—or once at the hospital—the decoy can run away."

Everyone was quiet, staring eagerly at me for a final decision.

"I don't think it'll be enough," Braylin said and everyone's eyes simultaneously shifted to him. "I doubt one person can distract all of the officials. It isn't like there will only be two."

"Let's just storm the building—overwhelm them with numbers!" someone in the crowd said, pumping a fist in the air, followed by a few other exiles cheering in agreement.

"If you want to get shot, sure," Paren said, the cheers immediately silenced. "We don't have enough weapons—that's the whole point of this. And as much as we hate the officials for blindly following Raine, they're just doing their jobs. Most of them have families and just want to work their shift and go home. There's no sense in us killing unnecessarily."

Some of the others nodded energetically, looking relieved.

“What if we just walk in?” I asked.

At this, those who wanted to storm the building and those who wanted a more peaceful approach all looked at me as if I grew a second head. Maybe even a third.

“Hear me out,” I defended. “What if a few of us steal uniforms from the officials? We can dress like them and walk right into the armory—we’ll say we were assigned the next watch, or shift, or whatever they’re called—Fabian?”

“Watch.”

“Thanks. We’d keep the group small so we don’t raise suspicion. When we can, we fill up the bags,” I raised the six large, black canvas bags from Zaire. “At that point, we need to get out as quickly and as carefully as we can. It won’t be enough weapons for everyone, but if those who are willing to carry weapons hug the outside of our group as we march on Fallmont, we should be okay.”

Everyone was completely quiet at this point—no one was even muttering a sound about the plan. Breaking the awkward silence, Bexa shot her hand in the air with an, “I’ll go.”

I smiled half-heartedly to thank her.

Cromwell waved, along with Paren, Fabian, and Skylar, who peered out from behind the door of the bedroom.

“No.” I glowered at her.

“Are you seriously being that childish?” she accused.

“No, I just don’t want you putting everyone in danger because you’re reckless.”

“I’m not reckless!” Her voice squeaked with the last syllable.

She paused for a moment, her face twitching as she gnawed on her cheek and stared me down. “Fine. I’ll stay here. Good luck finding someone else to go.”

“I’ll go,” Braylin offered.

I hesitated for a moment, knowing well that Braylin was clumsy. "Alright. We have our six." I tossed a bag each to Bexa, Cromwell, Paren, Fabian, and Braylin, keeping one for myself. "We'll leave when it's dark."

The next couple hours were spent as a small group, plotting with Fabian on where we could find official's uniforms.

"Is there some kind of uniform manufacturer?" Bexa teased.

"Yes, in Rockhallow. We don't have time to make that trip though—that's on the other side of Avid. It would be more practical to get our uniforms from Fallmont."

"You're insane. No way," Bexa crossed her arms and furrowed her brow.

"I can get them. I don't think they realize that I'm with you guys—they just haven't seen me around. I can say I was taking care of my dad—my dad hardly leaves the house anyways. They'd probably believe it. That's only if anyone asks anyways—don't worry about it."

I exchanged a concerned look with Bexa.

Before we could speak further, Skylar exited the bedroom and made a beeline for us.

"I'm sorry," she said to Fabian, who was clearly taken aback. His mouth hung slightly open as he looked at me for help.

"Um. I'm—s… what?" he managed.

"I'm sorry," she repeated. "I accused you of being untrustworthy, and I'm sorry. Can I come with you?"

Fabian let out a sputter and his eyes flew open wide as he looked at her in disbelief. He turned to me. "Is she joking?"

I flattened my lips and shrugged.

"Hell no!" he told her, letting out a single laugh.

"Why not?" she pouted.

"Because you tried to accuse me of being a traitor! You threw a damn fit in the bedroom. You're insane if you think I want you joining me."

"I'm good with a gun. And a knife. You need me."

"Like hell I do. I don't plan on hurting anyone. I plan on going in, smuggling some uniforms out, and coming back here."

"Smuggling from where?"

"City H—"

"Hah!"

"I'm sorry?"

"That's a horrible idea. Don't you know some officials?" she asked, her eyes wild.

"Yes, but they aren't just going to hand me their unif—"

"Duh. But do you know where they live?"

"Yes, but I don't want you hurt—"

"I won't."

Fabian groaned dramatically. Once again, he looked to me for an escape.

"She's got a point about City Hall being a dumb idea," I said awkwardly, feeling bad for not taking his side. "Houses might be a bit less risky. And if you get one uniform from one house, one from another, and so on… it's less likely anything will be noticed as missing right away anyways."

"If they all report missing items, that'd be a big problem," Fabian said.

"How many uniforms does each official get?" I asked.

"Seven."

"Don't take a ton from any one person and I don't think they'll notice," I said.

"So?" Skylar bounced energetically, rubbing her hands together with a dry sound.

"Fine. It's getting dark—we better get moving."

"Take this," I said, subtly sliding the Skeleton Key into Fabian's hand. "Skylar knows how to use it, but right now, I think you should be the one to hang onto it."

As the two slipped out the front door and into the growing darkness of the night, Cromwell turned to me and muttered in his deep, gruff voice, "Should we be working on a Plan B?"

"Would you say I look… *official*?" Skylar stood in the doorway, a wide grin stretched across her face. She was dressed from head to toe in an official's uniform, which looked slightly baggy on her thin frame.

As she stepped into the house, I could see Fabian behind her, his face exhausted and unamused as he grunted, dropping a large bag on the ground and throwing himself down on the frilly pink couch with a sigh.

"She insisted on putting it on while we were headed back," Fabian answered my unspoken question as I sat beside him.

"How'd it go?" I asked, hiding a snicker as I watched Skylar flaunt her new costume to the exiles.

"As well as can be expected. She was actually a lot of help. Considering the curfew, most of the officials were home. I knew of a couple that had watch around town tonight, so we targeted them, but one of them has a wife and kids. Those kids are going to need therapy, but Skylar kept them distracted long enough for me to slip in and slip back out with a couple uniforms. I managed to get six total from four houses. I know of one large guy on the force, so I'm hoping the one I took from his house is big enough for Cromwell. I also managed to get a badge to get us past the scanners—each official has two, so he shouldn't notice that one is missing. We should probably hit the armory first thing tomorrow night—any longer than that and we risk them all reporting missing belongings. It's one thing if just one person reports something missing—it would get written up as carelessness. If they all report it—we're screwed. We didn't take too many from any one person, but eventually they'll notice."

"What did she do to the kids?" I asked, disregarding the rest of his news.

"Don't worry about it—they're fine."

I grimaced at the thought of Skylar scaring some poor kids half to death.

Grateful for one more day to rest before leaving our ugly pink townhouse, I found a place to settle down for the night. Since the dream with Zane in the white room, I hadn't had another dream at all—I was almost starting to miss seeing Zane in my dreams, even though I always knew it wasn't real. *Maybe, soon, it can be real.* I fought the optimism, pushing it down and trying to ignore its existence entirely. *It's impossible. I was there. I saw what happened.*

TWENTY-THREE

Wednesday night, the six of us donned our stolen uniforms. We kept five of the weapon bags shoved into the sixth, which I would be carrying. I combed back my short, black hair, tying it into a nubby ponytail. Bexa followed suit, combing out her long, frizzy hair and gathering it into a neat bun. We had to look like actual officials, not some homeless criminals.

Cromwell stepped out of the bathroom, his uniform pulled tight around his arms and chest. Bexa and I suppressed laughter as he observed his arms in front of the crowd.

"If I sneeze, I might bust out of this thing," he said, tugging at the sleeve around his left wrist. "Let's get this over with."

"I'm coming with," Skylar proclaimed, trotting over.

"We don't have enough uniforms," I said.

"Oh, I'm not going *in* the armory," she said plainly. "But I will be waiting outside in case there's trouble. I'll have my gun. I'll keep hidden as close to the doors as I can. I won't move unless absolutely necessary, but it's stupid to go in there with no backup."

"You shouldn't be alone," I said.

"I'll go with her!" Cindee chirped, skipping forward. "I'm tired of being cooped up in the house all the time anyways."

"Oh goody," Skylar forced a cheesy smile, over-exaggerating a head tilt. "The Bubble Gum Princess is going to keep me company!"

Cindee full force punched Skylar's shoulder, replying to Skylar's yelp with a rapid bat of her eyelashes.

"Fair enough," Skylar groaned as she massaged her shoulder.

Our group of six grew to eight as we left for Nortown. Shouts of "good luck!" and "you can do this!" flooded the room as we closed the door behind us.

"Fallmont is that way," Fabian pointed to the left. "So Nortown is there…ish." He pointed right.

The walk took a few hours, but it was relatively calm. The air was still, except an occasional gentle breeze that would send a thin layer of sand rolling across the ground. As we neared the city, we slowed down and walked as close to the walls as possible to keep from leaving us in view from the gate for a prolonged period of time.

I handed Cindee my dagger. "Just in case. I'm hanging onto my gun though. Skylar has a gun, too. When you hear us leaving, leave some distance, but follow us out. If we're in there for too long, or if you hear anything suspicious, that's when you guys come into play."

She nodded, turning the dagger over in the moonlight, admiring the intricate etchings on the hilt.

As we neared the gate, I patted the uniform pockets, realizing something was missing. I felt my heart begin to race and my face grew warm.

"Oops!" Fabian whispered, reaching into his pocket and pulling out the Key, handing it to me. "Thanks for letting us borrow it."

My shoulders sunk in relief as I let out a sigh.

Once unlocked, we hurried in past the gate and raced down the street, hugging the walls of nearby buildings and crouching behind bushes and dumpsters when available. Fabian led the way; it was easy to tell he was nervous. He practically sprinted the entire way through Nortown, hardly looking back to make sure any of us could keep up. When we reached the armory, a large, glossy black structure with no signs of any kind, he finally stopped, pausing behind a pungent dumpster.

I held my nose as I joined him, trying to block out the smell of what could only be compared to sour milk and rotting diapers.

"This is the best cover we're going to find," Skylar told Cindee, who mirrored Skylar's disgust and disappointment, but nodded in agreement nonetheless.

The two crouched behind the dumpster, peering around the side.

"Ready?" I asked the others. I hurried away from the dumpster, straightening my posture and smoothing out my uniform.

Fabian, Bexa, Cromwell, Paren, Braylin, and I walked in solidarity toward the entrance of the armory. Even in the darkness of the street, we could see our reflections in the sleek black glass walls, all of us nearly marching in unison. I was the first to approach the door, reaching in my pocket for the ID badge Fabian and Skylar snagged with the uniform. I handed the bag over to Fabian as I eyed the metallic scanner affixed to the door. I turned the card over and swiped it across the sensor. A blinking orange light turned solid green and there was a faint beep, followed by the click of the door's lock. I turned over my shoulder to look at my friends before pulling the door open and peering inside. As I opened the door fully, Fabian whispered to me.

"Hand me the badge," he said, holding his hand out subtly at his side as he stood close to me.

Confused, I slid the card into his hand and he pocketed it.

We stepped into the facility's lobby—a spacious room with potted plants and stiff faux leather chairs seated around a tall desk. On either side of a steel door on the far end of the room, a couple officials stood, looking bored, but maintaining their attentive stances. As they spotted us entering the room, one of them stepped away from the door and quickly approached us.

"What are you doing here?" he asked. As he grew nearer, I could see his jaw was crooked, and he had a thin scar along his shaved hairline. I tried to read his face to determine if we needed to turn and make a run for it.

"Stauntwell asked me to take these newbies in for an hour watch," Fabian answered confidently. I could see him shift his shoulders, pulling them back proudly, authoritatively.

"Newbies aren't allowed in the armory," the official said, one of his eyebrows raised as he looked over each of us. We all stared back at him, unmoving.

"That's what I thought too," Fabian said, his voice casual as if talking to a friend or coworker. *Maybe he knows this guy from when he was an official?* "I prefer not to get into it with Stauntwell, so I figured I'd just bring them. No worries, man. I'll go ahead and take them back."

Fabian began to corral us, turning us back toward the door.

What is he doing?

"Wait—" the official called.

We turned back to face him, and he still seemed skeptical. Fabian looked at him expectantly, yet convincingly cool.

"I didn't catch your name," the official said.

"Carson," Fabian said, pulling out his ID badge and handing it to the official, who squinted in the dark at the photo and then looked up at Fabian for a moment. "Decided to go blond and get a cut since back when that picture was taken—long story. Was ready for a change."

The official handed the ID badge back, seemingly convinced. When he handed it back, I caught a quick glimpse of the badge, which I hadn't observed before. *Carson Blanchett*, the ID said in thick black font below a photo of a man with long, tight brown curls.

"Go ahead," the official said to Fabian, waving a hand behind him and the other official disappeared behind the door he was guarding. "Did Stauntwell give any special instructions?"

Fabian shrugged lightly. "He just said he'd like me to show them around the armory and then explain the different posts. These two are supposed to practice lobby duty," he pointed to Braylin and Paren. "The others are supposed to practice hall watch. He told me I need to stay, of course. I'll be quizzing them all on some of the other things they've been learning the past couple weeks while we're here."

"Stauntwell still making newbies recite the Upper Command?" the official asked, an amused smile stretching across his face and crinkling the corners of his eyes.

Fabian scoffed. "Wouldn't be training from Stauntwell if they didn't recite the Upper Command, brother!"

"Damn!" The official burst out in a deep belly-laugh. "My condolences, guys!"

The official patted Fabian's shoulder.

"We're just glad to have a chance to sit for a while," the official said. Other officials began to step through the door until they all collected in the lobby, falling back into the stiff faux leather chairs with grunts and sighs.

"Enjoy it," Fabian said. "And know that I am deeply envious." He laughed.

As the official began to step toward the chairs to join the others on their break, he turned on his heel to face us once more.

"What are the five statutes of the Upper Command?" he demanded in a booming voice that contrasted sharply with the amused smile on his face.

I felt my heart pause briefly before rapidly hammering against my chest. The five of us stood, frozen, staring at Fabian, who looked equally taken aback by this question.

A moment of silence passed, and the smile began to fade from the official's face slowly.

"They've only heard the Upper Command once," Fabian said. "Maybe twice. That's why I'll be practicing it with them tonight."

The official's face still continued to look increasingly serious as he looked over us all and then observed Fabian.

"Weapons are for protection," Fabian recited to us, locking urgent eyes with each of us.

"Wea—" I started slowly, trying to signal to the others to recite with me.

"—pons are for protection," we all repeated.

"These officials are my brothers and sisters," Fabian said. "I will defend them like family."

"These officials are my brothers and sisters," we chanted back. "I will defend them like family."

"Raine is the ultimate authority," Fabian said, his eyes fixated on mine in particular, pleading with me.

"Raine is the ultimate authority," we recited. I felt each word sting my tongue and throat like acid.

"Honor, integrity, and justice."

"Honor, integrity, and justice."

"Stand up for what is right and protect others from those who do not!" the official called, finishing the list.

"Stand up for what is right and protect others from those who do not!" we repeated, though each of us knew we had differing view on right and wrong than the officials.

"Have fun on watch!" the official said, finally taking his seat amongst the others.

We all nodded silently and followed Fabian as he made his way to the steel door, scanning his ID badge and letting me, Bexa, and Cromwell through as he followed behind.

"I'll come get you two when it's time to trade places," Fabian said, holding out a hand and preventing Braylin and Paren from entering the hallway. He looked apologetically at them as they resigned to standing guard at the steel door. "Stand guard."

Behind the door, there was a hallway full of more steel doors on either side. The ceiling of the narrow hallway had inlaid lights, casting sharp white circles on the ground at even distances along the length of the hall.

"Let's just start checking each door," Fabian said under his breath, scanning in at the first door. He pulled it open, revealing a room full of filing cabinets. "Nope." He shut the door and moved onto the second, which turned out to be a storage closet of office supplies and cleaning equipment. The third, another file room. By the time we reached the fourth, we finally saw something promising.

"What are those?" Bexa asked, looking at the strange, still machinery in the large room.

It looked as if the door opened to a factory within the building itself. The walls and floor were concrete, and monstrous machinery towered over us as we stepped into the room.

"Split up—if you find anything, come get me. I'm going to check the other rooms," Fabian said, disappearing back out into the hallway.

Cromwell ran toward the back wall, which was lined with large, sealed crates. He searched for a moment and returned with a crowbar, which he used to lift the lids from the crates. As he dug through their contents, Bexa went in search of a light source, as the room was only lit by a few small florescent fixtures crookedly arranged on the tall ceiling.

I cautiously stepped toward one of the gigantic machines, reaching out and feeling its smooth, cold metal with my fingertips. I traced the framework of the machine, following a branch of colorful wires around it. On the far end, I found a still conveyer belt. Below the belt sat boxes full of disfigured pieces, scrap metal, and mystery fragments. *We found where the guns are made, but where did they go?*

"Guys!" I heard Fabian's voice echo. "Come here!"

Immediately, I ran for the door, along with Cromwell and Bexa, who had found a small flashlight. At the door, Fabian motioned for us to follow him. We continued down the hallway, passing a few more doors. Fabian scanned the ID badge and opened the door for us, an elated smile on his face.

The room was about half the size of the factory room, but there was no machinery. Instead, each of the walls was lined with hard black boxes, each sealed and labeled.

"Are these—" I began, processing the sight before me.

"Yes," Fabian said, his voice uneasy. He removed the bag from his shoulder, pulling the other bags out from within and passing them to us. "Fill them up as much as you can manage—not so much that you'll be weighed down and can't run. We need to fill Braylin and Paren's bags too."

"Three," Cromwell asked, the thick muscles in his arm twitching as if calling attention to them.

"What?" Fabian asked.

"Give me three bags. I'll carry Braylin and Paren's bags." He reached out and took a second and third bag, leaving the rest of us to take one bag each.

We all ran toward the walls, throwing lids off containers and shoving weapons into bags. Cromwell came across boxes of ammo and, after verifying the bullets would suit the guns everyone was grabbing, he stashed a ton into his bags.

I lifted a lid on a larger box in my section of the wall, revealing black-hilted knives with basic black sheaths. I picked one from the box, delicately removing the sheath, revealing a serrated blade. *I can carry far more knives than I can guns, and no matter what, we aren't going to have enough guns for everyone—we simply can't carry that much. If I fill my bag with knives, at least most of our people can be armed.*

I pulled the box from the wall, dumping the contents directly into my bag. I tested the weight of it, ensuring I would be able to carry it. Confident, I replaced the box on the wall and sealed it back up before zipping my bag and slinging it over my shoulder.

As everyone was finishing filling their bags, a sobering thought struck me.

“Fabian?” I called.

“Mm?”

“How are we supposed to get out of here without all of those officials noticing our bags?”

“I have an idea.”

TWENTY-FOUR

We all followed Fabian out of the room and back into the hallway. He stopped before reaching the door to the lobby and he turned to me.

"I need you to cry."

"What?" I asked, squinting at him.

"I need you to walk out this door crying. Don't say anything. We're going to let Skylar and Cindee know we need a distraction, but in order to get out there, I need you to cry. I'll be with you—just trust me."

I groaned and rolled my eyes, setting my bag down. "Give me a second."

I tried to think about Zane, about Lamb, about Gwenn. Somehow, when I finally *wanted* the tears to come, they wouldn't.

"E," Fabian urged. "We need to hurry!"

I unbuttoned the bottom half of my uniform shirt, exposing my healing wound from the attack about a week ago. The green stitches were in place, but the gash was healing, albeit slowly. I let out a pathetic whimper before tugging on the green thread, seeing it lift my skin slightly. As I tugged, I felt tears well up in my eyes and I felt my chest lurch a little. I looked up at Fabian through blurry, wet vision.

"Perfect," he said, turning and opening the iron door, motioning for the others to stay back.

I wiped my eyes, smearing tears across my cheeks. Stepping back into the lobby, I let out a thick sniffle. The door shut behind Fabian as he hurried to my side, putting an arm around me.

"Hey," he said, loud enough for the lobby full of officials to hear. "You're still new! No one expects you to know everything just yet! That doesn't mean you aren't cut out to be an official."

Another sniffle, but this time I projected it by running my palm up along my nose. Now that my eyes got the message, it was easier to believably sob. I let my shoulders slump over as I cried. Looking briefly over my shoulder, I could see Braylin and Paren, confused as they stared at me. I subtly winked at them before turning back forward.

"I'm just going to take her to get some fresh air," Fabian said to the officials. "We were reviewing and she was struggling a bit. I think a quick breather will do her some good, and we can get right back to it. The others have instructions to treat the next few minutes like a true watch—no supervision. I'm thinking about pretending I broke in—see if I can shock them." He chuckled. "Good thing newbies aren't allowed weapons—I can't get away with that once they have guns."

The crooked-jawed official seemed worried as he looked me up and down, but he remained seated, allowing us to exit the building and walk toward the dumpster.

"What the hell happened to you?" Skylar said in a funny voice, her nose still pinched to block out the smell as we rounded the dumpster.

"We needed an excuse to get out of there for a moment. We filled the bags—we have plenty of weapons and ammo, but we can't get out without all of the officials noticing. We need a distraction," Fabian said.

"You didn't have a plan before now?" Skylar asked, squinting at Fabian.

"I thought they'd leave. I told them I was training the others as new recruits, and I figured they'd allow them to train without a bunch of onlookers. They just sat in the lobby and now I don't know what to do," Fabian said, his words hurried and his eyes full of panic.

"How many are there?" Cindee asked.

"Maybe a dozen," I replied. "Probably a little less."

"I think I know what could work. We'll give you five minutes to collect the others. Be ready to run. We'll meet you back home—don't wait up for us," Skylar instructed.

Fabian and I returned to the lobby, and I was sure to rub my eyes with a bit of extra aggression to keep them bloodshot. We walked back toward the steel door, and Crooked Jaw called out to me.

"Feeling any better?" he asked.

I nodded. "I just got frustrated. It's been a tough week. After tonight, I'll buckle down and write myself some flashcards to study."

"Great idea!" He smiled encouragingly and gave me a cheesy thumbs-up. "It gets better, I promise."

"Thank you," I said with a sniffle and a quickened nod, allowing Fabian to steer me toward the door again.

"I've got a couple things to go over with you all," Fabian said to Braylin and Paren. "Can you two join us?"

They nodded, maintaining serious expressions on their faces as they entered the hallway with Fabian and me. Once the door was shut, we picked up our bags as Fabian filled the others in. Just as he finished speaking, there was a blood-curdling scream in the lobby. Fabian threw the steel door open just in time to see Skylar and Cindee, their faces and shirts smudged with blood and their hair tangled. Skylar had a wild look in her eyes, and the blood on Cindee's face ran down her cheeks with her tears.

"You have to help us!" Cindee let out a heartbreaking sob.

The officials all stood from their chairs, hurrying toward the girls.

"They're coming!" Skylar wailed, turning behind them and pointing off into the distance. Without another word, the two girls took off running down different streets as if their feet were on fire.

"You!" Crooked Jaw pointed to some of the officials. "Go help the blonde!" He pointed to another group, demanding that they help the brunette. The rest took off in the direction Skylar pointed, under the impression that they were hunting down some deranged criminals.

"You and the newbies stay put! This is good practice!" he crowed to Fabian, who replied with a salute before Crooked Jaw bolted after one of the groups.

We all rushed to the door, watching as the three groups grew further from the armory. Cromwell passed a bag each to Braylin and Paren as we got ready to run.

"Let's go!" I instructed the others, who followed me down a separate street from the officials, keeping cover as best we could.

As we ran, Cromwell reached for my bag and I hugged it closer to me, throwing him a confused look as we kept running down the street.

"You're bleeding," Cromwell said, his voice steady. He pointed to my abdomen.

I looked down, nearly tripping over my own feet as I caught sight of my bleeding stiches, still exposed after forgetting to fully button my uniform shirt. The shirt flapped open and closed as I ran, as if playing peekaboo with my wound. I groaned, clumsily holding the bag out to him. "Thanks."

As we reached the city gates, Braylin threw them open, allowing us all to rush out before he slid them shut behind us.

A few hours later, when we finally reached the house, there was just enough sun below the horizon to illuminate the sky in a deep purple glow. Upon opening the door of the house, we were greeted with excited cheers from far more than the couple dozen or so people that we had before. The house was packed with people—possibly as many as fifty.

"H-how?" I stuttered, an involuntary smile forcing its way onto my face.

"They got two more trucks!" Eve cheered.

"How?" I asked again.

She shrugged. "Zaire said something about his business. He wasn't sure about the logistics of it all at first, but I guess they had two more fully functioning trucks available. Legend is driving one of them, and Astraea actually offered to drive the other. Legend and Zaire filled the two up with people and dropped them off here right after you left. Then Zaire took Trae with them to go pick up the other truck."

"Trae knows how to drive?" Bexa asked, looking amused.

"Not really," Eve chuckled nervously. "She figured it out well enough. They were going straight from their workshop to Fortitude. They should be back in a couple hours with three trucks full of people!"

My stomach fluttered as I thought of how big our army of exiles could get in just a few days. At that, I remembered my wound was bleeding earlier that night. I fully unbuttoned the uniform shirt to get a better look at the gash, but it appeared the bleeding had stopped. The areas directly around the stitches appeared inflamed and angry about my tugging, but no true damage was done.

After conferring with the new team members, thanking them for their sacrifice and willingness to join, as well as filling them all in on the plans, Skylar and Cindee returned.

"I was starting to worry!" Braylin said, hugging his sister, who was still covered in blood. "What happened?" His jaw dropped and he looked her over, panicked.

She giggled lightly. "I'm fine. It's just my hand." She held out her hand, which had a deep cut along the palm. "It was Skylar's idea!"

Skylar waved to him with a bloody hand.

"It was brilliant!" Braylin commended them. "I can't believe it worked, actually."

"As much as I hate to say it," Skylar said. "That was the easy part. What's coming is going to be much worse."

The next few days were spent in combat training. We began to fill multiple houses within the ruins—half of each house slept during the day and trained at night, and the roles were reversed for the other half. By Monday, our numbers had grown to 342.

I hadn't anticipated so many people joining us, but Zaire explained to me that it didn't take much convincing for the people of Fortitude to come to our aid—especially with Legend's influence over them.

Despite not having enough weapons for everyone, Cromwell, Paren and some of the other exiles worked together to train the others on hand-to-hand combat techniques and self-defense. Skylar and Fabian taught everyone how to shoot a gun—even though not everyone would have one, there was no telling how many people would have opportunities to acquire them once inside the city. Lastly, Bexa and I taught the others how to use a dagger, though I felt there wasn't much to teach except "stab" and "be careful of the pointy end."

"I want you to meet someone," Zaire said after one of his "shipments" of exiles. He guided me through one of the houses furthest from mine until we reached the kitchen, where a middle-aged man stood, stirring some ingredients into a large bowl. The kitchen smelled like onions and garlic, and the smell grew stronger with each stir. The man looked up from his concoction and smiled at me, reaching out a wet hand in greeting.

"Big fan!" the man said as I hesitantly shook his hand. "I'm Herb!"

"Herb is an official," Zaire said, keeping a hand on my back as if I might snap and attack the guy.

"Oh?" I responded.

"Herb is the one who is going to hook the camera feed up to the skyscraper screens for you," Zaire explained. "He wasn't able to get it hooked up in advance, but I think with our defenses, it shouldn't be a problem. He has a plan on how to do it, and he doesn't think it'll take but a few moments. He also has a contact on the inside who will make sure Raine is in her office. They're supposed to meet us at the gate."

"Oh!" I exclaimed. "That's fantastic! Thank you, Herb!"

"Pleasures all mine! Zaire is a great friend of mine—saved my tail once when I was a driver. I screwed a truck up *bad*—he fixed it up and didn't say a peep to anyone about what had happened to it. When I got some of your letters under my door, I really felt for those people—the ones whose stories you shared. I knew Zaire's brother was an exile, and I guess you can just say I developed a bit of a soft spot for you guys and your troubles. I think the prison system really is the way to go. In fact, if w—"

"Thank you, Herb," Zaire said, cutting him off with a gentle pat on the shoulder. "You'll be in the group staying close with Eos when it's time to march—I'll keep you posted."

Zaire and I stepped away and Herb went back to mixing his garlic and onions.

"He's a bit chatty," Zaire apologized under his breath as he escorted me back to my house.

"I can tell," I said. "It's fine. He's allowed to be whatever he wants if he's willing to help us."

"Right?" Zaire sighed.

After Monday, we requested that Zaire, Legend, and Astraea stop picking up exiles.

Tuesday evening, after spending the night in the ruins with us, Zaire and Legend began to question why we shouldn't collect more exiles.

"Are you sure we have enough people?" Legend asked.

"Pretty sure," Fabian answered for me. "Fallmont has about 200,000 citizens. Give or take. They have maybe 250 officials, but some of them are drivers who won't be in town, some are trainees, and some of them agree with us. So, let's say that leaves us with about 150 who are loyal to Raine, or at least are dedicated to their jobs. Fallmont is pretty large, and not every one of those officials will be even close to our path, as long as we are quick. We *might* come across about half of them."

"But what about citizens who are against us?" Legend continued to ask.

"What about the ones who are *for* us?" I retorted.

"Just trying to be logical here," Paren started. "Obviously there are going to be citizens who are against us. Some of them will lash out. Many won't. They don't have much for true weapons and they aren't trained in combat. There will also be a lot who have families and don't want to put themselves or their loved ones at risk. I think it's more likely we will have bystanders or people who hide. If you had kids at home and you saw an angry army of exiles storming down the street, would you throw yourself at the army?"

Silence.

"No matter what, speed will be our best friend. When we get there, move fast," Paren instructed. "We need to get all of our people in City Hall as quickly as possible, and make sure all entrances and exits are locked and guarded."

"Everyone here has some training now, and everyone knows the plans," I explained to them. "If we start adding more people now, they won't be ready in time."

"Why don't we just wait a few more days?" Zaire asked, leaning against the brick wall exterior of the house, almost losing his balance as a piece of rubble fell to the floor.

"Every day we're here is another day we risk them finding us first. Next time they surprise us, we might not be so lucky as before, especially if they are prepared and we aren't expecting them," I said.

"Then just move to different ruins every day so they can't pinpoint exactly where you are." Zaire was determined to find a flaw in my logic.

"Nope. We have too many people now. It's one thing to move among a couple buildings concealed in the ruins, but it's another thing entirely to move over 300 people across an open desert. At that point, we may as well just parade around with a big battle flag." I crossed my arms and I could feel my face growing warm. "We need to do this as soon as possible, and I think we have the numbers. Like Paren said—we need to act fast. We're prepared—they won't know what's coming until it hits, and then it'll be too late."

"You're talking like you plan on slaughtering the lot of them," Legend said, shooting me skeptical side eyes.

"Only if we have to. I'd rather not. The goal isn't to make the New Territory some kind of Fortitude 2.0. We want the normal citizens—we need them."

"Fortitude has normal citizens, too," Legend reminded me.

I rolled my eyes. "You know what I mean."

"So, when do we leave?" Paren asked.

"We should leave late tonight," I suggested.

"Make an announcement!" Braylin said. "You have an army that needs to be kept in the loop. Do you really want to have to go around and tell everyone individually what we're doing? Speak up!"

I groaned. The thought of a speech didn't intimidate me, but it certainly didn't excite me.

The crowd of exiles were simply standing around, talking amongst themselves. I cleared my throat awkwardly, looking at them all before me.

Nothing.

"What did you think that pathetic phlegm noise would do?" Skylar teased. "Speak up—don't be a chicken!"

"I'm not scared," I said, narrowing my eyes at her.

She crossed her arms and smirked.

"Listen up!" I shouted, projecting my voice as loudly as I could. The people nearest me in the crowd turned to look, but the furthest people continued their conversations.

"HEY!" I yelled, my voice echoing through the street. At this, the conversations died, and everyone faced me.

I looked at Skylar with a smug grin, but she just waved a hand as if shooing me.

"We leave tonight!" I commanded confidently. "Hours before daylight. We want to walk in the shadows. At dawn, things are going to change. We should reach the gates just as citizens begin to fill the streets on their way to work. Do not attack unless in self-defense! Unprovoked violence is *not* going to convince them that exiles are safe to rejoin the cities."

The crowd nodded in agreement, quiet chatter spreading amongst them.

"You know what team you belong to. We have quite a few of you designated for the lobby of City Hall; some of you are to guard the doors to the stairwells, the door to Raine's office, and Raine's office itself. Many of you have been assigned in pairs to the other doors throughout the building as added security, and to make sure there is always additional help near other teams in case of an emergency. You are all ready for this! We have trained you, you have practiced, and you know what we stand for! Don't let everything we've done be for nothing. Don't let everyone we've lost be for nothing." I felt my throat burn as I raised my voice even louder. "Innocent people have been suffering for years because of this corrupt system, and it's time to show everyone enough is enough! Who's ready to end this?" My voice felt gruff and raspy as I shouted the final words. The exiles erupted in shouts. Fists pumped in the air, others cupped their hands around their mouths as they yelled. I felt heat surging through my fingertips, my arms, and then my chest until it consumed me.

TWENTY-FIVE

Paren, Fabian, Braylin, Skylar and I worked together to determine how many people from each team would get guns and how many would get daggers. We distributed the weapons to each team, and since we didn't have enough weapons for every single exile, we designated them to the most skilled fighters within each team. Our makeshift team of leaders determined that Herb and I should remain at the very center of the mass as we marched the streets, allowing for the best protection possible. Herb and I were both to be armed with a gun and a dagger.

"I'm shocked you're allowing me to carry a gun," Skylar said, her eyebrows raised as she nudged me with an elbow playfully.

"You're talented, what can I say?" I smirked. "It'd be a waste if we didn't give you one."

"So, you trust me?" she asked. "Even after I snapped?"

"With my life," I said, looking directly into her eyes.

I saw the corner of her mouth twitch in a faint smile as she gave a single nod before checking her gun for bullets and wandering off to join her team, assigned the task of standing guard outside Raine's office.

"It's getting close, isn't it?" Paren asked, approaching me with his shoulders back and arms crossed, a scab on his elbow stretching at the edges as he did.

"A few more hours," I said, feeling my heart thumping in my throat.

"You did all this," he said, picking at his scab with a stubby, dirty fingernail.

I scoffed, shaking my head as I looked at my feet. "I didn't. If it were just me leading all of this, we'd all be dead by now. I'm just very fortunate to have friends that are smarter than me." I paused. "And better with people than me."

Paren smiled meekly, his eyes briefly meeting mine.

"If we're successful," I said, tasting pure hope on my words. "The New Territory is going to need a new leader. We're not just taking Raine down, we are convincing everyone that her ways are wrong. We need someone who will lead the cities the right way."

Paren's eyes narrowed as I spoke, as if analyzing every word.

"If the people will have you," I said, feeling my stomach fluttering. "Will you be the new leader of the New Territory?"

Paren's face was void of emotion for a moment. I opened my mouth to speak and clarify that there was no obligation, and that ultimately it would be up to the citizens anyways, but before I could utter a sound, he broke the silence.

"If they'll have me," he said, his voice cracking on the word 'me.' "Yes."

"I can't think of anyone better to lead them," I said, reaching out and letting my hand rest on his shoulder for a moment before I stepped away.

Nearby, I noticed Zaire and Legend. I trotted over, flagging them down.

"Are you guys marching with us?" I asked bluntly, clearly taking them both by surprise, as they replied with uncomfortable laughter.

"I'm sorry," Legend let his laugh die out into a weak chuckle. "What?"

"Are you guys marching with us? Simple question."

"Not simple!" Zaire retorted.

"Actually, it is. One-word reply—yes? Or no?" I asked, fighting to suppress an amused grin, enjoying their awkwardness.

"You know what?" Legend said, his eyes alive with excitement, seeming to sparkle despite the darkness of the room in the night. "Hell yes! We're with you."

"Oh," I said, genuinely taken aback.

"Did you expect us to chicken out?" Zaire asked, hands on his hips in defiance.

"I mean, not exactly 'chicken out,' but I didn't figure you guys were coming. You were both such a huge help, I guess I didn't picture you two actually marching with us."

"Ouch," Legend said, his mouth hanging open, yet still smiling. "Of course we're coming! We've been with you since the beginning of this mess, no way in hell are we missing out on the end."

Later into the night, we determined we had a few hours left until dawn—just enough time to reach the gates of Fallmont. Some of us worked together to gather up the teams, creating a formation in the streets of the ruins. Herb and I would remain in the middle. Those coming with to protect us while we're inside Raine's office need to stay inside the circle with us, extending outward to those who were tasked with standing watch at the doors of City Hall. Cromwell, the leader of the City Hall door defense team, volunteered to take the Skeleton Key to the gate, heading up the entire army. We followed him as he began to march down the street and into the desert once more.

As we walked, I looked around at my friends surrounding me. Skylar was in one of the closest circles around me. As I looked over to her, her eyes remained fixated ahead, her stride purposeful. Behind her, Paren walked proudly, head held high but his gaze looking almost sorrowful as he looked off into the dark distance. On my other side, a few layers further out from me walked Braylin and Cindee, their steps in unison as they pointed up at stars. They exchanged a few words and giggled at each other. I remembered how lost they were when they were separated, but here they were, helping lead a revolution. Somehow, they still took time to look at stars together.

My hand fell to my pocket, mindlessly feeling the last Dawn Letter through the denim. I kept catching myself repeating this action, as if I feared it could just disappear from my pocket. I tried to keep my thoughts clear, knowing that we have done all of the planning we could, and any additional planning at this point could only cloud my thoughts. Instead, I let myself feel the way my heels sunk into the sand beneath my feet with every step, each one bringing me closer to what we had all been waiting for. It was only a matter of time until we got to this point, and no matter how near or distant it seemed up until now, it had never felt as real as it did in that moment.

"When we get inside, as quickly as possible, head to City Hall! You know what to do from there!" Paren instructed as we grew closer to Fallmont. In my trance, his voice jarred me, sending a cold chill across my neck and back.

I looked up from my feet, spotting the gate looming in the distance. Realizing my breaths were fast and shallow, I tried to refocus on the sand and my feet, taking extra care to steady my breathing. *I've been tortured. I've been to—and escaped—every exile town and every city in the New Territory. I broke out of prison. I've killed people. I've blown officials up. I've been in Raine's office before. I can handle this.*

It was precisely that last visit to Raine's office that lingered in the back of my mind, reminding me that there was a very real possibility this could go horribly wrong.

"Are you going to look for him when it's all over?" Paren asked me. When he turned to face me, his expression turned from sheer focus to concern. I realized I had been staring a bit too intently at my feet.

"Um," I struggled for a second. "Of course I want to know if the rumors are true or not. I'm just not sure I'm ready to know, you know? And I can't be worrying about that right now—everyone is counting on me."

Paren smiled reassuringly. "It'll all work out. You can check after we win."

"How can you be so confident?" I nibbled on my cheek, pushing at it with my knuckle.

"Look around you," he beamed. "When was the last time you have ever seen so many people in the New Territory united under a common cause?"

In that moment, I realized just how many people surrounded me. In every direction, there were so many people that I couldn't see through them.

"These people all believe in you, they believe in what you stand for, and they're here to protect you for the sake of friends, family, neighbors, and even future generations. If you can't see how powerful that is, I think you're missing the point here," Paren said.

"Quiet down back there!" I could hear Cromwell hiss. "We're getting close to the gate—everyone needs to shut up."

Paren put a finger to his lips mockingly, throwing me a playful wink. I smiled back at him. By this point, the sun was beginning to linger over the horizon, setting the sky ablaze with stunning oranges and reds. The shapes of crimson clouds began to appear as the sun crept up ever so slowly.

As we approached the gate, I could see some of the exiles around me pulling out their guns. Almost as one mass, we all crouched ever so slightly, as if the couple inches height would somehow make a group of more than 300 people less visible. With everyone crouched, I could somewhat see Cromwell speak to someone through the gate. *That must be Herb's contact.* Shortly after, I saw him insert the Key into the lock. Seconds later, the towering metal gates were pulled open, allowing us to all flood into the street, rushing like water through a pipe.

The further into the city we ran, the more people began to appear on the streets, stepping out of their houses, no doubt on their way to work, just like any other day. Upon realizing the mass of exiles storming through the street, each one of them seemed to react with the same chain of expressions—confusion, realization, and shock. Some of the citizens, upon concluding who we were, began hurling rocks, garbage, and anything they could get their hands on at us. The few exiles that were hit by the projectiles threw a few expletives and middle fingers at Raine's supporters, but didn't miss a step. Other citizens were clearly our supporters— some applauded upon seeing us, others cheered things such as "Down with Raine!"

It was only a matter of time before we started to spot officials patrolling the streets. As soon as we caught their eyes, they immediately raised their guns. Instinctively, everyone around me picked up their speed, nearly trampling me as they raced for City Hall. It was as if we all felt bulletproof as a group until the sight of an official shattered us. I began running to keep pace with the group.

A couple shots rang out on both sides of us, followed by horrible screams. Some of the exiles tried to stop, probably to check on the fallen, but they were nearly run over in the process.

"Keep going!" I yelled at the top of my lungs. "We can't stop!"

As we neared the city center just outside City Hall, more shots rang out and then suddenly, there was a booming voice commanding the officials to cease fire.

"CLEAR THE AREA!" the voice commanded. "ALL CITIZENS EVACUATE!"

Another shot rang out, leading to an eruption of yelling and further gunshots. Citizens began to scream, running from our army as quickly as they could. As we approached the front door, I could see bodies of exiles strewn across our trail. A couple of them were still moving, albeit rather weakly.

Cromwell threw open the front doors; he and another exile held them open for everyone. I looked behind us and spotted a dark figure crumpled up in the city center. The man clutched a bleeding leg and, upon sitting up, I recognized the figure as Legend. I felt my eyes grow wide and I involuntarily gasped—half from shock, half from the force of the exiles pushing me and the others forward into City Hall, slamming the doors shut behind us all.

The employees in City Hall clearly had no idea of the chaos going on outside their building, as they all stood, stunned for a moment, before throwing themselves beneath the bank counters and other furniture in fear.

The few officials in the room raised their guns, but our army was too fast and too large. The outermost circle of exiles swarmed on the officials, acting fast enough to allow only a couple misfired shots from the officials' guns before completely rendering them defenseless.

Our outer defense team corralled the officials to the front door, which Cromwell and some of the others were holding steadily in place. They removed the officials' weapons and opened the doors just quickly enough to shove them out into the street, immediately pulling the doors shut with a startling crash. Cromwell locked the front door as the rest of his team formed a long line a few feet away from the door, facing it with guns aimed and ready. The rest of his team—the largest group of exiles— patrolled the lobby.

"Go!" he commanded the rest of us, sending us clamoring toward the staircase door. As I ran past him, he handed me the Key. Through the staircase, we came across two other officials. One of them reacted quickly, shooting one of our exiles, letting her lifeless body slip down a couple steps before it was stopped by the feet of our army, blocking off the rest of her path. Bexa and another exile threw quick punches, snatching their weapons before they could retaliate. Four of our team members escorted the officials to the lobby to wait under the guard of the main defense team, who decided not to risk opening the door to throw more unarmed officials outside.

As we approached the third floor, we began to funnel through the stairwell door. We had a team tasked with guarding the stairwell, blocking off doors to prevent people from other floors from making their way to the third floor or the lobby, but our group still remained large. Only a few could fit through the narrow door at a time, and while I was still a few steps down from the door's platform, I heard more gunshots followed by angered, animalistic yelling as the mass of us shifted and began rapidly spilling out through the third-floor doorway.

By the time I wriggled through the door, I could see six officials. Three of them were flailing on the ground as multiple exiles pummeled them. Others stood, pointing the officials' own weapons at them as the unarmed guards thrashed. I spotted Eve just as she sent her boot sailing into the cheekbone of one of the downed officials, sending a spray of blood across the ground.

"Stop it!" Cindee squeaked, pulling Eve away. Enraged, Eve shoved Cindee away and continued kicking.

A little further down the hall, one of the officials lay dead, her neck sliced open, blood pooling against the shiny white tile, reflecting the light fixtures above. The other two officials were being corralled down the stairs by a few exiles who had pinned their hands behind their backs.

"Stop!" Paren demanded, pulling Eve and some of the other exiles away from the official, who was letting out wet, gaspy breaths. "Take them downstairs, *now*!"

Some of the exiles reluctantly lifted the officials and carried them downstairs to the lobby. As I tried to get my bearings, I noticed a couple of lifeless exiles scattered around the stairwell door. I felt the weight of each lost life in my chest, forcing it down like a weighty pill. With a deep, shaky breath, I pointed toward Raine's office and, without a word of direction, everyone regrouped as they marched down the long hall.

City Leader.

I stared at the sign fixated just outside Raine's door, which was shut. Key in hand, I made my way to the front of the group, inserting the Key into the lock, twisting the dial gingerly, my hands visibly shaking. As I felt it form to the lock, I twisted and heard the deadbolt's *thunk*.

Paren and some of the other exiles barged into the room as I opened the door, immediately throwing themselves at Raine, who appeared to be alone in her locked office. Paren snatched Raine's arms before she could react, pulling her wrists aggressively behind her. His large arms flexed as he crushed down, ensuring she couldn't move.

Everyone stepped to either side, clearing a path for me to enter the office. I strutted into the office, locking eyes with Raine. Her always-flawless raven curls were tousled and frizzed by the sudden attack. She bit down on her maroon-painted lip, allowing it to roll back out from under her teeth as she narrowed her gaze and lifted a single eyebrow at me.

"I knew it was only a matter of time before I'd see you again," Raine said coolly. "I suppose you still managed to surprise me with your numbers." She held her chin high and head still as her eyes seemed to individually fixate on each exile in the room.

As I began to speak, Herb started to rummage behind some books on a lofty oak bookshelf.

"I gave you a chance," I said, my voice trailing off. "And you threw it away. Violently."

Raine pursed her lips, her pale skin crinkled around her mouth. "Even if you kill me, that isn't going to change th—" her gaze immediately snapped over to Herb, who had exposed a compartment behind some of the books on a middle shelf. He was toying with a fist-sized white sphere. He lifted a tiny panel on the sphere, exposing what appeared to be a miniature keypad.

"What do you think you're doing?" Raine asked, the skin beneath her right eye giving a single twitch as she narrowed her gaze at Herb.

Herb continued to ignore her, entering a lengthy code on the keyboard. A moment later, the white sphere began to glow blue. He placed it on the now-empty shelf, rotating it until he revealed a small black circle on one side of it.

"It'll be live as soon as you're ready," he said, giving me a nod to proceed.

I stepped in front of the camera, ensuring Raine would be visible over my shoulder in the background. I looked to my side, where Skylar and Braylin both gave me nervous, yet reassuring smiles. Pulling the folded letter from my pocket and smoothing it out on my pant leg, I held it in front of me, nodding once to Herb. He reached out, tapping the very top of the camera, which turned green.

"My name is Eos Dawn. By now, you've read the stories about exiles… no… *people* who were mistreated by Raine. Some of them are your family, your friends, your neighbors. There's no way you could be oblivious to the corruption anymore, but I have one final story for you."

TWENTY-SIX

As I read Zane's story, I felt my eyes sting and my throat begin to burn. Behind me, Raine spewed her dissention, "reminding" the citizens that I was a "deranged criminal holding her captive." When I concluded the letter, I gave a brief word of thanks for any citizens who supported us during this dangerous time.

"The hard part isn't over," I spoke clearly. "It has only just begun. With your help, we can rebuild our government under proper leadership, with a justice system that practices exactly that—justice."

I turned to face my friends again, wiping at the tears beginning to collect at the bottom of my eyes.

Skylar and Braylin pulled me into a hug and I let out a couple exhausted sobs, collecting myself quickly.

"See if he's here," Skylar whispered in my ear. "We've got this under control."

I pulled away from the hug and nodded at her. I left the office, where Skylar was ordering some of the exiles to escort me, some to patrol the hall with her, and others to keep watch on Raine, who was still being restrained by Paren.

At first, I was walking briskly down the hall, but the more I thought about what might be, the faster my feet carried me. As I raced down the stairs, I had to hold to the metal railing to steady myself. My escorts struggled to keep up with me as they dodged the bodies along the way.

Once at the bottom of the stairs, I burst into the lobby and raced to the door of the holding cell staircase, avoiding questions from the main defense team as they continued to patrol. I stumbled down the dark stairwell, trying to follow the blurred tiny lights along the edges until I reached the bottom, nearly missing the final step.

I whipped out my gun, spotting an official at the end of the hallway.

"Where the hell is he?" I demanded, spit flinging from my mouth as I gritted my teeth and aimed my gun at him.

He looked stunned, his hands thrown mercifully in the air.

"I don't know what you're talking about," he said, his eyes bouncing around as if trying to count how many exiles had burst into his hall.

"Zane Hess!" I shrieked, storming toward the man with my gun aimed at his chest. I could feel bile in my throat and my vision blurred slightly with tears. "You've got five seconds."

"I don't know what you're talking about!" the official pleaded. "We only have one prisoner in holding, and it's a female."

"Fine," I said. "Badge."

He slowly and carefully pulled out his badge, tossing it to the floor in front of me, my eyes and aim never leaving the man, I slid the badge behind me with my foot. My escorts began to scan into every holding cell, as well as through the doors to the long-term holding cell until each one had been checked.

"He's right," someone called to me. "There's only a woman here."

"I'm so sorry, E," another exile said softly.

I shook my head, slowly at first, and then more rapidly, feeling a searing pain in my chest and stomach.

"I'm gonna kill her," I decided out loud, turning on my heel and barreling back up the stairs, gun in hand.

My escorts raced after me, finally catching up as I reached the third-floor door again. As I stepped through it, it was slammed shut behind me. An official stepped into the way of the door, preventing my escorts from joining me as another official snatched my weapon and forced me to turn around. My skin went cold as I saw all the exiles in the middle of the hallway, their backs to the door and their weapons at their feet. Their hands were raised in the air. I stood for a moment gaping at the sight of their surrender.

"What—" I breathed softly as I approached them, the official with my gun following me from behind.

As I reached the front of the cluster, I realized what made them all set down their weapons.

In front of all of us, Raine stood proudly, a gun aimed at a person facing the crowd on their knees before her. I took another step closer, forcing myself to blink a few times to be sure it wasn't a dream.

The top of his head revealed a thick scar and a bald patch, making his hair nearly unrecognizable, but his eyes revealed exactly who he was.

Zane.

TWENTY-SEVEN

"Eos," he said breathily, a pained smile creeping onto his dirty face. His hair, once carefully styled with gel, was now greasy and flat. His face and arms were covered in small scabs and bruises, and his eyes seemed sunken in his face. Ragged grey clothes clung loosely to his thinned frame.

"How?" I asked, cupping my hands over my mouth and nose as I stared at him as if blinking would make him disappear.

Just then, a familiar figure stepped out of Raine's office. Once at Raine's side, Arke shifted her weight onto one leg as she smirked at me.

"Arke?" I stared back at her, trying to make sense of things.

She wiggled her fingers in a playful wave.

"Why?" I asked.

"I work for Raine," Arke said with a nonchalant shrug. "She promised to 'overlook' things for me. If I led the officials to your camp, she'd let my sister sneak back into the city to live with me."

The attack… when we blew up the officials. That must have been her. That's why she wasn't with us when we relocated.

"So, you really don't think all exiles are dangerous criminals?" Paren asked, his voice full of spite. "I mean, you clearly don't. Not if you're willing to let a criminal back into the city. Why aren't you willing to try the prison system again if you have that kind of logic?"

Raine narrowed her eyes. "It was an exception I had to make. I weighed the payout. One criminal traded for many."

"How…" my voice trailed off as I looked at Zane, falling to my knees unknowingly, facing him at eyelevel.

"Why are you so against the prison system?" Paren asked, his voice drowning out my confused mumblings.

"It's an outdated method of controlling crime and it isn't practical," Raine said, her answer sounding incredibly rehearsed. "Criminals don't deserve forgiveness. They aren't as human as the rest of us. To break a law is to go against human nature. The exile towns protect humanity. Our ancestors failed to recognize that our downfall—the entire war—was caused by animals like you."

"Criminals aren't lesser beings! That thought process is completely inhumane! The exile towns are outdated. Even still, as you can see," he motioned to the crowd of exiles, "it clearly doesn't contain us like you want."

"Move again and I'll put a bullet between your eyes," Raine said, her usual cool neutrality momentarily giving way to obvious hatred, her eyes squinting, fixating on Paren.

"You're the criminal!" one of the younger exiles of the group shouted from the front row. His eyes pleaded with Raine as he pointed a finger at her. "Why won't you even consider something different? You're worse than any of us!"

Bang.

The boy fell to the ground with a smack, his face against the floor as blood began to puddle.

A girl who had been standing beside the boy screamed as she threw herself at the boy, who was already long gone.

My eyes stung and I could feel bile burn in the back of my throat. I stayed, kneeling and staring at Zane, whose eyes were glossy and bloodshot.

"He didn't do anything!" the girl wailed, looking up at Raine from the floor, the knees of her jeans soaking up the red as she sat with a hand against the boy's cheek.

"He was a hostile criminal. I did it to protect myself and my people."

"Do you even hear how insane you sound?" Paren asked, his voice sounding gritty. I began to worry that Raine would see him as hostile, too.

I kept staring at Zane, his eyes never leaving mine. "Why—"

"I didn't know if I could use him later on. Save him as a trade-off to protect everyone."

"But you shot him. How—"

"I didn't kill him," Raine said, her eyes locking on me once again. "Simple as that."

"But you tried to," I said, still feeling breathless.

"Self-defense."

"We didn't touch you—we weren't going to hurt you. We just wanted to talk."

"And now?" Raine asked. "How many lives were lost today because of you?"

"I didn't want it to come to this," I felt my voice break in defeat.

"But you let it. In fact, you *forced* it to this point."

"You shot him for trying to propose an idea to you!"

"A dangerous idea—"

"No! You have no clue what's dangerous."

"I think I do," she said, her finger twitching against the side of the gun in her steady hand as she aimed it at the back of Zane's head.

"So, what's your plan now?" I asked her. "We've set down our weapons, but this isn't all of us, and the people of the New Territory aren't stupid. They know what you've done—they know what kind of monster you are."

"You're going to call off the rest of your people. Arke is going to get me exile reports, and I'm going to remind the citizens the kind of people they are following. They already know what kind of people you all are, but I think they need a reminder on just how wicked your sins are."

"Says the one with a gun to a man's head," I said, my lip curling involuntarily.

"If you're so fond of bringing back outdated methods of managing criminals, I suppose you wouldn't object to reinstating the death penalty," Raine said, slowly pulling back the hammer of the gun with her thumb.

I felt my lips part as my eyes darted between Raine, Zane, Arke, and the other officials in the hall, desperately trying to think of how I could save Zane.

"Pick. Hang onto your hope that the rest of your people will save you and you'll overthrow the government," she said with a stubbornly stoic face, as if all of this was nothing more than an inconvenience to her. "Or, save lover boy and give up."

My eyes locked onto Zane's. He visibly took a deep, shaky breath, keeping his head held high. "*No,*" he mouthed to me, his eyes sorrowful, a single tear leaving a clean streak in the filth on his face. "*Don't.*"

I tried to speak, even just to stall, but I could feel the words cling to my throat, coming out as muted sputters. My heart raced and I eyed one of the pistols on the floor near my knee. I clenched and unclenched my fist, knowing my mind was already made up.

Just as I was about to snatch the gun from the floor, there was a clatter down the hall behind Raine, just startling enough that Raine turned momentarily, giving me the split second I needed to grab the gun. I aimed at Raine and fired, sending the gun clattering from her hand onto the tile. The gun fired, sending a bullet down the hall as she fell to her knees, clutching her bleeding shoulder with a scream. My friends behind me followed my lead simultaneously, charging the officials, taking their weapons and rendering them defenseless with their hands behind their backs.

Skylar appeared from down the hall behind Raine, running straight toward us. She slid across the slick tile as she tried to stop, latching her fingers in Raine's curls to stop herself. With a pained squeal, Raine fell on her wounded arm.

"What kind of psycho are you?" Skylar screamed, tugging on a handful of Raine's hair at the scalp. "Do you think you're any better than any other criminal out here?"

"Skylar!" I called, scrambling toward her. "Stop! Killing her would be too merciful. I have something better—just wait. We need to get all of these officials and her down to the holding cells."

Skylar let out a furious snarl, releasing Raine's hair by using it to throw her head forward.

"Get up," Skylar spat.

Raine eased herself to her feet, and Skylar pulled her hands behind her back, bringing forth another pained cry from Raine as her shoulder wound stretched.

As the exiles upstairs began to bring all the officials and Raine down to the holding cells, reuniting with the exiles in the stairwell, I realized we were safe for a moment. I tucked the gun into my waistband and turned, seeing Zane still on his knees on the floor. He was rubbing at his messy hair, open-mouth staring at the entire scene. When he realized it was over, his eyes began to frantically scan the faces still in the hall until they met mine, and they instantly turned red and began to well up. I approached him, cautiously, afraid this was just another nightmare. As I reached him, I dropped to my knees and put my fingertips to his cheek.

It's real.

I threw my arms around him, pulling him in tight as I broke out in violent sobs. He pressed his palms flat against my back, pushing me closer against him as he buried his face in my neck, letting a couple hot tears trickle down my collarbone.

After a few moments in silence, blocking out everything and everyone around us, we pulled apart just enough to look at each other.

"Thank you," he said shakily.

"I thought you were dead."

"There were some days I wished I was, but I knew you'd win."

"What do you mean?" I asked.

"You're stubborn," he said, a tear getting caught beneath his eye as they crinkled in a smile. "I knew you wouldn't just drop the cause, especially not after what happened."

"There were a lot of times I wanted to give up."

"But you didn't."

"Neither did you."

"Thank goodness, right?" he laughed sweetly. "I make everything better, don't I?"

I laughed, running a hand under my wet nose.

"Cute," he teased. He pulled out the edge of his sleeve toward me in offering.

"Ew," I smiled, shaking my head.

He stood to his feet, holding a blackened hand to me and helping me up.

"You didn't ask how I'm still alive," Zane said.

"It doesn't matter. What matters is that you are."

"Too bad! Let me tell my heroic story!"

Zane and I walked carefully downstairs to join the others in the lobby as he recounted the shooting from his perspective. He told me how, when Raine shot him, he passed out from shock. He woke up in a hospital room with a bunch of stitches on the top of his head. The nurses told him he was incredibly lucky that the bullet wasn't any lower or it would have been a lot worse. Instead, the bullet grazed his scalp, resulting in a lot of blood, but not so much that he couldn't be saved. Once he had healed, he woke up one night in a high-security holding cell, where he spent an unknown amount of time before he was forced upstairs to be used as a pawn against me.

As we reached the lobby, the front doors were open and there was chaos in the street. I pulled the gun immediately from my waistband, pushing Zane behind me as we crept around the side of the door. When I peered out into the city center, I realized citizens and exiles were celebrating in the streets. I lowered my aim slowly, seeing some of the Fallmont-native exiles reunited with family and friends. As we stepped outside, there was a familiar voice calling out among the excited commotion of the crowd.

"Zane!" the voice called.

I squinted through the mass of people, spotting Gavin and Mallory wiggling their way through the crowd.

"Zane!" Gavin called again as he burst through between a couple of people. He ran straight for Zane, whose eyes lit in matched joy and surprise.

Zane jumped on Gavin in an enthusiastic hug. When he finally dropped from him, I approached the two.

"You know each other?" I asked Zane. I looked between him and Gavin, their eyes nearly identical as they smiled back at me.

"Eos," he said. "This is my brother, Gavin."

TWENTY-EIGHT

Gavin explained to us that he was transferred to Fallmont under doctor's orders shortly after Zane was exiled, allowing Gavin the best medical care possible. During his time in the hospital, he met Mallory, who had recently started working there. After intensive medical treatments for nearly a month, Gavin's health improved drastically and he was allowed to leave the hospital, but the government wouldn't allow him back to Eastmeade. They claimed it was "too dangerous" to move him back and forth in the event his health was to decline again. Mallory and Gavin moved in together, and after a short time, they decided to get married.

I left Zane for a moment, giving him some time to visit with his brother and his "new" sister-in-law while I searched for my friends. Noticing that I looked lost, Braylin came over. I almost didn't see him until he was directly in front of me.

"I caught it all on camera," he said proudly, holding up the camera ball, which was still glowing green. "Everyone saw what Raine did and said."

"Huh!" I let out an airy laugh, giving him a brief hug. "All of this," I motioned to the city center around us, full of people celebrating the revolution. "It's because of you. I don't know if the letters or the speech alone would have been enough of a tipping point, but capturing Raine's true behavior on camera—that did it."

Braylin's cheeks turned a vivid red and he gushed for a moment before clumsily pointing the camera at me. "Speech!"

I looked up at the skyscraper screens, showing all the buildings surrounding the city center, seeing myself in the middle of it, my short, black hair matted to my face, blood crusted over on my cheek.

I hesitated for a moment before waving at the camera. "Hey," I said awkwardly. My voice could hardly be heard over the noise of the street.

"Hang on," Braylin said, holding the camera closer to me, cropping in on my face far too close for comfort. "Try it now."

I cleared my throat, and the sound rang out through the city center as everyone grew rapidly silent, their attention turned to the screens. The people nearest me moved to face me directly.

"I—" I hesitated, looking to my side, seeing Zane, Gavin, and Mallory beaming at me. "I can't thank everyone enough. Your courage and your sacrifice made a difference. From this point on, we will work together toward reinstating the prison system. Because of each and every one of you, many innocent people will once again be reunited with loved ones, and future generations will know true justice."

I stopped, and everyone around me erupted in elated cheers and applause. I felt my face grow warm and I couldn't help but to smile.

Fabian, Skylar, and Paren appeared nearby, and the three fought each other to hug me first.

"Was that you who distracted Raine?" I asked Skylar. "You're the only one I saw come from that direction during all the chaos."

She nodded proudly. "I told you that you guys needed me!"

Fabian cleared his throat, shooting Skylar a playful side-eye.

"I threw a rock," she admitted.

"Well, whatever you did, it worked," I said. "Thank you."

"Hey!" Fabian said defensively.

Skylar groaned and rolled her eyes. "I threw a rock that Fabian gave me because he said he was going to use them as a weapon and I told him that was a stupid idea."

"Who's stupid now?" he said, poking her side.

"So," Paren started. "Where do we go from here?"

I smiled at my friends.

"Wherever we want."

6 MONTHS LATER

Before I could even open my eyes, I felt the hair on the back of my neck stand on edge. The sharp, piercing cry of a baby jarred me from my sleep, and I awoke with a jolt.

"Don't worry," Zane said, rolling his way off the bed without a second thought. "I'll get her."

I groaned, forcing my eyes to stay open, blinking back the bright sun cast through the windows.

"You don't have to get her every time," I called out groggily.

"She's my niece! I'm happy to help!"

Once I could tolerate the light enough, I threw the heavy covers from my body and sat up. I ran my fingers through my knotted hair, snagging on a thick tangle. Dazed, I waddled out to the kitchen, following the smell of apples and cinnamon.

"Morning!" Mallory chirped as she pulled a steaming apple cake from the oven.

"Cake for breakfast?" I asked, taking an extra-long sniff as I sat at the dining room table.

"It's a big day!" she said, setting the cake down and shutting off the oven. "What better way to celebrate?"

"I'm not complaining," I said. "Especially not about the cake."

Zane walked into the kitchen from the nursery, baby Leanne in his arms, sucking on one of her fingers.

"Do you want to hold her?" Mallory asked me, pulling out a chair and sitting at the table with me.

"Auntie Eos doesn't like babies," Zane reminded her in a baby voice.

"This one's okay," I said, looking at the rosy-cheeked infant as she pulled her finger from her mouth, a gob of spit dribbling onto her chest.

"You better go get ready while the cake is cooling," Mallory suggested with a sweet smile, taking her baby from Zane.

After we made ourselves look presentable, Mallory handed us both generous hunks of still-warm apple crumble cake, promising that her and Gavin wouldn't be long behind us to the trial.

When we reached City Hall, we waited outside for some of our friends. It was a cool morning, and there was a gentle breeze that occasionally swept through the air. A man in the distance called out to me, breaking the peace of the moment.

"Miss Dawn!" he called, waving an arm as he hobbled down the street. When he grew closer, I was able to make the man out as Mr. Montgomery.

I trotted out to him, offering him my arm, allowing him to stop running.

"Hello, sir," I greeted him. "How are you?"

"I'm a free man!" His deep wrinkles morphed around his smile. "They held my trial yesterday and determined my sentence was more than paid for. I'm free!" His voice squeaked gleefully on the word 'free.'

"Congratulations!" I said, beaming at him.

"Thank you so much for everything," he said, a thick tear bouncing at the corner of his eye, threatening to fall.

"It wasn't me," I clarified. Changing the subject, I asked, "Are you coming to the trial?"

"Of course I am!" He chortled. "Wouldn't miss it for the world!"

A tall blond in a pressed grey suit hurried toward the front doors of City Hall.

"Hold up!" I called. "President Paren, why are you in such a rush?"

Paren turned around, his cheeks red and a toothy grin on his face. "I told you to stop calling me that."

"Hey," I defended. "It was up to the people to call you that, and they did. I'm not to blame here." I shrugged playfully.

"It was a close race," he said.

"You're just being humble. The others didn't even have a chance."

"The others had experience." Paren chuckled bashfully, running a hand through his hair. "They used to work in City Hall with Raine. I don't think that kind of experience was in their favor. You were interim president prior to the election—the people were able to see what a great leader you are!"

"Some of the citizens would disagree," Paren said with a scoff.

"Well, they had a chance to vote, but you won anyways. If the people decide they don't want to be under your leadership, they can vote again in a few years."

Paren smiled. "I'll see you guys inside," he said. "I'm already running late. It was good seeing you both!"

"We should probably go get seated," Zane suggested. "They know where we're sitting—they'll join us when they get here."

Inside the courtroom, Zane and I made our way to our reserved seats near the front after helping Mr. Montgomery to his seat. A few empty chairs sat beside me. We waited, and I anxiously kept checking over my shoulder to see if they were here, but no luck. Just as the judge called attention, the doors opened and Braylin and Cindee scampered in, mouthing "*sorry*" to the judge as they hurried to their seats beside me.

"Where's Sky?" I asked her as she sat down, smoothing out her pink skirt.

"She said she couldn't do it," Cindee apologized. "It was just too much for her to be here. She decided to help set up for the gate ceremony instead."

I turned my attention back to the judge, who had already started.

"Your Honor and ladies and gentlemen of the jury," started the judge, a lanky woman with a tight ginger bun. "The defendant, Raine Velora, has been charged with the crimes of theft, violence, public disturbance, unlawful drug use, and perjury on multiple accounts."

The trial proceeded just like the many others that came before it.

"During her time as City Leader," the judge said. "Raine Velora has stolen freedom from countless citizens of the New Territory, including that of several minors—an act that is considered unjust and unlawful."

The jury scribbled on their notepads. I exchanged a look with Zane, who reached out and grabbed my hand. I smiled and my eyes traced over him. I missed his styled hair, and I hated the bald scar that reminded me of what Raine did to him, but I was also grateful for it—his life didn't end, and that scar was there as a reminder not to take it for granted.

"There are multiple accounts of violence inflicted by Miss Velora, two counts of which were against Mr. Zane Hess," the judge continued. At this, heads everywhere turned to stare, and he ignored them, facing forward. "One instance in which she forced her subordinates to use acid as a means of torture, and another instance in which Miss Velora herself fired a gun at Mr. Hess."

Again, the jury wrote frantically.

"How's the rehabilitation project going?" I whispered to Cindee, who greeted my question with a cheery smile.

"It's going really well! We should be ready to launch some of the programs next week! We've done research on programs that have been used in the past and have been able to build from the ones that showed some results. I think we've really got a great chance at success! If all goes well, we should be able to decrease recurrent crime by about 70% in the first year."

"That's fantastic!" I smiled at her.

The judge continued on, mentioning how Raine's actions allegedly led to the uprising in Fallmont, declaring her guilty of public disturbance and, ultimately, noise pollution.

"Are you still living with Gavin and Mallory in their tiny house?" Cindee asked.

"Not in that house anymore, thankfully," I said. "We moved into a bigger place, but we're still living with them. Zane really loves helping out with the baby, and I think I've gotten used to being surrounded by people. It feels weird being alone."

"We have multiple testimonies from officials and citizens claiming that Miss Velora, in fact, drugged some citizens against their will during their time in the holding cells to keep them submissive."

I turned to face Zane, whose gaze was frozen forward, his expression telling me that this was the first time he had heard of this.

"Did you know?" I asked.

He shook his head, never looking at me. "I just thought I was getting weak. They didn't give me much to eat or drink. I slept a lot. I thought it was my body shutting down. I had no idea."

At the front of the court room, I could see Raine sitting upright in her chair, her arms crossed and her brow furrowed. She didn't speak a word, and her lips didn't even twitch as she heard the accusations.

"Lastly, Raine Velora is being charged with perjury. Miss Velora has lied on countless occasions, including instances of false accusations in court, as well as several cases in which she ordered the exile of minors."

"Miss Raine Velora," the judge started. "You may speak on your own behalf now."

Raine's lips pursed. She shut her eyes briefly, took a deep breath, and stood slowly.

"I'm not going to stand here and tell you these allegations are false," she said with a somber coolness to her voice. Even from my place in the seats, I could see her eyes were growing red. "They're most certainly true. However, it is in the best interest of the jury and everyone present today to understand that everything I did was to protect the citizens of the New Territory. I did not make any of these decisions without careful consideration of the consequences, and I do not regret my choices."

There was hushed and nervous chatter throughout the courtroom. Raine continued to stand in place, as if ensuring she locked eyes with each juror before finally sitting again.

The judge cleared his throat before speaking. "Now th—"

"Additionally," said a young man in a suit near the front of the courtroom. The man stood to his feet as he continued. "The kidnapping of Zane Hess has proven that Miss Velora does not follow even her own laws that would have required Mr. Hess to receive a trial and proper exile for his crimes. Instead, Miss Velora held him captive in horrible conditions, lying to everyone about his well-being and whereabouts— even the fact that he was alive." He paused only momentarily for a deep breath. The judge looked unamused by the interruption, but she said nothing as the young man continued, speaking quickly. "Miss Velora's constant disregard for the truth for her own benefit, as well as the other charges presented to the court today, have proven that she is unfit for reentry into society."

"Sir," the judge said impatiently.

The man sat just as quickly as he had stood.

"Jurors," the judge said, breaking the brief silence. "If you would like to step out to discuss the charges presented, please do so now."

The jurors left the room in a single-file line, disappearing through a side door. Everyone waited eagerly and anxiously in silence, as if speaking would delay the decision.

"When's Arke's trial?" Cindee asked me.

"I think it's next Thursday, isn't it?" I replied, to which Cindee shrugged.

"Which town did they decide to keep her in until then?" she asked.

"Equivox, I think. I'm pretty sure they've moved most of them to Equivox anyways while everyone is waiting for the trials—harder to escape."

"Bellicose is tough to escape, too," Cindee said. "I thought that's where they were keeping Raine?"

"They were—and some of the other criminals. I think just the worst of the worst were there though."

"I'm so glad we were all able to do our trials super early." Cindee leaned back in her chair.

At the front of the courtroom, Raine turned her gaze, her eyes meeting mine as she stared at me with intense hatred.

"Face forward," a guard demanded in a growling voice as he tapped on the table in front of her.

Raine's head snapped forward again, but I could see her eyes fighting to resist looking to the side to see me.

Breaking the awkward tension of the moment, the jurors reentered the room, the sounds of their shoes tapping against tile echoing in the courtroom as they returned to their seats. They sat for a moment and each of them reached forward and placed papers in front of one of the jurors, an older woman with grey roots and overgrown chestnut hair. The woman rifled through the papers before nodding.

"We've made a decision," she said, standing.

The judge looked across at all of the jurors, who all nodded, their faces serious. The juror continued standing.

"We hereby declare Raine Velora guilty of theft, violence, public disturbance, drug abuse, and perjury. Due to the fact that her crimes fit into all five of the major categories of crime, we agree that a life sentence to Ironwood would be most appropriate."

"It's settled," the judge said. "Raine Velora, I hereby sentence you to life in prison."

Once the courtroom eventually cleared, we began to make the walk to the gates of Fallmont, where a massive crowd was already there to greet us. News of Raine's sentence spread quickly, and the people were clearly celebrating.

I searched for Paren, who left the courtroom before we could make it out. As I searched, I heard a steady clopping sound to my right. With a smile, I turned to face the source. Legend grinned back at me, beads of sweat forming on his dark forehead as he swung his crutches forward, propelling himself closer with every swing. Zaire moseyed beside him patiently.

"You're getting around pretty good on those!" I said. "I thought you weren't going to need them anymore?"

He let out an exhausted chuckle. "I'm still getting used to the replacement." He lifted the bottom of his pant leg, revealing a prosthetic from the knee down. "I'm still a bit... cautious."

"More like he's afraid the fake won't be able to support the weight of his fat ass," Zaire said with a smirk.

Legend shook his head with a laugh. "Shut up, I think the ceremony's starting." He swung one of the crutches out, smacking it against Zaire's shin, forcing Zaire to yelp.

"Good morning, ladies and gentlemen!" Paren greeted from a platform.

At the base of the platform, Skylar and Fabian stood in official's uniforms, their backs straight and shoulders stiff. Upon seeing me, Skylar shot me a twitch of a hard-to-conceal smile.

"For years, the gates of the cities have been closed off to the general public. Only officials, drivers, cross-city messengers, and those with special permission were granted passage. Today, in Fallmont, as well as our neighboring cities—Eastmeade, Rockhallow, and Nortown, people are listening to this speech and ceremonies are being held to break this long-held tradition," Paren continued, and I could see Bexa holding the camera ball. "If I may, I would like to call Eos Dawn to the platform please."

My body went cold and I could feel the panicked thumping of my heart in my chest. I stood there, frozen.

"*Go*," Zane urged, nudging me with his elbow.

Reluctantly, I stepped up onto the platform and joined Paren at his side.

"*What are you doing?*" I hissed under my breath.

Ignoring me, he continued his speech.

"I would like to thank Eos for her immense contributions to our society. If it weren't for her courageous acts, we wouldn't be here today to celebrate. On this day, we open the gates of the cities, allowing ultimate freedom throughout the New Territory. From this day forward, citizens will be allowed to go where they please, when they please. Eos," he said, turning to me, "if you will do the honors."

He handed me the Skeleton Key, and I looked back at him, confused.

"I had Zane sneak it from your room," he whispered, holding his smile.

I took the Key, running my thumb over its stained glass. Looking up at me from the crowd, I could see Eve, Astraea, and Cromwell. A few other familiar faces gathered together with my friends. Beside them, Bexa stood, sticking her tongue out and crossing her eyes at me. I suppressed a laugh and she stopped, smiling.

Everyone watched my every move as I carefully walked down the steps of the platform, approaching the towering metal gates of Fallmont. I took one last look at everyone behind me, their faces full of hope and, for once, peace. With a hand on the metal gates, I inserted the Key into the lock, twisting the dial until I felt the Key was in place. Slowly, I turned it.

Click.

www.ingramcontent.com/pod-product-compliance
Lightning Source LLC
Chambersburg PA
CBHW020458310726
48979CB00016B/2714/J